The Saffron Kitchen

**Center Point
Large Print**

**This Large Print Book carries the
Seal of Approval of N.A.V.H.**

The Saffron Kitchen

Yasmin Crowther

LP
F
CROWTHE

CENTER POINT PUBLISHING
THORNDIKE, MAINE

This Center Point Large Print edition
is published in the year 2007 by arrangement with
Viking Penguin, a member of Penguin Group (USA) Inc.

Copyright © 2007 by Yasmin Crowther.

The text of this Large Print edition is unabridged. In other
aspects, this book may vary from the original edition.
Printed in the United States of America.
Set in 16-point Times New Roman type.

ISBN-10: 1-58547-942-X
ISBN-13: 978-1-58547-942-9

Library of Congress Cataloging-in-Publication Data

Crowther, Yasmin.
    The Saffron kitchen / Yasmin Crowther.--Center Point large print ed.
        p. cm.
    ISBN-13: 978-1-58547-942-9 (lib. bdg. : alk. paper)
    1. Mothers and daughters--Fiction. 2. Iranians--England--London--Fiction.
3. London (England)--Fiction. 4. Exiles--Fiction. 5. Domestic fiction. 6. Large
type books. I. Title.

PR6103.R69S24 2007b
823'.92--dc22

2006033627

For my grandmothers,
Eleanor Powell and Khadijeh Assadi Moghadam,
and for Ella and Ali

Acknowledgments

Dearest thanks to John for being with me through it all, and without whom I would not have had the heart or the mind to write this book. Thanks also to Mark, my brother, for being my first hero, and to my mother and father for all they have given me—particularly my mother's stories of growing up in Mashhad and Assadieh. I am grateful to all my family and friends in Iran for welcoming me into their homes and for sharing their world.

I am greatly indebted to my editors, Richard Beswick and Pam Dorman, for believing in this book and for helping me to write it as well as I could. Thanks also to Toby Eady, my agent, for taking me under his wing, and to Jessica Woollard for plucking my manuscript from the pile.

I would also like to acknowledge Hanif Kureishi for helping me to start on this adventure; Neil McLean for all those Thursday evenings, climbing our separate mountains one sentence at a time; Emma Gervasio for working some bookish magic; and Nicola Bunting for helping me to carve out the space to begin. It would all have been much harder without the understanding of my colleagues at SustainAbility—thank you for giving me Fridays! Thanks also to those whose advice and support has helped me along the way, especially Bryony, and also Ernestine, Tonya Blowers, Michele Hutchison, John Fuller, Lauren Branston, Andrew Vickers, and the Nyman family.

I would very much like to thank Tom Anderson, who first read *Dover Beach* to me many years ago.

—YC

Ah, love, let us be true
To one another! for the world, which seems
To lie before us like a land of dreams,
So various, so beautiful, so new,
Hath really neither joy, nor love, nor light,
Nor certitude, nor peace, nor help for pain;
And we are here as on a darkling plain
Swept with confused alarms of struggle and flight,
Where ignorant armies clash by night.

—MATTHEW ARNOLD, "Dover Beach"

*I*n northeast Iran, on the plains of Khorasan, there is a village called Mazareh. It is a honeycomb of brown mud walls, where the foothills meet the plains, far from the nearest city of Mashhad, with its golden domes and minarets. It is home to forty families or more, whose generations have farmed the lands and tended the flocks of the once powerful Mazar family, who gave the village its name.

But *Mazareh* has a meaning of its own—"little miracle"—and it has had its own share of stars springing from the earth at dusk. It is a land of superstition, although the people are devout. If you go there now, you will find a new prayer house of redbrick being built to replace the slowly crumbling shrine on the village edge. If you look further, behind the old shrine on a summer day, you may find wildflowers, ragged poppies, laid at the foot of a stone traced yellow with lichen.

Look more closely, and you will see it is not one stone but two, body and torso, a stone woman who has stood there beyond remembering. You might pass by and never know she was there, but in the dark night, the wind breathes through holes in her body and she sighs across the land. She watches the passage of time. She is there now as the earth turns. Its currents lap through her. Rough or gentle, the blasts and blows of the seasons, the centuries, make her sing, although she has no mouth, no tongue, no voice of her own.

This is her story, one she might tell, should you care to listen.

1. London

A solitude ten thousand fathoms deep
Sustains the bed on which we lie, my dear;
Although I love you, you will have to leap;
Our dream of safety has to disappear.
—W. H. Auden

*S*trange not to know that you're alive or even
that you're about to die. That's what it must
have been like for my unborn baby. I'd been
kicked in the guts by my young cousin, as I hauled
him back from trying to jump over the bridge's rail-
ings into the cold green water rushing out to sea. My
mother's scream rang in my ears as she ran toward us
and the world froze: the churn of the Thames at high
tide, the rumble of going-home school traffic and the
tremble of the bridge. In that moment, my baby
started to die.

And then the world unfroze. The traffic rolled by as
if nothing had happened, and my cousin, Saeed, and I
clung together on the pavement. When my mother
finally reached us, she hauled Saeed to his feet, shook
him hard, and shouted in Farsi so that I half expected
him to make another run for the hungry river. But it had
claimed its life for the day. Saeed looked at his feet. My
mother shook her open palms at him and the sky, and
asked what she or his dead mother had done that he
should treat his life so lightly. Only when she stopped

for breath did she turn to see the spreading bloodstain on my pale blue skirt.

"Oh, Sara." She knelt on the wet pavement. "Saeed, find her phone." She pushed my rucksack toward him and out, onto the bridge, fell the rest of my life: my school books for marking, sixth-form essays on Othello and Desdemona, an apple, a bottle of folic acid tablets, cherry lip salve, my diary, a small photo album, and, beneath it all, my phone. One of them dialed 999 and I felt Saeed wrap his anorak around me, his thin brown arms goose-bumped in the cold and bruised from the bullying. I rested my head on my mother's knee between the convulsions of my body and cried for the lost life I had never known; for Julian, my husband, somewhere oblivious of it all; and for myself.

"What am I doing here?" my mother had asked in tears earlier that summer as she tidied her immaculate kitchen, her head shaking as she again wiped down the surfaces, rearranged the fruit bowl, and refused to sit down.

Her younger sister, my aunt Mara, was dead and my mother had not seen her for over a year. When I thought of Mara, I mainly remembered her laugh, how it had bubbled and rippled from her. Everything about her had been generous. Even when she was in a wheelchair with cropped hair and swollen with drugs, she was beautiful. And they had not had the chance for a final good-bye. More or less five decades and two continents, stretching from Paris to Berlin, Vienna, Prague,

Bucharest, Istanbul, Baku, Mosul, Kirkûk and Tabrîz, lay between my mother's life in London and her sister's death in Tehran.

It did not help that Mara's husband had already remarried. My mother had cried and shouted down the phone at the betrayal, full of her own guilt. Mara's two oldest children were already grown up, but the youngest, Saeed, was just twelve. He was tall but slight, with the dark skin of his father, a solemn, angular face, and large green eyes that rarely blinked beneath their thick lashes. He arrived on my parents' doorstep early that autumn and moved into my old bedroom, squeezing his stuff into the gaps my mother made, between the old clothes, books, toys, and photos that I had left or stored there over the fifteen years since I had moved out.

The following weekend, I had driven over to my parents' from my home in Hammersmith. It was a Sunday morning and I'd woken early, the window rattling in its casement with a dry wind that had blown up from the Sahara and Arabia before that, leaving sand on the window ledges and car bonnets, and bending the stiff old London trees in the night. I'd woken with Julian curled round me, his hand on my growing belly, and the warm air billowing through the window.

"Come with me for lunch, to meet Saeed." I rolled toward him.

"Next time." He stroked my back. "I've got a busy few weeks coming up. You go and do your Iranian thing and I'll get everything straight here."

"All right, but promise you'll come and say hello soon."

"I promise." He kissed my neck. "I'll miss your mother's cooking."

My parents' home was on Richmond Hill, large and set back from the road, far away from the rest of grimy London. The pine trees at the gate always welcomed me first, with their lemon green scent and the memory of childhood summers, scrambling up to the top branches, often away from my parents' arguing, to sit in the peace and dust motes with blood on my shins. I walked along the tidy, tiled, black-and-white path to the front door, which my father opened before I knocked.

We hugged. "You look well." He held me back from himself.

"How are things here?" I asked, and he rolled his eyes.

"Saeed's upstairs, settling into his room. He seems well enough. Your mother's in the garden. She wanted some quiet. A bit overwhelmed, I think."

"I'll go find her," I said, and he disappeared back into his book-lined study.

Along the hall, the house was full of the smell of her cooking, the soft, starchy scent of basmati, saffron, and roasting lamb. I went through the kitchen with steam on its windows and along the narrow blue corridor with its long cupboards full of henna, herbs, dried figs, and limes from her last trip home. The air was cool above the terra-cotta floor, before the steps down to the back door and into the garden.

I could hear my old tape player from behind the yew hedge and beyond the rose garden, the tinny sound of tombok drums and sitar. I passed the greenhouse, figs and jasmine growing up one side, overhanging the path, and found her on the bottom lawn, kneeling quietly, eyes concentrating on her hands, weeding and tidying. She was still beautiful at over sixty: high cheekbones and dark hair to her shoulders.

"*Salaam*, Maman." I spoke quietly but she turned quickly, startled, breaking into a smile as she saw me, eyes full of tears.

She wiped her face with the back of her hand, leaving a smudge of mud on her cheek. "Hello." She pushed herself up, a little stiff. "I've been thinking of Mara; how I wish she was here. We spent so little time together."

I hugged her, and she felt small and fragile. "I remember you and Mara both dancing out here to this music a few summers ago."

It had been a dance from their childhood, arms raised, sinuous, slow, small footsteps and hips shaken with mock sensuality, one almond-eyed sister to the other.

She smiled. "I'm not sure what the neighbors made of it."

We both looked out across the tidy clipped hedges.

Later, I went upstairs to fetch Saeed for lunch. Ten oak doors led off the large landing, lit from a stained-glass window that stretched the height of the stairwell to the west. I knocked gently before going in to introduce myself. He stood to shake my hand with a polite bow that made me smile. His courtesy was a contrast to the mischievous twelve-year-olds I taught back at school. "That's lovely," I said, looking over his shoulder at my old acrylic paints on the desk. He had painted a gazelle in full flight, amber and gold, with its front and back legs stretched out like a rocking horse. "What gave you that idea?"

He told me about an old Persian carpet that had hung by his bed in Tehran. "The gazelle used to be in the corner close to my pillow. When my mother was ill and I couldn't sleep, I'd trace it with my finger." As he talked, he held up his hand and drew the gazelle's outline again in the air between us.

My mother joined us then from the garden and rested her hand on Saeed's shoulder to look at the picture as well. "Mara drew beautifully too," she said. "When I first came to England, I used to send Elvis Presley tapes to her in Iran, and she'd send me her drawings of home, the village and our family." She closed her eyes in the yellow sunlight.

"Have you kept them?" Saeed asked, gazing up at her.

"In the loft somewhere. They made me sad. I missed them all so much. I'll show you them one day . . . soon. But come on, it's time to eat."

"Why did you first come to England, Aunt Maryam?" Saeed asked as we walked down the stairs, a child's curiosity in his voice.

"Well," she answered, keeping her eyes on each step, "I'd finished my nurse's training in Tehran and I couldn't go back to Mashhad. It seemed like an adventure back then. My father was pleased to send me, I suppose." Her hand slid down the oak banister, blue veins and white knuckles, faded cuts and scars from the garden.

Saeed followed behind her, turning to look at the Hansel and Gretel cottage in the stained-glass window as he passed.

In the dining room, my parents talked about the school he would start in a few weeks' time and his eyes flickered from one to the other. "Your English will improve," my father said, slicing the leg of lamb. "When Maryam first came here, she only knew a few lines of poetry, which was remarkable, but not much use."

Our eyes crossed to her face, cheeks flushed as she served rice on to the plates.

"My mother said you had your own English tutor," said Saeed.

Her hand hovered above the plate, grains of saffron rice falling on to the cream linen tablecloth. "Yes, that's true." She frowned, distant for a moment, rolling the fallen grains beneath her fingers, so they broke and smudged the linen. "It was a long time ago; another life."

My father leaned forward in his chair. "Are you quite all right, Maryam?"

"Yes." She held the back of her hand to her forehead. "Sorry, let me get a cloth and clear this up. It's all this talk of Mara, the past. You bring it all back, Saeed—the dead and gone."

He bowed his head as she walked from the room, and I squeezed his hand.

By the day on the bridge, Saeed had been at school for a month, and been bullied from the start. I had received an anxious call from my mother to say that the police had found him looking lost in King's Mall shopping center during school hours. They had taken him to Hammersmith police station until he could be safely collected. Her call came at lunchtime and, as I had no lessons that afternoon, I said I would meet them there in an hour.

I walked through Ravenscourt Park. It was a beautiful autumn day, with red maple leaves fallen on the path and a hint of woodsmoke in the air. As I hurried along past mothers pushing their prams, I thought of the child growing inside me, and of Saeed, here among strangers. Beyond the park, I walked along streets of smart terraced houses, gentrified in soft pastels, canary yellow and apple green, with sports cars in the road and lush curtains at the windows. Late honeysuckle and foxgloves still flowered in the small front gardens.

I tried to remember being twelve, Saeed's age. Fatima had come from Iran to stay with us at about that time. She had looked after my mother when she was growing up in Mashhad in northeast Iran. She would make me laugh, sitting on the garden wall with her skirt above her knees. She wore long powder blue bloomers underneath, with hidden pockets full of safety pins and buttons, and a small prayer tablet etched with the mosque at Haram. That had been 1978, the year before the Revolution. In the early days, during that spring over twenty years ago, Fatima had treated me as a child. Maybe the foxgloves had reminded me of it. She had brought a small bag of grainy black poppy seeds with her on the plane, and while she sat on the wall, bloomers in the sunshine, I ran up and down the garden in my school pinafore and white socks, sowing the seeds where they fell.

"They're from Afghanistan," Fatima had looked into my eyes while my mother translated, "near to where your mother grew up. They will still be here after we're dead." She had smiled and pinched my cheek.

By the summer they had grown into tall, ragged opium poppies, pink, red, and purple petals fluttering above the roses, stocks, and gladioli. My mother had shown me how to score the seedpods with a razor, sap oozing out to be scraped away and made into the resin her father smoked at the end of his life. "Don't tell your father," she whispered to me, and there in the middle of our herb and vegetable garden, I touched something strange and dangerous, a world where flowers became poison and smoke.

Fatima always wore a headscarf in those days, which would slip back over her badly dyed purple-black hair as the day passed, and I took to wearing one too, knotted like a gypsy's at the back of my head. She would pull me on to her lap and tell me I looked just like my mother when she was small, and how she had always been my grandfather's favorite and that was why he had chosen her to come to England.

"Do you miss your dad?" I asked my mother once.

"No. He's always with me, in my head."

I don't recall much, if any, talk of her mother.

Then, with the summer and the poppies, the bleeding started. One morning I woke up and there was a warm dampness on my nightie. I sat up in bed, put my hand down there and brought it back sticky and dark, not like the bright red blood when I cut my knee, but smelling strong: of inside me, I guessed. After that, once Fatima had found out, everything changed. I would run in the garden with my skinny legs in shorts, jumping through the water sprinkler, and she would bite the side of her hand and tut-tut, looking away.

"She's used to girls covering their bodies," my mother explained. "I used to bind my breasts down with a bandage, and look at you, wet through."

She had seemed angry somehow, impatient with me. Almost overnight, I became painfully self-conscious of myself, my body, its protuberances, shape, flow, and juices: all bad, all spoiling, all beyond my control. That had been me at twelve.

The houses grew scruffier as I turned onto Shepherd's Bush Road and the traffic grew louder, car windows rolled down and hip-hop bouncing into the street. I passed the Thai supermarket; the little old lady at the till by the door looked up and recognized me. She smiled and I waved. This was my patch—past the off license, delicatessen, and newsagent's. Brook Green stretched out on the left, the parched plane trees dropping their skin-colored leaves where a group of tramps and drunks always gathered on two benches facing each other. You could smell them from a few yards away. The same lone woman was usually in their midst. She was worn but ageless, thin in tight jeans, with white flaking skin and thick Afro hair. I crossed the street if I ever saw her walking toward me, asking for money. I guess it was her patch, too.

Then, at last, the police station came into view on the right, its blue lantern left above the door from another time. Beyond it was the fire station, opposite the library and before the PoNaNa nightclub, where girls in stockings and school uniforms hung out on Friday nights with hairy-kneed young men dressed like schoolboys, tongues hanging out like wolves. God knows what Fatima would have made of it all. I wasn't sure what I made of it myself. I half admitted I hoped my baby would be a son. Life for a boy somehow seemed less messy; there was less to go wrong than with a daughter.

Up the steps and inside the police station, smelling of linoleum, I saw my mother and Saeed, sitting side by side on a bench in the hallway. Both looked straight ahead, not talking. I put on a big smile and walked up to them. "Hello, mischief." I ruffled Saeed's hair and he pulled away, eyes full of angry tears that I hadn't seen before. "All right, Maman?" I asked.

"The shame of it." She shook her head as if she had dirt in her mouth. "Why have you brought me here, Saeed? What would your mother say?" Her hands rubbed over each other, and there was a fleck of spit on her chin.

"Come on, lighten up." I knelt beside Saeed. "Don't worry, she's just a bit upset. She doesn't like places like this. It's not you." I reached out and rubbed her arm. "Let's get out of here. How about going to the river and seeing if we can find some tea?"

We walked in silence toward the squall of the Broadway, awash with exhaust fumes, sirens, and the distant shudder of the flyover heading toward Richmond and Heathrow. Saeed walked slightly apart from us. His anorak hung off his shoulder and the laces from one of his shoes dragged on the ground. He shrunk into his collar, and his new, short haircut left him looking cold and diminished. My mother was detached, with a weary resignation in each step. Her mouth was pinched and plum lipstick bled into her wrinkles.

We reached the riverside and turned right, passed the redbrick mansion block and boat clubs. It looked barren, abandoned by the weekend crowd of rowers and boozers. The traffic rumbled over the bridge, glorious khaki green and gold in the late afternoon, shadows and light playing off the water. A tall timber mast stuck up from the riverbed, about thirty feet into the flow, with an owl carved into it, like a totem pole where seagulls circled. It looked out over the tides, downriver to Putney, Battersea, Westminster, Greenwich, and away. I pointed it out to Saeed, and he smiled with sad eyes.

We arrived at some trestle tables outside a pub. The

door was ajar but it was lifeless within. "You grab a seat," I told them, hunting for chocolate biscuits in my rucksack, a weapon of last resort with my junior classes. "I'll see if we can get coffees."

Inside, I persuaded a New Zealander, looking lost and cold in his surf garb, to organize some filter coffee. Waiting, I looked over my shoulder through the large windows and watched my mother staring upriver, Saeed reading the side of the biscuit packet. Then she focused on him, her mouth moving, as I relaxed and rubbed the taut skin across my belly. Eventually she reached over and took Saeed's chin in her hand. I smiled, waiting for her to stroke the side of his face: poor boy, all would be well. Instead, she drew back her hand and slapped him so hard his head jerked to the side. I felt as if I had been hit myself and hurried outside, stumbling hard against the door. Saeed was backing away from the table, his hand holding his cheek. He flinched as I put my arms around him. I could feel him shaking.

"What are you doing?" I demanded of my mother, her thick-veined hands trembling on the table, her cheeks spotted pink. "He's bullied at school and then he comes home to this. You're supposed to look after him, protect him."

"And make him weak?" she replied. "You don't understand, Sara."

"No, I don't."

"When I was a child, if I was weak, I was punished. It made me strong. When I humiliated my father, he

24

humiliated me. It made me strong. Look at Saeed. He's weak at school and you tell me to pity him. That won't make him the son Mara wanted, the grandson my father deserved, the nephew I want." Her voice caught in her throat.

"I can't listen to this. Saeed, why didn't you go to school?"

He sat, half turned away, and spoke quietly, slowly: "This morning I went to the bus stop, and got on the bus at the back. I was tired as I don't sleep well here. It was warm and I fell asleep. When I woke up, the bus was in Hammersmith. I tried to find your house, Sara, to wait, but I got lost. A police lady in the shopping mall helped me."

My mother shook her head. Saeed's face was wet with tears. He leaned forward and rested his head in his hands. Our coffees were brought out and I sat watching them both. I couldn't quite believe what had happened. "Come on, drink up," I said. "I'll drive you two home."

Saeed stared at me, his eyes flooded and simmering. "I don't want to go home with her." He wouldn't look at my mother.

"You didn't mean it, did you? You're really sorry, aren't you, Maman?"

I needed to hear her apology as much as Saeed did, but she looked over my shoulder, toward the moored houseboats, their walkways and nodding geraniums.

"It's not the first time," he whispered.

"What isn't?" I asked, frowning.

"That she's hit me."

I turned to my mother.

"He's too weak." She blew on her coffee, her hands trembling.

Saeed stood up and walked away from the table. I tried to hold on to his sleeve, but it slipped through my fingers. "Come back," I said softly. He walked slowly at first, but when he was out of easy reach, he started to run toward the bridge. "What have you done, Maman?" I asked, and made to follow him, walking briskly and then trying to jog as Saeed ran up the steps.

I put my hand under my belly, breaking into a sweat. My mother pushed herself up from the table and turned to follow us, as I panted up the steps with my eyes half closed. Saeed had made it to the middle of the bridge and stood there as I drew closer. He looked at me like a frightened animal, and then glanced down at my mother, still on the riverside. The railing was low and he suddenly leaned forward to swing one leg over it. At that, I heard a shrill cry of distress from my mother, a deathly scream, as she saw what was happening, and I felt a surge of adrenaline shoot through me. I flung myself toward my little cousin, balanced a few yards away, and grabbed him as he wavered. With all my weight, I pulled him back on top of me, his foot kicking into my gut as we crashed down onto the pavement. I felt a cramp like life being wrung out of me, and clung to Saeed on the damp ground.

A little while later, I heard sirens straining to clear a way through the clot of traffic around the Broadway. I kept my eyes closed and disappeared inside myself, away from the violent shivering that ground my teeth and bent me double.

When I woke up, pale blue light flickered across my eyelids and I lay still with my eyes closed. I could be dead. I listened to the distant traffic, insistent horns and screeching brakes mingling with echoes from the depths of the hospital: its trolleys, swinging doors, births and deaths. I must be quite high up, I thought, above the menagerie. Nearer, I heard the soft squeak of shoes trying to tread quietly, and whispers. I could smell lilies. I didn't want to open my eyes, but I was still breathing: I felt the rise and fall of my rib cage. Beyond the heavy scent of pollen and disinfectant, I could smell something acrid: my own skin and the dried scent of panic. I ran my tongue over my parched lips and licked the salty tears pooled at their edges before I felt a hand on my forehead and a kiss on my mouth.

"My beautiful wife."

His words twisted through me and I opened my eyes, lifting my arms to hold him. With a rush, everything seemed to hurt: my knees and hip where I had fallen, my nails where they had torn against Saeed's uniform, the back of my head where it had cracked against the pavement, and my ruptured, hollow inside. Julian rested me back on the pillow and laid his finger across my lips. His skin was gray, his blue eyes shrunken and red.

"I don't want to see my mum," I whispered, my throat tight.

"You don't have to." He stroked my face.

"Take me home?" I asked.

"In the morning, if the doctor says so."

"Do they know what it was?" My hands were cold and clammy, holding his.

"A boy." Julian's voice cracked as he rested his head beside mine.

We stared out of the window into the orange dusk.

That night, I dreamed of my mother. I was standing at the French windows to the rear of my parents' house. They opened onto a small sandstone patio with three steps down to my mother's rose garden, a neat maze of flower beds cut into the mossy grass. The roses were just past full bloom: fat pink, red, peach, and yellow petals, browning and curled at the edges. There was a breeze and it blew the petals from the flowers, twisting and tumbling in the air and across the lawn where my mother walked slowly toward me. She kept stooping to gather the fallen petals in her arms, but they blew away almost as quickly as she could bend to reach them.

"Maman," I cried out, "come quickly."

But her gaze was distracted by the flurry; rose petals blowing and spiraling around her. Then, as if from a children's story, from behind the yew hedge at the bottom of the garden emerged a soot black and amber-striped tiger, its soft paws heavy on the dewy English lawn, moving straight toward my mother as she heaved herself too slowly up the steps.

"Don't turn round!" I cried, as the tiger drew itself

back on taut, sprung haunches. "Come," I called to her with my arms open, and the tiger bounded into them.

I woke up, the pillow sodden beneath my neck and hair matted against my face. Soaked with sweat, I wiped the chill wetness from my skin with the back of my hand and looked into the gray light of an early dawn. I wanted to go home. As life woke up around me, I closed my eyes again. I could scarcely bear to see it: a new day beginning, indifferent, inexorable. I felt old. I left my breakfast of dried toast and orange juice on the tray. The smell of it brought bile into my mouth. My dad arrived as I lay there, trying to send my mind somewhere else, to a parallel universe of happy endings.

"Hello, darling," he said as he bent to kiss me, looking like he hadn't slept. "I brought some proper coffee and a croissant, your favorite."

"I'm really not hungry, Dad. But thanks."

"Nonsense, try a mouthful for your old man," and he broke off a small piece and held it to my mouth.

I let the pastry go soft in my spit and closed my eyes before swallowing.

"And another."

I opened my mouth again.

We sat like that silently for half an hour, and he fed me like he would a sick bird, crumb by crumb. At the end we smiled at each other. He reached into his coat pocket and pulled out a small, pale brown cloth dog, its fur worn through and one ear stitched back with green thread.

"Ted." I laughed and winced at the same time.

"He's a bit the worse for wear, but he's seen you through some tough times."

I held the small toy up to my face and breathed it in, the smell of powder and the drawer in my old room full of discarded makeup and perfume. "Thanks, Dad."

"Your mum's devastated, you know."

"I guess so," I replied. "Did she tell you what happened? Hitting Saeed?"

"Yes, enough." His face collapsed at the recollection. "She's decided to go back to Iran for a while. She feels so guilty. I don't think she can bring herself to see you."

"I don't think I can face seeing her right now. I wouldn't know where to begin." I heard him sigh. "Are you all right, Dad, with her going away?"

"Yes, it gives everyone some time to sort things out. But I hate to see you all so upset. I keep thinking I should have been able to do something."

"It wasn't your fault."

"I don't know. Maybe I should have seen it coming. She's not as young as she was, and Saeed's taken his toll, waking up in the middle of the night in tears. I think he made her homesick and exhausted all at once."

"How is Saeed now?"

He shook his head. "It's just about all he needed."

"I don't know why it happened." I felt my own tears coming again.

He took my hand. "She's a complicated woman, Maryam. Sometimes she's a mystery to herself, let alone to me." He had shared these words before, other times when she had seemed to crack around the edges, a stream of Farsi shouted from the landing before the door to her turquoise room was slammed shut, emerging full of regret hours later.

I closed my eyes as he sat on the side of the bed. It started to rain and I listened to the soft fall against the window. The doctor came and drew round the curtains, as my dad waited for Julian in reception. "You're about fine to go home," he said as he prodded and probed. "Have a checkup with your own doctor in a week."

"What about my baby?" I asked.

"Not much to see." He studied his hands. "Early days. You could do a blessing. That sometimes helps."

I looked at him: graying temples and long, thin fingers. "Thanks." I rested back against the pillow.

Julian arrived a short while afterwards.

"Sorry I'm late," he said. "I just needed to hand off some work."

He had brought fresh clothes and drew the screen round again. I sat up as he untied the blue paper gown and gently helped me to stand and step into my jogging pants and jersey. It felt strange to be on my feet again, as if it had been an age and not just a day since I had fallen.

I leaned against him as we walked slowly to the car. I longed to get home, and hugged my dad good-bye beneath the heavy gray sky.

Sitting in the kitchen a day or so later, my fingers traced the knots and swirls of the tabletop. Julian was upstairs. Everything seemed shabby in the dull light. The air was dirty and motionless and I wished it would rain. Creswell, our black Labrador, nosed at the back door to get into the garden. I pushed myself up and walked over the cold tiled floor to lift the latch. There was a green blanket on a hook above our boots and walking shoes, and I wrapped it round my shoulders, kicking on some flip-flops. Outside was the long, narrow garden with a high beech hedge on one side and a tall, dark wood fence on the other, overhung with honeysuckle in the summer and ivy now. There were lavender and rosemary bushes beside the door, and I bent to rub my hands through them, smelling their sweet, sharp fragrance.

I walked along the mossy sandstone paving to my bench at the bottom of the garden beside an acer that dropped red sycamore seeds in spring but was bare now. The bench was part of a maple trunk with a seat hewn into it. It was dry enough and I perched on the edge before sliding back and tucking my feet under the blanket. Our neighbors' terraced houses stretched away on either side. I felt flooded with fatigue.

The telephone rang inside and then stopped. Julian called my name. I sat still and closed my eyes, hearing the squeak of the back door, then his voice. "What are you doing out here? Aren't you cold?" he asked. His hair was tousled, glasses perched on the end of his nose as he watched me, near and far away at the same time. "Come on, I'll make some tea. Your dad's on the phone."

I uncurled my legs and rubbed my calves. "Be along in a second."

Inside, the kettle was already rattling on the hob as I went through into the sitting room and sat on the edge of the sofa.

"Hi, Dad, how are you?" I said.

"That's what I should be asking you."

"Oh, I don't know. Glad to be home."

"Yes." I imagined him standing by the phone in his study, surrounded by all his legal magazines and papers. "I'm taking your mum to the airport tomorrow morning. She's been into town today and got her tickets from Iran Air."

"How is she?"

"Quiet. She wants to be on her own most of the time. I'm staying out of her way. She knows where I am. You know she loves you very much, Sara."

"Yes." I thought of her room at the corner of the house, its turquoise walls and the smell of her perfume, lilies of the valley. "How long's she going for?"

"She's got an open-ended ticket, so it could be anything between a fortnight and a month or so. You know what she's like. I can't pin her down."

"Yes, I know." Growing up, life had been punctuated by her occasional trips back to Iran. I'd make my own way to school as dust gathered in the corners, house plants wilting and sheets unchanged. My father would do his cheerful best until she returned, laden with presents, gold bangles, and pistachios.

"I suppose I should be used to it by now." He

laughed, tired. "It will be good for Saeed and me to get to know each other better. Go for some walks, you know. And I could do with a pair of young hands in the garden."

"I'll come and see you both in a few days," I said. It was quiet on the other end of the line. "Tell Mum good-bye for me."

"Yes, darling, take care."

I put down the phone and looked at the black-and-white photograph from my parents' wedding on the sideboard. It was in the mid-sixties outside the Chelsea Registry Office, everything shiny and black with rain. In the background my mother was wearing a short white wedding dress, thin gauzy material floating round her thighs. She was looking away from the camera, to the side of the frame, her hair in a short bob and her veil flying high above her, caught in the wind like a sail. In the foreground my father was running toward the camera, his eyes wide and cheeky like a schoolboy's behind horn-rimmed glasses. He was in a dark Beatles suit, holding out a black umbrella as if he thought his new wife was right beside him, sheltering from the rain. He had no idea she was far behind, in a world of her own. I touched the glass covering the picture before turning back to the kitchen and the smell of toast.

Julian and I sat opposite each other across the table. I didn't want to meet his eyes. He rested his hand alongside mine, cupping it against the wood. My other hand warmed on the mug of tea. Over his shoulder, the wall

34

was a dull mushroom sort of color. I had liked it at first, the self-effacing softness of it in a kitchen which part of my mind still remembered as always flooded with soft green light, full of the garden's reflections through the window. It felt more like a moldy greenhouse at that moment.

"That wall could do with a lick of paint," I said.

Julian twisted his head round to look at it, and I watched the tendons stick out on the side of his neck. He faced me again with an overindulgent smile.

"Yeah. Why not?"

I saw how he watched me with a new, anxious, careful love, as if I might crack and splinter at the wrong word. I'd seen my father look at my mother in the same way.

"You know how you were supposed to go to New York next week?" I asked.

"Yes," he said, "I'm trying to reorganize it."

"That's not what I mean." I squeezed his hand. "I think you should go. It's lovely you're here, but some time on my own might be a good thing." He frowned, trying to peer into me, and I smiled gently. "It will be all right."

"Are you sure?"

"Yes, I've got so much to think about, all that's happened."

"Your mother?" he asked. "She never hit you, did she, Sara?"

"No," I looked through the window, "not as far as I remember. She would get cross sometimes, out of nowhere. Once, I must have been about eight, I was playing in front of her dressing table on my own, and put on one of her scarves, knotted beneath my chin. I had her bright red lipstick smudged all over my face." Julian smiled. "She was so furious when she saw me. She said the scarf was her mother's and I should know better. She scrubbed my face until it was sore, but the worst thing was that she got out the kitchen scissors and just lopped off my ponytail, so my hair was really short. She said I wouldn't play with makeup if I looked like a boy. You should have heard me cry."

Julian shook his head.

"It only happened once and she felt really bad afterwards. It's funny now."

"But still, damage was done." He reached for my hand as we sat together in the late afternoon, waiting for life to begin again.

My father phoned the next day to say she had gone. He'd spent the afternoon with Saeed, looking for windfalls in the garden. They were going to bake an apple pie.

"Sounds good," I said. "I'll come and try some, after Ju's left."

"He said you thought some quiet time would be good. You'll be all right?"

"Yes, fine. What about you?" I heard him sigh. "What's up?"

"Oh, I don't know, Sara. I went into your mother's room when I got back from the airport and sat in the middle of all her stuff. She'd left behind her address book, half English, half Farsi. The only thing of mine was that glass paperweight I'd given her, with a red rose in the middle. I sat there and hated myself for giving it to her—a dull, heavy thing with a dead flower inside."

I frowned. "It will be all right, Dad."

"Yes, sorry, darling, I know."

Later, I sat on the bed and watched Julian pack. He was quiet and methodical, opening and closing the doors and cupboards we had rubbed against for the five years of our married life together.

"We should go away when I'm back," he said.

"Yes, by the sea. I'd like that." My legs stretched before me and he gently rubbed one of the high arches, a habit of tenderness, before bending to kiss my forehead.

The next morning he was gone.

I sat at the foot of the stairs in the empty house, Creswell staring up at me. "How about some tea?" I began, and went to fill the kettle, staring out of the window above the sink. I could hear London's rumble beyond the walls and gardens, the clatter of the Tube as it came overground on its way to Chiswick, the roar of planes on their way down the Thames to Heathrow, the distant drill of roadworks and car doors slamming. I listened to the sigh and creak of bricks and floorboards as a blackbird outside whistled urgently, beautifully through it all, and the water came to a boil.

There was a card on the windowsill from work: *Get*

Well Soon. It had arrived with a bouquet of flowers that I'd put in Julian's study, not wanting to see them, already wilting in their vase. Next to the card, beside a basil plant and a clay pot of pens, was a small glass jar with a black lid. It was dusty and left a fine powder on my fingers as I picked it up. *Zaferan* was written on the side in my mother's hand, black ink on a white label. It was half full of orange, red, and ochre stamens, complete or crumbled: saffron from crocuses. I twisted the lid and lifted the jar to my nose, and it was as if I breathed in an essence of my childhood. There was something about the smell: earthy, sharp, sweet and delicate. I thought of my mother: she would already be in Mashhad. It was a city I knew mainly from photographs and stories she had told me, and also from summer holiday visits when I was very young. I put some saffron in my mug and poured on hot water, watching it slowly turn amber.

I had a memory from when I was a small child of going to Dover with her, just the two of us. We had found our way down to the shore, the cliffs behind us, white and yellow against the blue spring sky. She had sat on a blanket and brought out a small red book. She had only ever shown it to me on a few other occasions.

"This book brought me here, Sara, from far away." She had put her arms around me with tears on her face, not just due to the salty air. "Let's think of Maman's home," she had kissed my cheek, "and wish it good thoughts."

"What thoughts?" I'd asked, and she'd smiled then.

"Ah, love, let us be true to one another."
I'd frowned at her and sing-songed, "True to one and other," thin and shrill into the air, lost over the white-tipped dark sea.

"Where are you?" I said aloud in the quiet kitchen. I closed my eyes.

2. Maryam's Past

While my dust was being tempered in the mould,
The dust of much trouble was raised;
I cannot be better than I am—
I am as I was poured from the crucible.
                                    —Omar Khayyám

*M*aryam had gone to the hospital with Sara and Saeed in the back of the ambulance. She held Sara's hand as it grew limp, her face pallid on the stretcher, deaf to the siren's wail in the rush hour. Maryam rested her own head beside her daughter's, tears running into her mouth. She stroked Sara's face, its stillness, and thought of another hospital ward when she had been half Sara's age, military police at the door. "Send your mind to Tehran," the kind Doctor Ahlavi had told her all those years ago. Where was Sara's mind now? Maryam screwed her eyes shut. What had happened? She stood on the tarmac as her daughter was taken away to casualty, and Saeed looked on through the thin veil of evening rain.

"She'll be all right. She's in good hands," a porter

told them. "Do you want to sit down, lady?"

Maryam shook her head, lost, trying to frown her way back to the reality of the day.

"Can I get you a taxi?"

She nodded in her daze, beckoning to Saeed, and they waited on the curb, dandelions and moss cutting through the chinks and cracks of the pavement.

In the back of the cab, Maryam's hands began to shake. Saeed still had Sara's mobile phone. "Should we call Uncle Edward?" He spoke in a whisper.

Maryam nodded, reaching for his hand, but he flinched at her movement, shrinking into the corner of his seat. "God help me," she said, feeling a numbness beneath her skin. "Forgive me, Saeed." She looked at his downcast face, her father's nose, Mara's eyes. "I didn't deserve to have you in my care. I deserved no family." She rested her forehead on the cold window, her breath coming fast, misting the glass, before she pulled herself together and reached gently for the phone again. This time Saeed handed it to her and she dialed. Edward was home, and she told him what she could in a breaking choke of tears.

"I'll call the hospital now," he said. "Why didn't you stay with her?"

"I don't know." Maryam bent her head to her knees. All those years ago, none of her family had stayed with *her*.

Edward was waiting for them as the taxi drew up at the end of the path. He hugged Saeed gently and saw that his school blazer was ripped at the shoulder, and that there was a graze across his cheek. Maryam hurried past them both, her hands held before her like a blind woman's. She stumbled up the stairs and into her turquoise room, where she knelt on the floor by her dressing table and reached for the drawer beneath her mirror and its tumble of scarves inside, soft silks and cotton. She held them to her face and remembered her sisters' laughter and the noise of the bazaar. "I should never have left." She heard Edward's tread at the door and looked up, a dull ache in her temples.

He sank into the easy chair. "I called the hospital and Julian. She's going to be fine, Maryam, but she's lost the baby." His eyes glazed, focusing on the middle distance, hands in his lap. "Why?" He turned to face her and Maryam closed her eyes, fighting to hold herself still, to quell the tremor that tore silently through her veins and tendons.

"I don't know." She searched for some sense. "I've been so tired. Saeed has brought back so many memories, crushing memories, with his chatter and tears." She tipped her head back to stare at the ceiling. "Sometimes I wake in the night and, for a moment, I'm not sure where I am: here or there." Her eyes scanned the room, its careful decor, before resting on Edward's face, his pale blue eyes. "I wake from dreams and I think I'm in Mashhad or Mazareh, but I'm not. I'm here."

Edward bent forward and laid his finger across her lips. "Enough, Maryam."

She looked at him and struggled to remember some-

41

thing good: Sara teaching her to ride a bicycle when she had been about thirteen, running along behind her, their laughter in the spring breeze, May blossom fallen on the grass. "You can't do anything," Sara would half tease. "You can't ride a bike, play tennis, or make pancakes." Maryam would pinch her cheek playfully. "But, daughter of mine, I can ride a camel, beat you at backgammon, and eat watermelon with my bare hands."

In a way, they had learned English together. Her eyes settled on a photo of Sara as a toddler, one hot August when the three of them had driven to the seaside, with towels and a picnic hamper in the back of the car. They had stopped for a break in a lay-by beside a meadow. Sitting on the grass verge, Sara had pointed at things and Edward had said their names. Maryam had repeated them as well, also learning new words— swallow, barley, dragonfly, ladybird. She remembered lying on her side, taking the photo of Sara chasing a butterfly, her fingers outstretched. Edward had caught it for her and cupped it in his hands. It had opened and closed its wings, resting there, cornflower blue like a fallen, fluttering piece of sky.

"I wish I'd been a better mother," Maryam whispered.

"She's alive." Edward reached for her hand. "You did all you could."

Maryam didn't know if that was true. She just felt herself wrapped up in old knots that could only draw tighter.

• • •

Later that evening, Edward took Julian to the hospital. "Better you stay here for now," he had told Maryam before checking that Saeed was all right, quiet in his bedroom where he was painting again.

After Edward had gone, the house was silent and Maryam found herself crossing the dark landing to unlock the door to the loft. She trod slowly up the bare wooden stairs and switched on the electric light, kneeling to reach into the space behind a stack of rolled-up carpets and rugs. All alone, she pulled out a battered gray briefcase and sat on the dusty floorboards to undo the locks. It opened. On top was a layer of jewelry boxes, and she looked inside each one in turn. Beneath the cotton wool were rings from her father— turquoise, pearl, ruby, and gold—one for each year she had not seen him, always arriving around her birthday, until his death. All she had ever wanted was his forgiveness, but he hadn't spoken to her since the day he had banished her. *You are no longer my daughter.* She put her head in her hands and remembered going up into the loft with Sara when she was a child, how the rings had hung loose and heavy on her little girl's fingers. "I'm a Persian princess," Sara had said with a gap-toothed smile. Maryam turned the jewels in her hand. She didn't want to remember the price she had paid, or to think what the gems might mean if not an apology or a peace offering. Surely her father would not have mocked her with his gifts: a payment to stay away, out of sight. She would never know.

She remembered how Sara would call out from the loft's leaded-glass window, down to Edward cutting the grass around the apple trees below. "Hubble bubble mischief," she'd shout in her excited, fluting voice, and he'd blow her a kiss in reply, before calling back, "Mischief. Who planted all these damn poppies everywhere?"

Maryam wiped her cheek with her hand, her eyes swollen with crying. Beneath the jewels were Mara's letters, tissue-thin airmail paper and thick brown envelopes, yellowing at the edges, with stamps peeling away, the proud Shah and his peacock throne. She opened them carefully, taking out pressed flowers and knots of grass over forty years old, sent when her sister was still a child. Mara's chatty Farsi scribble ran across the pages, and it was as if Maryam could hear her voice again. She unfolded her sister's charcoal-and-pencil sketches, seeing again the outline of faces and places she had dreamed of her whole life.

She held the paper to her face, trying to breathe it in, as an autumn wind blew round the edges of the house. It moaned and she remembered the plains of Mazareh, her family's village, where she had spent her childhood summers. A large stone woman had stood in the red dust of the nearby foothills. It had always been there. As a young girl, she would rest her cheek against the cool stone and put her fingers in the holes chiseled through its face and torso where the wind breathed from across the barren hills.

"It's been too long," Maryam whispered, and from

44

beneath the letters and pictures she slid out a slim, faded red leather-bound book. Her fingers flicked its pages and the intervening years fell away. She could hear Ali's voice reading, his lips moving over the English words and lines—*The sea is calm tonight*—as they had once moved over her in the days before her life had first begun to fall apart. It was why she had come to England in the first place. She was still falling apart, she saw that now.

Her breath was heavy and ached in her chest as she closed the book and put Mara's drawings aside for Saeed. Slowly, she locked the jewels back in the briefcase and hid it again behind the pile of rugs. She turned off the light and made her way downstairs. In the sitting room, she sank onto the sofa and waited for Edward. He had never punished her, not once, she thought. He always made her feel safe. In a way, it was why she had married him. She looked at Sara's picture above the fireplace. "Now I've lost you, too." Her head sank back, her fingers running over each other. She fell into an exhausted sleep.

Hours later, Edward returned from the hospital to the silent, gray house. In the soft light of the sitting room, he took the book from Maryam's hand, remembering it from when they had first met. He stroked her hair from her face and fetched a duvet, tucking it over her shoulders before sitting on his own at last, in the dark. He cried.

In the end, he had failed. All those years of trying to hold her up through her nightmares and tears, the

45

places where she floundered and the past she could never fully share with him. In the early days, when they were just married, the bleak moments wouldn't last long: a few hours before she would reemerge, sweet and smiling, and he would hold her even closer. But it grew worse after the Revolution and her parents' deaths. Her collapses were less frequent, but deeper and darker. She would emerge from them in a daze, blank eyes wandering down to the garden, peering at him as if she scarcely knew him, flinching if he tried to touch her. Then finally it would pass. He always hoped each time would be the last.

"I'm sorry," she'd say, resting her head on his shoulder. "I fall over in the gaps."

"As long as you're still here." He'd kiss her forehead.

The next morning she talked of going back to Iran for a while, and he nodded, as gray as the dawn. "Whatever's right for you and Sara." He felt he could do no more.

And so they spun apart.

A week later, Maryam arrived in Tehran and stayed for a few nights with an old nursing friend, Parvin, in a tenement block at the foot of the Alborz Mountains. She woke each morning to the churn of riverwater beneath her window, an icy swirl of yellow leaves. She half told Parvin what had happened, and half just waited for time to catch up with her, as they sat with the cafetière on the table, watching the brown city awaken beneath the snow-capped mountains.

They remembered when they had been student nurses in Tehran with their smart white uniforms during the day and chic Western outfits in the evening.

"We had a party, didn't we?" Parvin smiled. "Although I think it was a shock for you, coming from Mashhad. You had never shown your ankles to anyone!"

"I grew up in a religious city and my family was strict. It wasn't easy to escape."

"You're not escaping from Edward now, are you?" Parvin teased, and Maryam shook her head, looking out to the green glow of a floodlit mosque in the distance, eerie in the dull light of early morning.

"I ran away *to* him," she answered. "I was running from something else: another life, or the idea of one. But still, it has been inside me all along, and now it has brought me back here."

A few days later, Maryam flew from Tehran to Mashhad, along the spine of mountains that ran across the north of the country, through the ancient province of Khorasan. There she stayed with Shirin, her niece, the daughter of her elder sister, Mairy. The last time Maryam had visited Mashhad, three years before, it had been to bury Mairy in the catacombs below the mosque at Haram, alongside their mother and father. Now Mara lay there as well: both her sisters, all the family of her childhood, dead and gone. Shirin was polite to her strange, foreign aunt, who was awkward and old-fashioned in her Iranian customs, her scarf forever slipping from her hair. "Don't whisper," she told

47

her sons as they peered from behind the door at the walking myth of their mother's and grandmother's tales.

Maryam left as soon as she could, bowing her thanks, away from the hush whenever she walked into a room, Shirin's smart friends looking up with their polite, quick smiles.

"A smile like a knife," she heard Fatima's voice whisper in her head.

"Welcome, Fatima," she whispered. "You were like a mother to me."

From Mashhad, Maryam set out on the last stretch of her journey to Mazareh. It was the first time she had returned to the village since she was a girl. As she sat in the taxi, she remembered the same trip from forty years before, when it had taken over an hour on horseback to reach the first foothills. Mashhad had been a provincial town then. Now it was a sprawling city, where cranes and construction work crawled up the gray slopes into the shadows cast by the hilltops. It was November, the month she had left.

The motorway stretched ahead between the hills to the open plains and mountains of Khorasan and the Turkmenistan and Afghan borders. Maryam stared into the bright light of the horizon and her eyes watered, as she carefully checked with her fingertips that the white cotton scarf still covered her hair. She had rejoiced at this journey as a child, her escape from Mashhad's strict rules and gossip for whole summers in the mountains, among the villagers who had farmed her family's land for generations. She watched the foothills approach, earth the color of amber, saffron, and ochre, and felt the home she had left in England recede far behind, with its neat hedges and lush lawns of overwhelming green.

They passed huddles of people at random fuel stops. Small, dirty children carried buckets of water and sponges to wipe red dust from the passing windshields. Trucks laden with sugar beet rolled by in clouds of grit. The horizon was blank save for an occasional brickworks or factory blowing black smoke into the white sky. When Maryam thought of Sara, which was most of the time, the roar of the bridge that day filled her head, along with the smell of her daughter's blood on her hands. "Forgive me," she whispered, a running chant in her mind, as she reached for the backpack Edward had given her for the journey. Inside she touched the spine of her book from the loft, as she had done many times since leaving London, remembering how its cover had once been red as berries, in the days when she had been young, when life had been redeemable.

As the taxi turned off the motorway, Maryam saw the fat outline of a Persian moon, yellow in the blue sky above the mountains. The road ahead was narrow, white and empty. She wound down the window and breathed in the silence, and the chill air from the snow-line. The taxi lurched over potholes as the dusk softened, pinpricks of light appearing in clusters as night fell. The car eventually reached a scratched sign by the side of the road: *Mazareh*. She had found it again, its mud and straw walls, its smell of sheep and rosewater.

The past brushed Maryam's skin and it was as if she saw her younger self, about sixteen years old, headstrong and restless, walking forward through the dusk and across the decades to welcome her: "Greetings, I am Maryam Mazar, and the seasons are changing." She had left behind that voice long ago. It had been 1953, the last time she had left Mazareh. She heard her lost world calling and opened her arms to the dead and gone and to a place called home.

I am Maryam Mazar and the seasons are changing. Snow coats the foothills outside Mazareh and the wind is biting. I am almost looking forward to returning to Mashhad. They will bring the sheep down from the summer pastures soon, and the place will smell of shit. Today I worked with Hassan, our new chief farmer, in the fields, pulling up sugar beet. I filled many baskets and my hands are rubbed raw. Hassan said they will not have me back in Mashhad, that I have become a peasant and lost my fine manners. Maybe it is so.

Later, we sat around the kerosene heater as the children played and laughed, chasing each other with the dead sheep's eye that rolled pupil-up in Hassan's soup. It made me think of the old house in Mashhad, the spying servants, the constant inspection—that everything is just so. I feel like an insect stuck in amber there, an old bee's wing trapped in honey. But still part of me longs to go back. I am ready for my books, for Ali to walk me to school and chaperon me home again, and for him to tell me everything he is learning as my father's assistant. He will test me on the Koran and we will learn clever poems to recite to each other. It will be winter here soon and they won't want another mouth to feed.

Tomorrow, Fatima arrives to prepare for my return to Mashhad. I have missed her over the summer. She has looked after me my entire life: I have grown up under her kitchen table, reading my books and listening to her chide and chatter with the maids.

Fatima's truck approached in a cloud of dust in the late afternoon. It heaved along the uneven track, twisting between the untidy honeycomb of straw-and-mud homes to the large square of hardened brown earth at the center of the village. It was full of children who had just finished school and were excited by the promise of a new visitor. They pushed and pulled each other, laughter and diesel fumes filling the air as Fatima climbed out and the truck groaned. It was good to feel her solid arms around me again.

"They are waiting for your cakes," I whispered as she watched the children jostle.

They shouted as she lifted her parcels from the back seat. We opened one on the ground, full of sweet cakes, pistachios, almonds, and honey. Then there was silent chewing and grinning as little brown hands helped themselves and the children sat on their haunches, stickiness all over their mouths and mine.

I smiled at Fatima. She took my chin in her hand and

shook her head. She said I looked like a boy with my red cheeks and sun-browned skin. "Your father will not be pleased," she teased, and held a finger up in mock warning. I pretended to bite it, which I think shocked her a little.

As we walked over to Hassan's house, where I have been staying, she said, "When will you grow up, Maryam?"

"When it means I can be free."

She has asked me this question for ever and I always give the same answer.

In many ways, she has helped me hide my growing up: binding my breasts so they do not show and washing the rags when I bleed, keeping it secret so that everyone thinks I am still a child. She has helped keep me safe for myself, as if I am her own daughter, and in some ways, I am.

I made her fresh tea, and as we sat and drank she told me the news from Mashhad. She said my father's new wife would have her baby soon and that we must pray for it to be a boy. I do not like Leila, the new wife, who lives in the main house that used to be our home; and I do not want another sister. I already have two, not counting the one who was dead when she was born.

When Fatima had rested, we walked slowly to the low slopes at the edge of the village. It was growing dark and the cold crept in with the shadows. We sat on the stony ground and I leaned against her, warm in our Afghan coats made from last year's sheepskins. "Tell me about my sisters," I asked. The three of us are threaded together by our blood and by the first letter of our names: the Mazar sisters, Mairy, Maryam, and Mara.

She spoke first of Mairy, who at nineteen is three years older than me, and already has three noisy children by our cousin Reza. At her birth, Mairy was put on Reza's knee as his future wife. I know this is not unusual, but I have always felt it must be a terrible thing to have your life decided moments after your first breath. Mara is my baby sister, and everyone's favorite. She is all freckles and curly hair and blows kisses in her sleep. Fatima says she is full of mischief. I cannot wait to see her again.

I asked about my mother and Fatima gave a sigh, which I know means she will not tell me everything. She does not need to tell me. It has been a long time since my father came to our part of the grounds to see my mother, his first wife. Fatima told me only that she overheard Aunt Soraya, my father's sister, telling my mother that she had grown to look like the Russian peasant she was born, and no wonder she is unwanted. I thought of my mother and tried to remember her being happy. I could not.

As I listened to Fatima and watched the stars fill the vast, darkening sky, I knew that I did not want any of their lives. I felt it in my belly, although I still do not know how my life may be different. I shed tears for them and for myself on Fatima's shoulder as she stroked my hair, and the sheepdog chains rattled nearby. It is a familiar sound that I will not hear again for many months.

The following morning, Ali arrived from Mashhad to take us home, and so the summer drew to an end. As soon as I awoke, Fatima set about preparing me for our return. She poured buckets of cold water over my head and scrubbed my skin; the water tasted of salt and earth. As I sat next to the kerosene heater to dry, she pulled the comb through knots in my hair. It had bleached auburn in the sun, which she thinks is bad. "You're like a peasant." She rubbed oil into my skin until the room stank of jasmine and I felt sick. "Quiet those stormy eyes." She held a finger up at me. "What's the worst that could happen?" She unfolded a pale blue chador from her bag and wrapped it round me and over my hair. When I went outside, the children pulled at it and laughed, but I could not chase them as I would normally have done. Hassan was different as well when he saw me dressed for home: he twisted his hat in his hands and would not look me in the eye. Just the other day we had picked sugar beet together, laughing, the plains stretching endlessly to a haze on the horizon where the mountains rise. I have heard him sing in the black and empty night by the open door, his bony farmer's hand against his face and his voice harsh but lyrical in the dark.

I was so pleased when Ali arrived. He brought me a book of English poetry and the pages smelled good. "Your father sent this for you." He bowed, glancing up through his fringe with a smile. I knew it wasn't true. He had smuggled it out for me, and for a moment we held each other's eyes.

In the early afternoon, we had our last lunch together, sitting on spread-out rugs in the courtyard of Hassan's home, his mother, sisters, Fatima, Ali, Hassan, and me. We ate mint and cheese wrapped in flat bread, still warm from the village kiln. As they talked, I leaned back against the wall and looked up at the pale blue sky. A cool autumn breeze breathed over us, carrying something sad from the mountains: a promise of rotting leaves and dried roots after the summer has gone. I watched Ali run his fingers over the crumbling brown earth. In the spring, saffron would grow there again, darkest purple petals and stamens the color of blood.

Afterwards, Ali asked quietly if there was time to visit his mother, and I nodded. His family has always lived in our village, although his father is long dead, and his mother now frail. I also wished to bid her farewell, with her silver hair and papery skin, and so in turn I asked Fatima if I might accompany him. She smiled her indulgence in a way that would not be permitted in Mashhad. She knew Ali may not see his mother again.

Their house lies in the middle of the village, through a wooden gate and across a small, bare courtyard where they keep chickens. The low afternoon sunshine filled the main room, and we sat cross-legged together, a stripe of light across the mud walls. His mother rested on cushions beside the samovar in a huddle of red and green patched blankets. Ali is her youngest son, and I watched him prepare her tea, her hand trembling to hold the glass as his sisters moved around us, carrying their children, nodding to me. His mother is Kurdish, and Ali has her once green eyes and golden skin. Sometimes I see the village girls look at him from behind their hands. They say he is lean and strong from having grown up on the farm before being sent to help my father in Mashhad. "You have such fine manners now," his sisters teased.

I smile in secret when I walk beside him here at Mazareh, where it is as if we are equals. It will change when we return to Mashhad and he is our servant again.

"I would like to hear you tell Maryam Mazar your story of the fireflies," his mother prompted softly, the smile of a girl still at the edges of her mouth.

"It's a foolish story,"—Ali reached for her hand— "but if it pleases you." He turned to me with a smile and something sad in his eyes. He began: "When I was a young boy, when my father was alive, I would work with him and my brothers in the fields. In the early evening, we'd irrigate our square of crops, letting water run through the channels that grew dry and dusty in the day. As my father pumped the water, I'd run from corner to corner of the field, making sure there were no blocks to its flow—no sleeping dogs or sly, thieving diversions. One night, our work complete, I lay on my back beneath a sky full of stars. When I sat up again and looked across the crops, it was as if I saw more stars growing from the earth we had watered. I touched my head to the ground and whispered a prayer, for I thought it was a miracle, and ran home. I called my father, who was washing the day's dirt from his hands, and to my mother to come and see the stars rising from the ground. As we stood on the field's edge, other villagers joined us, and my father tousled my hair. 'They come for you, Ali,' he said. 'Fireflies over the water.' 'And are stars fireflies over the sky?' I asked, and he pinched my cheeks and said maybe that was so. We fetched candles and left them in the earth to thank Allah for the fireflies, from wherever they might come."

He looked back at his mother and she brushed her hand against his cheek. "When you were young and your father was strong," she sighed, and we sat quietly together.

Later, as we prepared to leave, his mother took my hands and kissed each palm. "Look after each other, and may the world bring you both kindness and light." Her voice quavered, and I bent to kiss her hand as well.

"I will pray to see you when next summer comes."

She smiled and held her son's face against hers for a long while, tears in the corners of her eyes, before holding him back and bidding us both farewell. Ali's head was bowed as we left.

By the time we returned, Fatima had packed our provisions in the truck. She climbed in front, with Ali driving, and I sat in the back to look through the dusty window. The villagers fired shotguns in the air as we pulled away, and I watched the village recede for as long as I could. I knew how hard it would be to believe it had ever existed when we returned to Mashhad.

The journey from Mazareh takes about five hours. The roads are rough and herds of sheep can block the way, especially in the valleys at dusk when shepherds look for shelter for the night. I watched the shadows lengthen from the smooth-domed hills and took one last look at the vast plain stretching behind us to the Masjed Mountains and other distant countries. Lights from the villages came on slowly and clustered in bright, receding pinpricks in the dusk. I tried to remember the names of the mountains—Gossemarbart, Tomor, Shilehgoshad—and was rocked to sleep by the potholes, while warm air blew in from the engine.

It was late when we arrived at the high iron gates of my family home on the edge of Mashhad. Golam sat outside, as always of an evening, and rolled back the gates for us. He has worked for my father as long as I can remember, with no teeth and lines on his face like the valleys. We nodded at each other through the window as he closed and locked the gates behind us again.

Inside, my mother's and sisters' quarters were already dark, but a soft light shone from my father's study. The night was silent and the air smelled moist and fragrant after the dry plains of Mazareh. The paving stones and soil were wet from Golam's watering, sweeping, and tidying at the end of the day.

Fatima called me to come and have a hot drink in the kitchen with her before going to bed. I was half asleep from the journey as I crossed the grounds, but I still saw the hot, red glow of a cigarette above the bench beside the courtyard fountain, which was dry in readiness for the winter. My father stood in the shadows. I went to him and bowed my head, reaching out my hands to be taken in his. He bent to kiss me on each cheek, and I smiled, warm with his welcome.

"Maryam. So Ali has brought you home safely at last." He spoke quietly, and I met his eyes, hoping he did not mind my brown skin. "You will tell me your stories of the summer in days to come. I will call for you." He flicked the cigarette on to the wet ground and turned back to the house, his heels clicking on the paving stones.

Ali followed, turning to smile over his shoulder, the whites of his eyes vivid in the dark.

"Goodnight, Baba," I called and made my way to Fatima and her warm kitchen.

As always, it was as if I had never left.

School has not started yet, but Ali came this morning to help with my reading. We sat in the kitchen with Fatima. No one can understand us when we do not speak Farsi. I brought out the book of English poetry that he gave me in Mazareh. It is cherry red, with letters embossed on the cover, small enough to slip in the fold of my sleeve.

Ali read the first lines of a poem called "Dover Beach." He told me it is a place in England, near the sea, with white cliffs like a fortress. My father has always said Ali has a gift with languages. Sometimes I watch him in secret as he listens to the radio's foreign crackle, with a dictionary in his hand. I like to hear the strange English vowels in his voice when he reads aloud. This morning, I made him repeat the lines of the poem more than I needed, before I tried as well, practicing slowly. I like it when he corrects my pronunciation and we watch each other's mouths. We finished the first five lines.

The sea is calm to-night.
The tide is full, the moon lies fair
Upon the straits;—on the French coast the light
Gleams and is gone; the cliffs of England stand,
Glimmering and vast, out in the tranquil bay.

Last night I crept outside and slept on the roof. The long, dark corridors and closed doors give me bad dreams. On the roof, with enough blankets, I can pretend I am still in Mazareh. I prayed to the moon, which hung fat and white over my head. It must have been a bad thing to do as today has been difficult.

After I cleaned myself in the morning, I went to watch Fatima bake in the kitchen, slapping the flat bread to the inside of the kiln wall. The doorbell rang. Instead of waiting for the maid, which I should have done, I pulled my scarf over my hair and ran up the stairs and across the marble hallway. Nobody was there to see me. I opened the door and kept my eyes lowered. It was a young man in a cream suit and shiny brown shoes. He looked over my head and asked for my father. I know that he looked over my head because I have learned to see out of the corners of my eyes even when I am staring at the ground. He followed me to my father's study and I knocked gently until I heard his reply. Inside, the air was full of thick smoke spiraling to the ceiling. The man entered, and I was left outside to shut the door and hurry away.

Later in the afternoon, I was watching Mara chase lizards when my father sent for me. I looked at my reflection in the window to tidy myself as I walked back to the main house and his rooms. He was reading on low cushions by the samovar, and put down his paper before beckoning me to sit beside him. I could see Ali at a desk in the side room and wondered if he could hear us as I sat carefully and my father asked about the farm and my studies. I made him laugh and pinch my cheek with stories from the summer, as well as telling him about serious matters, like the village's need for a new water pump and that I hoped to stay at the head of my class when the term starts. I can see this makes him proud, even though maybe he wishes I were a boy. Sometimes I do, too.

He asked if I had talked to the young man from that morning and I protested I had not. He told me he was the son of a nearby merchant and landowner and—he spoke slowly—that he would like me for a wife. As he talked, I looked at the elaborate engraving on the samovar. I had first learned about blistering heat by touching the curling silver flowers and peacocks as a child.

"What do you think, Maryam?" he asked.

I brought a hand to my face, took a deep breath, and looked at him. It was hard to meet his eyes, so I turned my head and spoke to the table, saying that the man had looked straight past me and that he must be rather rude not even to look at me when he wants to marry me. This annoyed my father. He said it had been a sign of respect to avert his eyes, and that I knew it. I shook my head, a frown like a clamp on my brow as the room twisted around us. My skin grew clammy and I looked through the high window before turning my gaze back to my father. I felt trapped.

He put his hand on my arm. "Hush," he whispered, which steadied me for a moment. "You are young and full of nervous excitement. Think on it for a while."

As I got up to leave, he took my hand.

"Maryam, maybe it's time to put these childish ways behind you."

He made me feel ashamed and angry. I wanted to run but could not.

I sat quietly with Fatima until it was time for bed.

I have a new half brother, with a fat red face and black hair, born wailing into the dawn. His name is Shariar. My father is glad he has a son, and so am I if it means he will forget about me and the man with the shiny brown shoes, for a while at least. My mother just sits on the wall smoking her American cigarettes and swearing in Russian when she thinks no one is listening. She is tired.

Ali comes every day now and walks me to school. This morning we stopped next door at Aunt Soraya's and she gave us both nougat for the walk. She is my father's sister and on her third husband. The others died, but she is rich and finds wealthy suitors quickly. She likes to wear long black chadors made of the lightest, softest materials. "This is silk from Paris, Maryam," she says, "somewhere I doubt you will ever go." She likes Ali and pinches his cheek until it is red and white between her finger and thumb. "You're a lucky boy," she says, "to have that job with my brother. You should be tending sheep, and don't you forget it. I'm watching you, Ali." She wags her finger at him. "And you take care to walk two steps behind my niece when you take her to school. I see you two talking over your books. I don't miss a trick." This always makes me angry, but I never want her to see that I care.

Today, I thanked her for the nougat and Ali followed me on to the dusty street. "Two steps behind, mind you," I whispered softly over my shoulder. I kept my eyes to the ground for the rest of the road leading away from my family's house, past my grandmother's home, and I looked at the feet of my father's groom as he walked by in the opposite direction. We eventually came to the shortcut through the orchard where Ali keeps two paces behind but we talk quietly on our way, ducking under branches and over the rough, stony earth.

"What's the capital of France?" he asked.

"Paris, where I will never go."

"What's Nelson's Column?"

"You always have impossible questions, Ali. I don't know!"

He told me then about Trafalgar Square in London, and the statue of a sailor on a column that stretched into the sky. I said I wished I could read my father's books as freely as he did. I know he steals into the library when my father takes his afternoon nap. Ali has told me that my father doesn't read many of the books on the shelves, because Ali himself has to cut most of the pages open with a knife. We talked about all the books my father has received as presents.

"People want to impress him," I said, "to keep in favor."

"Or to get the hand of his clever daughter," replied Ali, which made me angry.

"Two paces behind," I snapped, and felt a little ill all day at the memory of it.

Fatima and I have been to pray at the tomb of her son. It would have been his birthday. Years ago, my father arranged for his burial in the catacombs at Haram, the mosque around which Mashhad has grown. It is one of the holiest sites after Mecca, and Fatima is proud he is buried there, but uneasy as well. She is a cook and something disturbs her about her baby's bones resting with the grand families of Khorasan. I lent her a beautiful chador that my mother no longer uses: black cotton with embroidered beads, shiny like lizards' eyes. We walked quickly together through the streets of the bazaar to where Haram rose up like a gold and turquoise fist, its dome punching through the dirt to the sky. It was busy, but we found a corner of earth near his tomb and Fatima knelt down in the dust, whispering her prayers. I stood beside her. When she got up, I put my cheek to hers, wet and smelling of figs and sweat.

Her baby is dead because of me. My mother was forbidden to nurse me and I was given to Fatima instead. I sucked her dry and her own baby died. When I found out years later, my father said that her son had been born weak anyway. I know that is not true. I killed him before I could walk. It was the first thing I did in my life. Fatima should hate me, but she loves me.

School has closed early for the last few days. The teachers told us that there have been protests far away in the streets of Tehran, and that we must go home in case the trouble spreads here, but I found the streets quiet as I wandered through the bazaar. Most of the stalls were already closed until the evening, and the goods had been covered with dusty tarpaulins and heavy canvas or padlocked into wooden chests piled against each other. The traders were drinking black coffee in small groups, or sleeping on mats in the shade.

One of the stalls belongs to Ehzat, Fatima's cousin, and she was just beginning to tidy away her sacks of herbs and spices: turmeric, tarragon, nutmeg, and cinnamon. I sat on her stool and listened to her hum and chatter half to herself and half to me. It was suddenly a warm afternoon, a lost summer day in late autumn, and I felt my eyes close as I listened to her talk about how this was her busiest time of year as families prepared to feast before Ramadan, and how she was still waiting for Fatima's orders. Between phrases, she clucked her tongue against the roof of her mouth, while shaking her head at me meaningfully. I tried to follow her gossip, but found my eyes wandering to the shadows and dogs sleeping in the shade, remembering fragments of English poetry. I swallowed a loud yawn and Ehzat clucked even more loudly and shook a paper bag of dried figs at me.

"Come on, daydreamer, take these home: some for your mother and some for Fatima."

I shook myself awake and thanked her. Her hands were warm but callused when I squeezed them goodbye.

I took the bag of dried figs to Fatima, who put them in a pale blue bowl and told me to take them through to my mother, promising to bring along some fresh tea. She told me off for my heavy sigh, and said I should be more dutiful about keeping my mother company, especially as I did it so rarely. I pulled a face, and she made to chase me with her tea towel, which made us both laugh so hard that we had to sit down and catch our breath.

I knocked on my mother's door, and entered when I heard her soft, whined *salaam*. She was sitting cross-legged on the floor in the corner of the room, sewing. Her lips were pursed and her eyes tightly focused on turning a hem for one of Mairy's children. I sat and waited for her to finish. The room smelled musty. It was her smell, like a cupboard of clothes that has not been opened for a long time. I listened to the birds outside in the trees, chasing each other noisily, as my breathing slowed. I was glad when Fatima bustled through the door with the tray of plates and cups rattling as she put it on the floor. My mother shook her head and looked up blankly as if she did not know who I was. I tried to smile into her vacant eyes.

"Maman, Ehzat sent these for you. She remembered they're your favorite." I pushed the bowl toward her and watched her pick out a single dried fig: hard and light brown on the outside; shriveled and red where it had split open and you could see the flesh inside. She put it in her mouth so her cheek stuck out and took a mouthful of tea.

The figs were sweet and chewy. Fatima and I took one each as well. We couldn't talk, but looked into our teacups, sucking and working our jaws noisily.

My mother asked about my lessons without looking at me, and I told her how the term had started well. She said that I must leave school soon, then surprised me by asking if I'd thought more about the marriage my father had proposed. I felt the air ebb away inside me. I hadn't expected him to tell her about it. I looked directly at her: tight, dry lines ringing her eyes, and the rash on her neck, not quite covered by her scarf, where she absent-mindedly scratched herself when she sat on the wall outside, like a bird that might blow away, sucking on cigarettes and no longer noticing anything.

"I don't want to get married and be like you or Mairy," I replied.

She put her hand to her face and stroked her eyebrows, then the raw skin on her neck. I chewed another fig and Fatima sat quietly in the corner, away from us.

"You don't want to be like her," my mother nodded at Fatima, "working to have a roof over your head."

I looked at the tight set of her lips. I could remember her singing to me when I was little, a soft voice barely more than a whisper. She would rock me to sleep.

"I'd like to have a profession," I said to the tea leaves in my cup, "like a nurse."

"Huh." She picked up her sewing again.

I finished my tea and looked over to Fatima, frowning that I wanted to leave. We stood and I leaned to kiss my mother good-bye, but she turned her face away.

"You'll see sense sooner or later," she said, to me or to herself, as we put the cups back on the tray and left the room.

"Why is she like that?" I said outside to Fatima, who hushed me and said she was just a little lonely and tired before her time. Deep inside I felt a barbed knot of sorrow for her, that she isn't happy; and for myself, that she is so far away from me.

This morning, Fatima sent me to visit my new half brother.

My father's second wife, Leila, was sitting up in bed. She is about the same age as Mairy, and has a red mouth and long, dark hair that curls over her shoulders when her head is bare, as it was today. The room was full of blue, early winter light, and she smiled at me with her wide brown eyes. I tried to smile back. She was rocking herself gently to and fro, with the baby wrapped in a blanket curled over her shoulder. I breathed in the creamy scent of milk as she lifted him up and away from her, fast asleep, with long eyelashes on his cheeks and a mouth as red as hers. She laid him gently beside her and stretched a hand out for me, pale against my tanned skin. She spoke quickly, quietly, about how little she had slept, how tired she felt, and how she missed her sisters. Her voice was unsteady although she laughed sometimes, her fingers fluttering about her face. I balanced on the edge of the bed and told her about school. She asked about Ali: "Your handsome English teacher," she said, with a light smile in her voice. I returned her gaze and said he was well, as were my lessons. I am sure my cheeks shot red, but she looked away through the window.

It was near lunchtime when we heard my father in the hallway outside. I stood as he entered. Almost without noticing Leila or me, he rested his hat on the foot of the bed and leaned over the sleeping baby, a hand on either side of the small, warm body. "Shariar, my son," he said to himself, while Leila and I waited quietly, her hand keeping hold of mine. He shook his head before approaching Leila and cupping the side of her face in his palm. Her cotton nightdress was damp with her milk, and she tried to cover herself, folding an arm across her breasts like a wing. "When will the wet nurse come and give me back my wife?" He patted her cheek. Before she could answer, he turned to me and I lifted my head. "You have a brother, Maryam, how about that?"

I met his eyes. "I'm glad you are happy," I replied. I thought of my mother on the other side of the grounds and how he must have come to her after the birth of her daughters: one, Mairy; two, dead; three, me; four, Mara. "I'll leave you to rest." I excused myself, easing my hand free of Leila's.

It was good to be outside. I sat on the steps and felt the winter cold in the ground.

"You have nowhere to go?" I heard Ali speak.

"Just thinking," I replied, tilting my head to look at him.

We heard a sound come from inside the house. It was my father's voice, and Ali smiled gently before turning away to walk back into the grounds. I watched him go into the bright daylight and blinked. His silhouette was etched black and white on the backs of my eyelids.

My father came out and rested his hand heavily on top of my head. "Walk to the gate with me, Maryam," he said. "Tell me the kitchen gossip."

I stood and brushed the step's grit from my clothes. "We were sent home from school yesterday, because of the trouble in Tehran," I began. "Will it come here, the trouble?"

He walked tall and straight, one hand holding the wrist of the other behind his back. He told me not to worry while telling me nothing at all. He said he hoped I would think less about the outside world, and more about my own future and marriage. I could not see why the two need be so separate.

Eventually we stood still, and he looked over my head to the gate that Golam was opening for him. Looking into his face, I wanted to grab both his arms and shake him, and insist that he look and see me. But he just pinched my cheek and said he hoped I would not disappoint him. I let him go. My eyes were weary, so I closed them and sank for a moment into comfortable blackness.

Later, I went to find Fatima and sat quietly in the kitchen helping her split beans.

Ehzat arrived in the late afternoon and sat on a low stool at the corner of the table, gently biting the side of her hand and watching Fatima move about her kitchen kingdom. Low sunbeams fell through the half-open door and cast long shadows on the hearth and tiled floor, scattered with fallen onion skins and coriander stems. A black cauldron of rice bubbled slowly and filled the air with soft, starchy warmth, while two chickens turned gold on the spit. I leaned on the table, my chin on my forearm, and pretended to read.

Ehzat and Fatima whispered and occasionally broke into swallowed laughter. Fatima would bend double, hands on her hips, while Ehzat covered her face and shook silently, before clucking loudly and pushing her scarf back behind her ears, from where it had fallen over her eyes.

They made me smile. I tried to imagine them as young

girls, sharing secrets and making mischief. I had heard the stories of their childhood all my life, but many of them seemed to change from one telling to the next, so it became impossible to know what was real and what was myth. Over the years, the story of the village chief with four wives changed so that he acquired several more, and at last count he had almost a dozen. The dappled cow that gave birth to twins one season now regularly produced quadruplets, while the woman cast out into the night for her sin grew to hold a far harsher fate. They had told me the story of this woman, Zohreh, as soon as I could sit still on Mairy's knee and listen, which was before I could talk. As we grew, we would hold on to Ehzat's hand and ask for the story about the wild girl. Ehzat would shake her head in resignation and fix us with her eyes. "Watch her fate is not yours," she would always begin, and Mairy and I would grasp each other in excited dread at what was to come.

Once upon a time, there had been a woman in the village where Fatima and Ehzat grew up whose entire family had died in an earthquake on the other side of the country. The ground had yawned open one night and swallowed them whole, grinding their bones into the bricks, dirt, mud, and mortar where generations had grown up and lived for as long as anyone could remember. The woman who had been left behind was so racked with grief that when she gave birth to the child she had been carrying, the baby girl was born deaf and dumb, as if to protect her from ever hearing or speaking of the horrors that had befallen her family.

"Little did they know . . ." Ehzat would say, and pause, looking into our wide eyes, before continuing.

The girl, Zohreh, grew up to be beautiful, with green eyes and black hair that slipped in ringlets from her scarf. Strangers to the village could not help but stare at her, and she would look at the ground until they turned away. Years passed, and she grew even more beautiful, but still she had no voice. While her face promised she would sing like a nightingale, the sound from her mouth was as dull and shapeless as the wind's moan. Her mother grew old with grief and eventually died from the sorrow inside her, and Zohreh was left on her own. She tried to ask for help from the neighboring villagers, but they could not understand the unformed sounds that came from her lips. She grew more wild with no one to care for her, and children began to run away whenever she approached.

One spring day, when the shoots of the trees were a sharp green, some women in the village noticed Zohreh's belly had begun to swell. As she was not married, and yet beautiful, as well as dumb, each of them was filled with envy, anger, and fear that it may be the result of her husband's complicity. They pushed and corraled Zohreh until she broke away and ran with tears and spit on her face straight to the head farmer. She fell at his feet. The village women had followed and looked at him, accusation in their eyes and "whore" on their lips. He looked down at Zohreh and up at the gathering; pity, lust, anger, and fear flickered across his eyes. He bent down and wrapped Zohreh's loose hair, smelling of rain, around his fist and pulled her up like a dog. She covered her face as he dragged her to the square in the center of the village and brought the first stone, whispering like the wind, down on her soft skin and bones.

In the beginning, when I was very young, Ehzat had let Zohreh escape to the hills, where she bore a beautiful blond and blue-eyed daughter. Once, Zohreh even conjured up an earthquake to swallow the village in revenge. But as I grew older, Zohreh escaped less lightly and her punishments became more severe. At the end of the tale, Mairy and I would sit with tear-streaked faces.

"So don't you be deaf or dumb to your parents' will," Ehzat would finish, wagging her bony finger at us in the dark kitchen.

"But she couldn't speak," I would protest with loud sobs.

"But what could she have said?" Fatima would try to soothe.

As I sat and watched her with Ehzat in the kitchen that evening, many years since the first storytelling, I still did not know the answer to her question.

Mairy's birthday approached and today she asked me to come to the bazaar with her to buy fabric for a new chador. It seemed a long time since we had been on our own together. She left her children with our mother, and soon after breakfast we wandered out of the house and grounds.

It was still early, bright and clear blue with dew like broken glass on the ground, the lingering cold night air blushing our cheeks. We had the whole morning before us, so instead of turning left into Mashhad, we turned right toward the edge of town and the first gentle foothills, squinting against the white light of the low rising sun.

An old man sat by the roadside with a wooden barrow of fruit, sucking his gums and waiting for the day to begin. Sweet orange clementines and gaudy red pomegranates balanced on top of fat watermelons, striped dark and lime green, one sliced open so its pink flesh and black seeds winked juicily. He cut a thin slice for each of us, and it was sweet and sticky on our faces and fingers. We bought a small bag of fruit, and set off smiling, bumping into each other and trying to wipe our fingers on each other's clothes.

As we left the last buildings behind, we began to walk slowly up the side of a low hill that overlooks the town. The ground was loose with gray-brown slate and dry thistles, and so we made our way carefully, catching hands when we lost balance. Our slipping laughter bounced off the stones and filled the crisp air, along with the shrill birdsong that swooped around us.

Partway up, we came to a large boulder, warm in the first heat of the day, and clambered on top with faint perspiration on our skin. We sat and looked out over the valley that cradles Mashhad to the snow-topped mountains beyond. Our breathing slowed and I yawned in the fresh air, while Mairy broke open a pomegranate and we picked out the translucent ruby seeds, letting the juice burst on the roofs of our mouths.

I asked Mairy what fabric she wanted to buy, and she replied that she would like enough to make new chadors for us both, although she said I should get the plainest material as I was so much prettier than her. I gave her a shove and told her not to talk nonsense. She laughed and said again, "But look at you, Maryam. You are beautiful." Then she pulled a long black strand of hair from my scarf and curled it round her finger. "You're the prettiest of us all. I have heard Father say so."

I looked at her and she leaned forward to kiss my cheek. "I would rather be plain and useful than pretty and ornamental," I replied, shaking my head.

She frowned and laughed at the same time and asked what I meant. I sucked on the pomegranate seeds and stuck my nail into the clementine's rind so juice sprayed into the air.

"Well, if I were plain," I continued, "people wouldn't assume that all I wanted was to marry, and they might find it easier to think I could be happy some other way."

"By doing what?" she asked.

"Teaching or nursing," I suggested.

She frowned again, more in bemusement. "But that's for old maids, Maryam, or if your family can't provide for you. We have everything we need."

"But do we have what we need, or know what we want? Or do we just do as we're told?" I asked. "Look at those mountains. Why can't we just go there one day and walk along the valley floor, all the way to Afghanistan? I'd like to sleep in the poppy fields."

"Maryam, you have nice daydreams"—she pinched my cheek—"but you know we can't leave the country without permission from our father or my husband."

I saw the weight of this bow her head. "But *you* dream too, don't you?" I asked.

She pulled a smile back on to her face. "No, I'm happy here, Maryam. I know the order of things. I feel safe. But it's all right for you to want something a little different. All I hope is that you don't get lost in your mountains and valleys. It would break Father's heart, you know that."

"But I wonder if I can be even the smallest bit different and not break his heart."

She didn't answer, and we leaned back on the rock. The sun grew warm on our faces and for a while we closed our eyes and dozed. When we opened them again, our mouths were dry and we stretched and finished the fruit before sliding off the rock and starting back toward town, where the bazaar would already be busy. As we made our way down the hill, I pointed to a strip of dry brown grass running like a carpet along part of the slope. "Look, Mairy." I pulled her hand. "Shall we roll down?"

She laughed. "No, it's hard. We'll get covered in dirt and bruises."

"Oh, come on." I was determined. "Nobody can see."

"Look at your eyes," she said, her voice catching the moment's glee. "The sun's gone to your head."

"Come on, please," I pleaded, but without waiting for her reply I lay down and pushed against the slope. The hill and sky spun round and round, brown and blue, earth and sun, and the smell of soil filled my lungs. The ground was hard and the stones stuck into me, but I laughed and groaned until I stopped spinning and lay on my back, panting into the sky, covered in dry grass with dirt under my nails. Mairy knocked into me then and we laughed so tears streamed from our eyes, and we had to hold ourselves to stop the ache of our bruises and delight, picking the dirt from each other's face.

Slowly we made our way back into town. The hill-rolling had shaken something loose, and Mairy started doing her impersonations of our household, which she hadn't done since before she was married, when we shared a room together. She stood in the bazaar, examining the various stalls and their goods like Leila, fluttering her eyelashes for a bargain; or like Fatima, clucking and complaining about the poor quality. I had my hand in my mouth to stop myself laughing aloud when I saw Aunt Soraya's maid, Ahmeneh, watching us. "Shush, Mairy," I whispered with a nod of my head. "She'll get us into trouble with her stories to Soraya." We both looked at her until she turned and left. I felt like I had eaten something sour and couldn't spit it out. Mairy rubbed my hand, and we linked arms and moved to the next stall.

"Let's buy something lovely for Fatima and Mara as well," I said, trying to shake Ahmeneh's stare from my mind.

"Yes, and Mother and Father, too."

"And Ali," I wanted to say, but did not.

Mairy smiled in front of the bolts of cloth, rolled up and falling over each other. She ran her fingers over the soft silks and cottons. We unfurled the lengths of fabric, laying them against our hands.

"You should have the rose, Maryam, it's your color," Mairy said.

"And you have the sapphire," I replied. "It will bring out the gray in your eyes."

We felt a childlike pleasure as the parcels were wrapped and handed into our arms: a buttercup yellow cotton for Mara, sea green silk for our mother, and a bright lime and pink fabric for Fatima.

"She'll say we're dressing her like an actress." I laughed.

For my father, we peered into the traders' hessian sacks and bought a small parcel of black tea twisted in knots and mixed with drying jasmine petals, white and yellow and scented like a summer night.

We made our way home, and I felt like I had flown high into the sky, above it all. We both did, and we hugged each other in the courtyard, agreeing to give Father his present together in the early evening. We returned to our separate rooms.

We met again in the kitchen at dusk and spun Fatima around in her lime green and pink fabric, her cheeks red with delight. She brought honeycomb from the larder, which she usually saved only for special occasions. We licked our fingers and watched the fire, as the room filled with the smell of baking.

Before the evening began, Mairy and I linked arms and made our way through the garden to our father's rooms. The air was sharp and cold. As it was still early, we thought he would be on his own, and so Mairy knocked lightly on the door and went in without waiting for a reply. We found the air inside already full of smoke, and walked around the pillar to find Father and two other men I did not know bent over the low coffee table. Ali was there too, sitting slightly apart.

Before we could retreat, our father looked up, impatient at the interruption. "What are you doing here?" he asked.

Mairy went forward with the jasmine tea while I hung back, Ali and I watching and yet not watching each other. "We went to the bazaar today, and brought you this gift," she said, and handed it to him with a smile.

He looked at the parcel, took a deep breath, and passed it to Ali. "Take care of this." His tone was abrupt, dismissive, and Ali looked down at his hands, his knuckles white, as my father turned his attention to me. "I see you have a new scarf, Maryam," he said, "like a pink butterfly." He talked as he would to a child, but it was before strangers, and I am not a child. I looked away.

"A present from me for my sister," Mairy replied. "But we're sorry to interrupt you. We should go. Good evening, Father, gentlemen, Ali." She led me outside, where I breathed deep and blew out the heavy smoke from my lungs. My hair and new chador stank of tobacco. "Are you all right?" she asked.

"I just need some air after that room." I tilted my head back to the stars, and threw my chador wide like a cape, before running the length of the courtyard, my hair falling loose over my face and shoulders.

"Stop it," Mairy whispered. "Cover yourself. There are strangers in the house."

"Just once more." I ran through the cold, clean night and felt my scalp tingle as my hair was lifted by the breeze. The tension fell away. As I ran back to Mairy, arms outspread, skipping over the cracks in the paving stones, I saw Ali step outside. I stumbled into her, covering myself again. She did not see Ali, and for a moment he held my gaze from over her shoulder, in the dark.

A day or so later, I was called back to my father's office. I arrived early and Ali opened the door. We both smiled before his face quickly grew serious again. He made to retreat to his desk in an alcove off the main room, a tight frown about his brow and eyes. I called after him that I hoped he had not forgotten my English lessons, which made him turn and smile again. We looked at each other's feet. He coughed and said that each day now felt like a game of chess, the country's affairs being as they were, but that he was learning much from my father. We had not spoken of politics before. Nobody spoke to me of such things, and I wanted to ask him more but was anxious about my father's return. I said I was glad, and we both fell silent, not sure what to say. He asked if I would like to wait for my father and showed me into the main study before bowing and leaving me alone.

I closed my eyes for a moment and breathed in the quiet order and solidity. The air was still and everything was in its place. There was a warm scent of newly waxed wood and I skimmed my hand along the side table, pausing at each of the framed photographs tilted there. A picture of my father with the Shah had pride of place. His army hat was pulled low over his dark eyebrows and deep-set eyes, still piercing in the brim's shadow. Another showed him robed in white on his return from Mecca, surrounded by our relatives and friends. It had been a wonderful feast. The women and children ate after the men, and even though I had been small, I remembered my father carrying platters of steaming basmati, gold with saffron, to serve me and my sisters. Then he had picked each of us up in front of everyone. I was so excited I cried, and Fatima had to carry me outside to calm down. My mother followed to see that I was all right, and I could still remember her soft smile and scent of lilies of the valley, from the time before his marriage to Leila. My favorite photograph showed Father in Mazareh in his casual clothes, sleeves rolled up in the heat. He was laughing among the villagers. I reached out to touch his face and my finger smudged the glass.

I wanted to be worthy of him, but not only through marriage. I hung my head, and closed my eyes, sensing his arrival moments before the door opened and he broke the silence. I turned to him, a little guilty at having been alone with his image and my thoughts. I knew he wanted to hear an acceptance of the wedding proposal, along with a smile and some gratitude for the arrangement so that he need worry no more about his troublesome middle daughter. He threw his coat across the desk and sat heavily in the armchair. I waited quietly until he looked up and sighed. "What news, Maryam?" He pressed his palms down on the table, staring at me for an answer.

I held his stare. "I'm glad you are well, Father." I cleared my throat. "I hope you know I want to do what's right for you and the family, but I think I should also do what's right for myself." His hands bunched into fists on the desk. "I have thought hard and would very much like to be a nurse, to train in Tehran. Then, I promise, I will come back and marry."

He leaned on the desk and stood up. "But you are the daughter of a general. Do you think you can go and clean up shit in a hospital ward?"

My hands clasped together. "And help people who are ill," I replied as he moved toward me.

"Maryam, you don't understand. The future isn't safe. You must marry."

From deep inside, I found a voice: "No, that isn't the only way."

For a moment I believed his face would crack into a smile, that he would throw his head back and laugh like in the photograph, recognizing my defiance as a gift of his own blood. He did not.

He took my shoulders tightly in his hands. "You would deny my will?"

"I will not marry that man."

"Why not, Maryam?"

"Because I don't know him and because I have yet to live myself."

He could not contest what I had said, and we both knew it for an instant, but it didn't last. "I will not listen to this nonsense anymore, Maryam." I felt his spit on my face before he raised his hand and slapped me, my head jerking to the side. "Get out." His ring had cut my lip.

I stared at him, lifting the edge of my sleeve to my mouth. A spot of blood spread on the white cotton. As I backed from the room, I held my father's gaze before turning to open the door. Ali remained hidden in his alcove, but he had heard everything and looked straight at me. My legs and hands began to tremble, but I shook my head as he made to come forward. He pressed his palms together, his eyes on mine, and strengthened by his stillness I managed to leave. I closed the door before sliding to the floor against the wall outside.

I do not know how much time passed until I rose and went looking for Fatima. She was hanging washing in the courtyard and I sat on the wall and watched the dripping water fall to the stony ground. She gave me oil of cloves to numb the pain in my mouth.

After a little while, Ali came with a gift of sherbet flavored with rosewater. My lip was swollen, but I could lick my finger and dip it in the paper bag to taste the sweet powder, with tears in my eyes. He taught me another line of our poem: *Come to the window, sweet is the night air*. It was good to sit together. The mosque's call filled the falling dusk.

In the days that followed my father's anger, an uneasy quiet settled over the house and town. The papers, whichever you chose to read, told of impending turmoil or triumph in Tehran. Fatima shook her head and said the bazaar and Haram breathed with a new discontent. My father's office grew busy with a stream of visitors deep into the night. I watched their reflections in the windows and listened to echoes across the courtyard.

Ali was away for much of this time on errands, or if he was around, he always seemed to be kept at bidding distance by my father. I tried to ask him questions with my eyes, but he shook his head and would not speak with me. "Have you not had trouble enough?" he whispered once under his breath. I knew he meant to protect me, but it still made me feel like a child, and as the days passed, a strange, watchful silence grew between us. It left an ache in my bones.

Fatima said it was all men's business, a vipers' nest, and that I should be glad to be out of it. I was not. I felt trapped, excluded and ignorant, with questions no one would hear. I thought often of Zohreh, the deaf and dumb girl in Ehzat's story, and wondered whether I would ever be permitted to use the voice with which I had been born.

• • •

A lone woman among the men who came to my father's rooms was Aunt Soraya. Her voice scratched along the marble corridors and through the thin night air. Wrapped in her black silks, with heavy kohl eyes, she watched the swirl of politics and sprinkled it with her own interests, or so I imagined. Lying in bed, waiting for the morning, I decided to try and speak with her.

After school the next day, I went straight to her house, carrying a small box of Fatima's sweet cakes. There was a low marble seat built into the wall in her garden, overhung with honeysuckle, and for a while I stopped and rested there, hidden from view. It seemed a long time since I had savored such stillness. I peered into the box of cakes and chose one for myself, letting the honey soak under my tongue. I would have liked to rest my head on my hands and sleep a little in the stir of the afternoon, but the clock chimed from inside Aunt Soraya's hallway. I wiped my mouth and winced. I'd forgotten the cut, still tender from my father's slap. As I walked along the gravel path, two black guard dogs growled and bared their teeth for an instant before recognizing me and sinking to their bellies on the ground. I bent to stroke them, resting my face against their smooth, soft flanks. They had sucked milk blindly from my fingers years ago when they first came from Mazareh. I left them lying in the sun and went to the door. The bell chimes were swallowed deep in the house.

The maid, Ahmeneh, answered. Her narrow eyes flickered from my head to my feet. She showed me into the reception room with its stretching carpets and formal chairs, upholstered with strange tapestries of women in wigs with bare throats. I knew that Aunt Soraya had brought Ali to this room and told him that bare skin is a French fashion called *décolleté*. I liked the sound of that word in my mouth, but did not understand how anyone could pray at Haram and then sit on these chairs. I balanced on the edge of one, and hoped that would not be so bad.

Aunt Soraya eventually approached with a rasp of gold bracelets and brush of suede shoes across the marble floor. I stood when she entered. Her eyes glittered as she offered me one cheek, then the other, and I kissed both dutifully. I handed her the box of cakes with a small smile and bow of my head. She lifted the lid and her mouth creased. She said it was sweet of Fatima to try so hard with her village recipes, and that one day she must come and learn from Ahmeneh to bake proper cakes, "patisserie," she called them. I looked at my hands folded in my lap.

We made some polite conversation about my family. She wanted to know what we thought about my father's new son. I told her we prayed that he would be handsome, brave, kind, and clever. She snorted at that, but I kept my eyes fixed on the embroidery of a powder white woman in a sky blue dress on a swing.

After a little while, I turned the conversation to the reason for my visit. I started by saying that school had closed early several times in the past month because of fears of unrest in the town. Then I mentioned that our house had grown suddenly full of strangers coming and going, visiting my father deep into the night. I said I could make no sense of it, and saw Aunt Soraya look at me thoughtfully, her head tilted to one side.

"So that's why you bring me cakes," she said with a smile, looking from the corner of her eye. Maybe I had learned to do that from her. "You are interested in politics and the ways of men. But no happiness lies that way. Iran is like you, Maryam, a beautiful virgin in the world, surrounded by suitors, and much may be won or lost in the choices that are made."

"But why must we choose at all?" I asked with desperation in my voice. She watched me, and for a moment I imagined she saw herself as she had once been.

Her mouth seemed to soften and she rested her hand with its gold and turquoise rings on mine. "We, Iran, you and I, are not strong. We cannot be alone in this world. We must choose one ally or another, one husband or another if we are to survive, let alone prosper." I stared at her long, pale fingers. "Iran has been made love to by London, Moscow, Washington, all in their turn. Each fears we may ally with another. The Americans don't want the Communists to take us to their bed." She smiled at my blush. "Come, Maryam, you aren't so innocent. You forget I too was once your age, with your beauty and curiosity." She laughed with a quick intake of breath. "Anyway, now the British have been thrown from our oil fields, and their revenge is to isolate us from the rest of the world, to boycott all trade, so that no one will buy our black gold. The wells at Abadan are rusty and creak like old men, and the coffers are nearly empty." She leaned forward. "Mossadeq has grown a sick old man whom the world mocks—the 'blanket prime minister,' they call him. We need a strong leader to make strong alliances and secure our place in this world." She raised her eyebrows in narrow black arches, and I returned her gaze.

"But what have Mashhad and my father to do with all this?"

She drew her hands back into her lap. "I will tell you a little, Maryam, and then you must ask no more questions, go home like a good girl and do your father's will. Do you promise?"

I looked at the floor, which she must have taken for consent.

"There are rumors that the Shah has allies who plan to topple Mossadeq. There are more rumors that there will be uprisings across the country. There are simmering pockets of unrest wherever you turn; people are troubled and unhappy. The nationalization of the oil fields hasn't changed their lives or set them free as they had hoped. The role of the army and where it places its loyalty will determine who is held to account, who wins and who loses." She paused. "Mashhad is an important religious bastion, you know that. So your father is kept busy these days. There is much to negotiate, and he's a powerful man."

I waited for more, but she stood and faced the window. When she looked back, her face was its usual distant mask. She walked forward and leaned to tap my lip with her finger, hard enough to hurt. "Maryam, don't be troublesome in these difficult times. Marry well and learn to be wily. You are wise enough."

I didn't know how to reply.

As she turned to leave, she knocked the box of Fatima's cakes from the table, and soft, sticky flakes of pastry fell to the floor. I knelt to pick them up.

"Leave it," she said from the door. "Stand up, girl. It's only good for animals."

I left the pastry on the ground. It felt like a betrayal, but I let myself out and ran home.

The cut on my mouth healed slowly, and left a purple bruise even after the scab fell from my lip. I heard nothing more from my father, and Ali remained distant. "It's for your own good," said Fatima, shaking her finger at me.

One afternoon I was talking with Mara in the courtyard in front of the main house, when our doctor emerged from my father's rooms. He was the only stranger who could easily approach and speak to us without a chaperon. He got down on one knee and gently asked Mara about the game she was playing. She said the stones were oil drums, and we were working out whether to trade them with the Russians or the Yanks. He raised an eyebrow at me, before noticing the bruise on my mouth. He asked if it hurt, and I shook my head. "Come to the surgery tomorrow morning," he said, "and I will make sure your brain hasn't been knocked loose as well." I smiled from behind my hand. It seemed a long time since anyone other than Fatima had shown me such kindness.

The next morning, Ali walked me to the clinic in the middle of Mashhad. Groups of men loitered in the bazaar, and the coffee shops were swollen and loud with argument. We walked quickly through it, and I whispered over my shoulder that I knew something of what was brewing from Aunt Soraya. Ali did not reply, and when we arrived at the clinic he avoided my eye and waited on the steps outside.

A fan ticked constantly over my head in Doctor Ahlavi's room, throwing shadows against the walls. He looked at my mouth and asked what had happened. I told him I had stumbled in the night and fallen against the door frame. He nodded, and asked whether my mouth was likely to get me into any worse trouble than a split lip. I whispered that I didn't understand. His frown knitted his eyebrows together, and then it all spilled out of me in a tumble of words and tears. I said I didn't care for trouble, but that I was tired of being spoken to as a child or treated as a chattel to marry, when all I wanted was to go to Tehran and train to be a nurse. He handed me a tissue and I tried to steady my breathing. His eyes were gentle but firm, and I grew quiet under his gaze. Then he spoke softly: "Show you can be an adult, Maryam, and people will treat you as one. Can you be trusted?"

I frowned at the question. Then he surprised me by asking if I would like to assist in his surgery, if my father would agree. I shook my head in disbelief. "Yes, of course," I answered, not quite believing what I had heard.

He stood then and shook my hand, which few men ever did, and said he would do his best, but no promises. He waited for me to leave, but I just stood there with my hand on my mouth. I felt as if he might disappear before me, this small man with kind, close-set eyes. "You can go now, Maryam," he prompted, and I shook myself, apologizing and thanking him several times as I backed from the room. His mustache twitched.

I told Ali my news as we walked back, and although he said little, I knew he was pleased, and perhaps glad that I did not bother him with other questions.

At home, I hurried to tell Fatima, and she looked happy and sad at the same time.

Two days later, my father sent a message that I should go to the surgery for a couple of afternoons each week after school. I was filled with new purpose. I wore a white uniform and felt neat and proud. I registered people's names and took care of their notes and the inventory of supplies. Doctor Ahlavi let me help him tend some of the younger children when they needed a cut or bite to be dressed or stitched. I watched his hands carefully, the delicate movements of his fingers on their flesh like a musician. I wiped the children's eyes if they

cried, and learned to dress and clean a wound, or prepare for an injection. Sometimes when I was concentrating, he would turn his head and remind me not to
hold my breath, as it would not help for his assistant to
faint. He was very kind.

A favorite part of my day grew to be the evening after
the surgery closed, when Doctor Ahlavi would tell me
what I had done well and where I needed to pay more
attention. His two small daughters would come with
his wife and play, taking turns to listen to each other's
heart with the stethoscope. I would bring in some of
Fatima's sweet cakes, and we would sit together on the
floor and eat them with strong black tea, while Doctor
Ahlavi ran through my duties for the next day.

One evening, Ali arrived early to walk me home
and I asked Doctor Ahlavi if he might join us rather
than wait on the steps outside. After a pause, he
nodded and brought Ali in, so we all sat together,
each speaking of our day without a care for the rest of
the world. It felt like one of those end-of-summer
afternoons in Mazareh that I never want to end,
willing the sun not to slip away and its warmth not to
creep into the shadows.

My father had granted me these moments, this
freedom, for which I was grateful, but I knew there
would be a price to pay. He hoped I would tire of my
nurse's uniform and soon come to his point of view. He
should have known me better than that. I expected him
to eventually bring it all to an end with another confrontation, but that was not so.

A few days later, Doctor Ahlavi told me I need not come in the next day, but promised to send word when he needed me again. I felt fragile walls crumbling around me, and asked if I had done something wrong. He made me sit down in his room and told me there was much trouble in the capital because of tension between the Prime Minister Mossadeq and the Shah. He said even the streets in Mashhad would not be safe until it was resolved. I asked what he thought would happen. He shook his head, said only Allah knew, and made me promise to heed his words and stay at home.

It was dark when I shut the surgery door and Ali rose from the step. I told him that I knew times of trouble were upon us. He met my gaze and we walked toward the bazaar side by side. The streets narrowed approaching the copper market, overhung with awnings that threw long, dark shadows. Near one of the popular coffeehouses, a brawl had broken out. We heard shouts and the sound of breaking glass and stray dogs, before a group of men piled round the corner in front of us. Ali took my arm above the elbow and we both felt the heat of the other's skin for the first time as we ran down an alley stinking of urine and shit. It wound away from the noise. At last, feeling safe again, we slowed to walk in silence, and Ali guided us back to the familiar road home before slipping into his place two steps behind.

I glanced over my shoulder. "You must be careful tomorrow, Ali. You must stay at home and teach me more of our poem. Do you promise?"

He said he would come in the morning.

I could not sleep and a fever broke across my skin. Everything was changing.

I woke with the mosque's call as I do every day, and this morning I wished to pray with my mother, but could not find her. Her maids were packing some of her clothes, and one of them told me, "Your father has ordered us to shut up the house for a few days. We must all prepare to leave town. They expect unrest in the streets and it won't be safe."

I went to find Fatima, my head aching with the clamor of the previous day. I had chewed my lip in a night of little sleep and dark dreams, and it was sore again. In the bustle of the kitchen, Fatima put her hand to my brow and told me to hold some ice to my lip. I sat still in the corner, watching the maids scurry over the flagstones, busy with their baking and packing of provisions, breads, and cold meats. I was jealous of their freedom and excited laughter, Fatima chiding in their wake. I put my head in my hands and felt a sinking sickness in my belly that only grew worse when Ali arrived. The unrest and upheaval would give my father every reason to insist I now marry.

Ali said he could not stay long as he was expected with provisions at the barracks. "No," I whispered, not wanting him to go. I took the book from my sleeve, and felt the fever rise again. I tried to watch him speak, his lips forming words in a growing blur: *Begin, and cease, and then again begin*. The room and its faces began to lurch in my mind. I felt heat behind my eyes, and could scarcely lift my hands, reaching for the table to hold myself upright as my head fell back. "Fatima," I heard him call, far away. I slid from the chair, his arm catching me as a dark sea flooded my eyes.

"Oh, Maryam," Fatima's voice echoed in my head. "Ali, you must take her to her sister's quarters. There's no one else and there's no time. They must look after her today and take her away from Mashhad." She rested her hand on my brow. "I can't take you with me, Maryam. It isn't fitting for you to come to my family. You shouldn't be so excitable. Ali, I hope this is just a young girl's faint. Hurry, one of the maids will accompany you and talk to her sister. Then come straight back for these provisions. Her father will be impatient in town." She stroked my hair from my face and I wanted to hold out my hand to her, to let me stay, but I could not.

Ali carried me like a dead creature, the weight of my body in his arms. I felt the warmth of his skin again. He and the maid must have laid me on my bed in the chaos, although I do not know if they spoke with my sister to let her know what had happened. Half awake, I only heard the maid tease and giggle with Ali. That made me cross and I crawled beneath the sheet, wanting to hide and disappear from the world. I fell into an uneasy sleep.

When I awoke, it was midafternoon and the house was silent. I lay quietly for a few minutes and watched the bars of light fall through the slatted shutters. There was a jug of water on the table by my bed and I filled a glass before swinging my feet to the floor. I was still feverish, and the cool terra-cotta tiles made me shiver. The water tasted of salt against my dry lips as I listened for familiar sounds—Mara laughing, Mairy's children fighting, servants walking across the courtyard—but it was quiet.

I dressed and slipped outside. The sky was a dull white but still hurt my eyes. I found the kitchen abandoned, with the floor half swept. When I called for Fatima, my voice was lost in the corridors. There was flat bread on the table and I folded it with some mint and cheese and stood in the silence, before anxious curiosity pulled me through the house, out through the front door and across the courtyard to the boundary wall. I stood at the barred gate that led to the street. It was bolted and padlocked from the outside. As I shook it, a truck rumbled past in a flurry of dust toward the center of town. It was full of people where there should have been livestock or crops. A few seconds later and two more trucks followed.

I was locked in. I realized everyone must have gone and left me behind, and so I headed back to my room and dressed in some old clothes and sandals. Then I made my way to the part of our boundary wall that backed on to a passage between our house and Aunt Soraya's. Thick ivy and vines roped across it, so it was easy to get a foothold and clamber over the top. I felt lightheaded when I dropped down on the other side. Thick spiderwebs caught on my clothes and I heard lizards scratching in the wall's crevices. I wiped my hands against each other and saw that Aunt Soraya's house was still too, with its shutters bolted from the inside.

I walked along the road with my head bowed like a peasant. More trucks passed and covered me with dust. As I came closer to the heart of the town, I heard shouting. Not one voice, but many. I hurried along the narrow road that Ali and I had used to escape the previous evening. Indistinct and angry chants carried in the dry wind with the raw trill of women's rage or grief. I pulled my scarf over my face, and rubbed the grit and smoke from my eyes.

The trickle of people hurrying past grew to a flood as I came closer to the bazaar. Mothers clutched their children, crying or wide-eyed at the clamor behind them. Looters carried what they could—carpets, radios, cloth—treading over watermelons smashed green and pink in the dirt. I was breathing fast and felt the crowd of bloodied clothes and kicking feet spin around me. I tried to steady myself but my arms reached out hopelessly. At last I pressed my back against a wall and tried to slow my breath, coughing with dirt and fear. I could smell acrid panic in my own sweat.

A small boy was screaming in the dust a few feet away, and I pushed forward to lift him in my arms. His weight and heaving chest somehow steadied me. The end of the passage was in sight, and it was easier to go forward than back. We reached the open ground of the bazaar, with its trampled awnings, overturned tables, and broken pottery shards sharp on the earth. The small boy and I huddled together in an alcove, his hot breath and tears against my neck, my hair pulled and clenched in his tight fists. Above the clamor, I heard the wail from the mosque pierce the late afternoon.

Then, from nowhere, Ali was beside me. "What are you doing?" he shouted, grabbing both my arms and pulling me to my feet, the small boy still gripping my neck. The bazaar spun. He took my hand and I followed blindly, holding on to the child. We ran through a twisted rat run of passages and alleys, the shouts gradually diminishing, and at last up a short flight of steep steps into a small, quiet room. Ali told me to stay there and then he immediately left.

The little boy had passed out exhausted in my arms, and I laid him down on a narrow couch. At last his face was still. There was a bowl of water and I gently wiped his skin before I washed myself and lay down on the couch as well, curled around him. I saw the room had no other doors, and was bare except for a thin rug on the floor, the couch, a kerosene heater, and a mattress rolled in the corner. For a while, I slept.

When I awoke, the room was lit with candles and the little boy was playing with some blocks of wood on the floor. Ali was sitting on his haunches on the other side of the room. I pulled my shawl close and sat up, blinking and trying to focus in the flickering light. The only sound was the whisper of rain outside.

"I must get home," I said at once.

Ali shook his head. "Not yet." He explained it was still dangerous in the streets, and my home was deserted anyway. My father had sent all the servants back to their villages. My sisters and mother had gone north to my brother-in-law's family, and my father had taken his new wife and son to the army barracks.

"I was left behind, on my own," I said.

"Maryam, you're always fighting to be on your own. You'd be the last one for them to worry about. Your sisters will think you are with Fatima, and she will think you're with them."

"But where am I?" I asked.

"My home," he answered, and in response to my fearful eyes he promised that nobody had seen me and that I'd be back before my father spread the news and my family returned the next day.

"What news?" I asked.

He said my father had received telegrams that afternoon: Mossadeq had fled and the Shah was on his way back from Rome. "Your father is pleased."

"But there were many people hurt today," I replied.

"That's the price of fighting for what you believe in."

"And what *does* my father believe in?"

Ali frowned. "Tradition, I suppose."

"In spite of all its blood and misery? It makes me feel so dirty, Ali, all this. As if we're trapped in the past and can't think for ourselves." I thought of the meetings he must have seen in my father's smoke-filled rooms, and regretted that the ash and dirt would work its way beneath his skin as well.

"But Maryam, what can you and I do?"

"I don't know," I answered, as we both thought of the day's turmoil.

Ali stood up to stretch then, and asked if I would mind if he washed. I shook my head and looked away, not wanting him to see me blush. I heard him pull his smock over his head and saw his reflection in the polished jug beside me, the gleam of his shoulders and back as he bent over the water I had used. When he finished, he asked if I was hungry and I nodded.

"What will happen to him?" I asked of the little boy.

Ali said he had sent a message to the child's father, who lived nearby. He would fetch him before the morning.

"I can't stay all night," I said quietly as the streets circled outside.

"If you'd been sensible, you wouldn't be here at all." The town was full of fighting men, he told me, trucked in from the countryside and looking for trouble. "You risk your life or worse if you go out there tonight."

"I'm sorry." He had already risked a great deal by sheltering me. I thought of the people who would enjoy rumors that dishonored my father's name. He had enemies enough.

Ali unfolded a cotton sheet on the floor for bread, cold meat, and cheese. He took a jug from the window ledge, and filled his cup with red liquid. "*Salamatee*," he said, raising it in truce.

"What is it?" I asked, kneeling opposite him.

"A little bad wine." He smiled and offered me the cup.

I hesitated before lifting it to my lips, smelling the yeast and grapes and tasting its rough sediment on my tongue. I wanted to spit it out, but swallowed and felt its gentle warmth in my throat. *"Salamatee."* I raised the glass as well, and handed it back to him.

The little boy had fallen asleep in the corner, and Ali tucked a blanket round him. We ate in silence as his sleeping breath rose and fell in the soft light. My eyes were weary, yet at the same time I was alert to any sound outside, and to Ali there with me. With a smile, he asked if I would like to practice the next verse of the poem. I told him I didn't have the book, but he said he knew it by heart and I could repeat after him. I was relieved to break the silence with our ritual, but an equal longing and fear crept over me as we held each other's gaze, our mouths forming new words, all alone:

The Sea of Faith
Was once, too, at the full and round the earth's shore
Lay like the folds of a bright girdle furl'd.

Our voices were low and we breathed each other's sounds as we spoke the looping words. He smiled when I asked what "girdle" meant and shook his head, saying it would be improper to tell me. I replied that there was nothing proper about our situation and we may as well make the most of it. He said it was a woman's garment like a belt worn against the skin. We whispered the words again and I thought of the call to prayer from the minaret at Haram, like a ribbon twisting and binding the town, silky and blood red.

The dishes lay empty between us. Ali filled the glass

again and handed it to me. I could hear sly muttering in the back of my mind, imagining what people would say if they could see me alone with this man, a servant of my father, whose family worked his land. I was afraid and defiant at the same time, and took the glass again.

"What would become of you, Ali, if my father walked in now?" I asked.

He looked up at me through his fringe. "He is far away," he replied.

You would be beaten in the dark. The thought stood silent in my mind.

"What do you want to do, Ali, with your life?"

He gave me no answer.

"You must want more than to serve my father. Don't you want to travel: to Paris, Trafalgar Square, and Dover Beach?"

His eyes were dark and the candles guttered. Our shadows crept round the walls as he spoke in his quiet, firm voice. "You're a naive girl, Maryam. You know nothing of my life or its choices."

I felt as if I had been slapped again, but met his stare. He told me how his mother and father had spent their lives in my family's village, how his brothers still farmed the land, and how Allah had smiled on him when he was brought to Mashhad to work for my father. He had been just a child and had longed for his own family and the air of Mazareh, but choked back his tears to make them proud of him. He had learned to make the honey-colored tea with jasmine petals that my father loved, to change charcoal in the hookah, to sweep the floor and sprinkle the carpet with rosewater, and to make sure the room was always warm enough, or cool enough. He had learned to dip pens in ink and practiced writing his name in sienna swirls on parchment. He had learned to write letters for my father, seal them with wax, and keep his accounts. He sat on the edge of my father's meetings, and when they were over and the guests had gone, my father would ask Ali's opinion and he would listen to it. There were anger and tears in his eyes as he told me all this.

"Your father has given me a world I never dreamed of. He has given me books and language and his trust. He even allows me to teach his daughter poetry, to sit next to you day after day. And now here you are, like a spoiled, lost child, and I protect you, and the price, Maryam, what could be the price I pay for giving you this protection? Everything." His skin was taut across his face and his veins blue-gray in his temples as his words sank between us.

I knelt and held out my hand to touch his face. He pushed it away.

"Ali." I spoke softly and reached again across the dirty plates. I laid my palm against his cheek and this time he pressed his hand on top of mine, hard against his skin, so that I thought we must brand each other. Then he pulled my face to his and I felt a peace roll over me as his mouth touched mine. I fell forward and he took my weight as the plates clattered to the side. The little boy stirred in the corner, his hands clutching the air, then returned to sleep.

"How did you find me today, Ali?" I asked.

He was watching the crowds from the rooftops, he said, carrying messages back and forth for my father. "I would not have missed your face."

I closed my eyes and held the peace for another moment. "My father will have missed you."

"No, it will be all right, Maryam." He said he had not been apart from my father for long, and that the day's outcome had already been decided. My father's attention was elsewhere.

I shook my head. My father has eyes everywhere.

His lips touched my cheeks, hair, mouth. "We haven't finished our poem," he whispered.

I put my fingers to his face as he spoke and felt a dark sorrow bleed within. I repeated the words after him, although I could hardly breathe:

But now I only hear
Its melancholy, long, withdrawing roar . . .

He pushed my head back and I felt his mouth on my throat, his hands pulling open my clothes. I tried to close my eyes against the black swirl of my mind, a memory of praying with my mother and Fatima holding me in her arms. They had left me behind, I thought, every single one of them.

Retreating to the breath
Of the night-wind.

My shoulders were bare, and he eased away the bandages, his lips on my skin. I shuddered as we lay against each other, pulling away as his hand moved down over my belly. I shook my head. "No, Ali." He held me close and we fell asleep as the rain poured in its torrent outside. If only that moment could have lasted, but slowly the room grew chill, silent with dark dreams, and I awoke wretched. None of this would be borne.

"I must go, Ali, now while it's dark," I pleaded, covering myself.

He urged me to be still, that it would look suspicious in the black night and it was still dangerous. We would go as the day broke. So we sat beside each other, waiting as the candles guttered and burned out.

At last dawn crept upon us. There was a hard rap on the door, and my breath left me like a blow. I cowered in a dark corner. But it was just the little boy's father, and Ali handed him out gently, still sleeping, through the scarcely open door. They exchanged few words. I had wanted to kiss the small boy goodbye. It already seemed a lifetime since I had picked him up from the mud. As the man's footsteps disappeared, Ali whispered, "Come, we must go now."

In the rain, the alleyways and roads had turned to mud, and dirt the color of dung flicked up against my bare shins as we walked. I kept my chin bent tightly against my chest and so noticed no one and nothing. We made our way through the orchard, and the smell of dew on the leaves made me want to cry. I did not look up as we passed Aunt Soraya's house, and I did not see Ahmeneh watching from the upstairs window as Ali unlocked the bolted gate to my home.

Inside the courtyard, I touched his hand but could not look him in the eye, and stumbled away without a word. I heard the gate close again and the bolts rasp shut. I was locked in again.

I knelt in the shower with my head on my knees as the water fell over me. Then I crawled to bed and waited for sleep.

I cannot fully remember the following hours and days. That morning, sleep closed over me like the waves of the sea and I plummeted down, any light on the surface fast and far receding from sight.

I awoke gripped with fever. The walls of the room heaved and ballooned as I shivered in my sweat, my tongue stuck to the roof of my mouth and my lips torn and tender. The house was silent, although I could scarcely hear with the thud of blood in my ears. I tried to call for Fatima but my voice was trapped in my belly and could not crawl into the air. I dropped my feet to the ground and stumbled outside. Sunlight pricked my eyes as I made my unsteady way to the kitchen. It was as if my mind rolled away from my body, lost in a thin line of ants, shiny black creatures crawling over rotten fruit. I heard noises as I approached. Some servants must have returned. I couldn't stop shaking. As I reached the threshold, my legs twisted and bent beneath me, and the world turned black.

I don't know how long it was before I heard fragments of voices: "Hush"; "Quiet." A cloth was passed over my body, in and out of its cracks and crevices. Then I felt the cool metal of a stethoscope beneath my breast, and a thermometer stabbed under my tongue. "Maryam, what have you done?" I heard Fatima click her tongue against the roof of her mouth. Humming. A brush passing through my hair.

Days passed and the edges of my body returned. I felt the rise and fall of my chest, the soft stroke of Mara's fingers on my cheek. I would lie against Fatima as she put morsels of food in my mouth: fresh bread, cheese, a slice of apple. The tastes burst on my tongue. I do not know how long it was before I opened my eyes again and saw the early evening light through the window. I lay still and watched the dust spiral. A cockerel crowed in the distance, and seemed to be answered from a minaret.

When the door scraped open, I saw Fatima. Her skin sagged gray and loose on her face, and her eyes were full of tears when she saw me look up from the pillow. I wanted to speak but she put a finger to my lips. She sat with me, stroking my hair until I slept again.

Doctor Ahlavi returned the following day and helped me sit up. He shone a bright light in my eyes, and took my temperature and pulse. I scarcely recognized my own body: the bones of my wrists and hands stuck through my skin as if it would rip. Fatima stayed in the room as he examined me. I stared blankly at him and he gently pinched my cheek. "I am waiting for you to come back to my surgery," he said. I smiled weakly and thought I heard Fatima say those days were gone.

No one else came to see me. Mara sometimes played quietly in the corner, but otherwise I was left with myself and the silence. After a day or two, Fatima began to share the kitchen gossip, although her large smile had shrunk to a flicker, and her familiar belly laugh, shaking her bosom and wobbling her neck, had gone. She avoided talking about the recent uprisings and it almost seemed as if they had never happened.

"And Ali?" I asked one afternoon, my strength returning.

"Ali has gone," was all she said.

In my memory, deep in my sinews and bones and blood, I felt a collapse that might never end. "Where?"

She told me not to worry and that we would talk more when I was stronger. I started to protest, but Fatima shook her head and insisted, "Be still." I lay back on the pillow as the turmoil of that evening ran again through my head. Part of me clung to the hope that he had gone to visit his family, or was on an errand, but deep down I recognized the finality of Fatima's words.

My father did not visit me.

A few days later, I was able to walk outside. The late autumn air was fresh and sharp after my sickroom. It was quiet in the courtyard and I sat with Fatima on the low wall of the pond that ran along the front of the house. "What has happened?" I asked. She shook her head, but then began, steeling herself. She started to explain.

The day I collapsed, Fatima had just returned to the house from her brother's home. She was checking the larder, she said, fond of its cool fullness; eggs and butter, cheese and cold meats stored on its shelves. She had heard a clamor in the kitchen, and hurried back, expecting the noise to be some foolishness or excitement among the maids after the tension of previous days. Instead, she saw me on the floor with a purple bruise already appearing on my cheek. I had been wearing only a nightdress, and my legs and arms were sprawled and bare where I had fallen. Fatima pushed back the huddle of servants and knelt beside me. My skin was chalky white, she said, clammy against the back of her hand, and beaded with sweat. She folded a tablecloth beneath my head, checking for blood from my ears, nose, and mouth, and covered me with a blanket.

A maid was sent running into town for Doctor Ahlavi. The streets had returned to some calm, but it still took him over an hour to arrive. He checked for any broken bones and told them it was safe to move me to my bed, before asking Fatima what had happened. Only then did she realize that I must have been alone the previous night, as my mother, sisters, and father had still not returned. But she hid her worry, and told Doctor Ahlavi I had been feverish for a few days, and that she had barely turned her back that morning before finding me collapsed on the floor. He was not entirely convinced, but Fatima made excuses about the distraction of recent days, saying that nobody was quite themselves. This seemed to satisfy him and he left instructions for her to tend me.

My family returned that afternoon, and Fatima said the house was busy, with windows thrown open, rooms swept and perfumed. I slept through the clatter of arrivals and cleaning. Fatima told me that each of the servants had a different tale to tell of the uprising. She herself had spent the time baking bread and sweet cakes for her brother's family, far from the storm. Others spoke of bands of men fanning out across the countryside, offering a week's pay to any villager who would go to Mashhad and march for the Shah. She said some men never came back and that the newspapers were reporting hundreds dead in pitched battles in Tehran.

Since the uprising, my father had spent nearly all his time at the barracks. He disappeared from the early hours until the depths of night. Fatima told me she would wake in the blue-black before dawn to prepare his breakfast of boiled eggs and bread, which she left on a tray outside his room. Ali had also been absent in those first few days of my illness, and Fatima had assumed my father was keeping him busy in the town.

"So we became a house of women," she sighed.

My father's two wives stayed distant at opposite ends of the grounds. Ramadan and its still calm of fasting rolled over the daytimes, broken only by the cries of the muezzin, waiting for dusk to eat again. Nobody, it seemed, wondered where I had been during the uprising. They were more concerned with my fever and, Fatima said, maybe all would have been well if it hadn't been for Aunt Soraya.

One evening, shortly after I had first fallen ill, Aunt Soraya had swirled into the house with her black chador floating and billowing in her wake. She made straight for my father's rooms. He was not home yet, but she was determined to wait, and summoned tea and nougat. The maid told Fatima that Soraya was pacing the room, rubbing her bony hands together with her mouth set tight, in a scowl or a grin she could not tell. She had hissed at the maid to get out, with a sheen of spit on her chin.

My father returned shortly afterwards, slamming the door shut. The maid crept back outside and heard his low voice reverberate through the heavy wooden door, and Soraya's rising response, shrill as knives being sharpened. Soon the door opened again and before Soraya left, the maid heard her whisper, "Brother dear, you must protect our name. Tolerate no shame."

I closed my eyes. Fatima asked if I wanted to tell her anything, but I shook my head. I thought of Ali's face, his dark eyes reflecting light back to me, his mouth showing me how to form words, how to taste each other. Fatima continued.

She said she had grown ever more troubled by the maid's report of Soraya's indignation. So the next day, after she had tended to me, she made her way to the kitchen door of my aunt's house with an empty clay honey pot and a basket of fabric from the bazaar. Ahmeneh was mixing flour and water to bake bread.

Fatima greeted her from the threshold and Ahmeneh responded with her thin smile. Fatima entered then and stood beside the table, scattered with broken eggshells. She put down the pot and sighed that she had run out of honey, what with making me hot drinks to calm the fever, and that she would be most grateful to borrow some spoonfuls to tide her over until the next day's market trip.

Ahmeneh fetched and poured out some amber honey, marbled with bees' wings and broken torsos. When she had finished, Fatima suggested they should have some tea and Ahmeneh brought out two small glasses, filling them from the samovar on the stove. Fatima said she drank her tea loudly through a sugar cube, and only when she had finished did she look Ahmeneh in the eye and ask her directly if she had any household gossip to share. She said she would not put up with malicious rumors, at which Ahmeneh hunched her narrow shoulders and sucked on the air like a fish. Fatima's impersonation made me smile.

Fatima knew Ahmeneh might need a little persuasion, and so she leaned forward to place the creamy silk fabric from the bazaar on the table. It was embroidered with shiny thread and pearly sequins. Ahmeneh brushed the eggshells away with the back of her hand to clear a space. She touched the material with the tips of her fingers, and Fatima whispered that she would put the other women in Haram, even Soraya, to shame if she prayed in a chador so fine, so sophisticated, so French. Ahmeneh tried to pick it up, but Fatima pinned it firmly to the table with her elbow. The two women smiled at each other before Ahmeneh sighed and fetched more tea from the samovar. She began her story.

The morning after the protests, she had been standing at an upstairs window, watching skeins of smoke drifting up from the riot's debris, when she saw Ali and what appeared to be a peasant woman walking along the road. She had just released the dogs into the courtyard as they had been locked in the house for the night. The dogs recognized and ignored Ali but growled at his cowled companion, until the woman held out her hand, turning briefly toward Soraya's house as she did so. At the precise moment when the dogs had recognized the woman's smell, Ahmeneh told Fatima she had clearly seen my face. She watched Ali unlock the door into the grounds and saw us both disappear inside before Ali came out alone a minute or so later. Of course, Ahmeneh concluded, she had told her mistress as soon as she returned home, as she had only my safekeeping and the family's good name in mind.

Fatima said she threw the fabric in Ahmeneh's lap and left without a word.

Then she asked if I still had nothing to say.

I took hold of Fatima's hands in mine. "I will tell you what happened that night and then you will help me speak to Ali."

Her face perspired. "No, Maryam. It's too much. Ali has suffered enough."

"I must see him. You know that." I looked at her,

tears spilling down my face. "What has happened to him, Fatima?"

"What were you doing?" she whispered. "The fire burns you like anybody else, the sea drowns you, sickness makes you weak."

"I know," I answered. "But you should trust me not to burn myself, know that I won't hold my hand too close to the flame. Please don't listen to rumor or gossip."

She cupped my cheek in her palm. "I believe you, Maryam, but rumor casts long shadows."

"If you believe me, help me. Tell me what has happened, how I can see Ali and if I can calm my father's anger." I held my head in my hands.

"Very well, let me tell you about Ali." She began again.

After she had spoken to Ahmeneh, she returned home before setting out to find him. She took bread and cheese, but there was no answer when she called at his home. She was about to leave when she heard a noise inside, soft like an animal. She lifted the latch and tried to push open the door. The bolt had not been completely closed and so she nudged it easily aside. Ali was lying on the ground with his face turned to the wall. He made no movement as she knelt beside him, his hand curled against his cheek. She slowly lifted it away and his body flinched. His hair was matted with blood.

"I could hardly make out his eyes," she whispered, "swollen and blind. His hand was like a claw, curled up on itself, and black with dried blood." My mind grew heavy, sinking with her words. "I left him and went straight to the pharmacy to get spirit and salt for his cuts and arnica for the bruises. I fetched water and trickled it between his lips, split open like ripe fruit. His clothes stank of sweat, urine, and blood. I undressed him and found some clean sheets, tearing one to soak with spirit. He had a gash at the top of one thigh so deep that I could put my fingers inside. I returned day after day, and so my hours were filled with caring for you both."

I sat still. A thin crescent moon had appeared in the blue sky. My ribs were taut and it seemed as if my breathing had stopped. "My father's men," was all I said.

That night, I lay in bed and thought of Ali. I tried to remember all the times we had spent together. I had known him all my life. My body was still weak from the illness but my mind grew sharp and clear as I thought of the next day. Time passed slowly, but I was used to being left alone and thankful for it. I slept little and sat up with the gray morning, to dress slowly and wait for Fatima to bring me breakfast. The black crows cawed coarse and loud from the treetops and I was glad when the door grazed open and Fatima pushed her way inside.

"You're still not yourself." She rested her hand on my brow.

"I'm fine," I said quietly. "Fatima, has Ali seen Doctor Ahlavi? He needs proper care, you know that.

And I need to see the doctor as well." She shook her head. "Please, Fatima, arrange for us both to see Doctor Ahlavi later today."

She placed some bread and black tea beside me. "I will take you to the doctor in a few hours, but then ask me no more. What would I do if your father or Soraya challenges me? I have no other life to go to, Maryam." She left the room with her head bowed.

The sun was high when she returned, carrying a woollen shawl to wrap round my shoulders. We left by a side entrance and walked slowly. I was still light-headed and felt as if my body might float away without Fatima's sturdy arm round my waist. The fallen leaves in the orchard crunched under our feet, and the bare branches looked like bones reaching into the sky. A single apple hung high up on a bough, yellow and pink and out of reach. I thought of how Ali would have shaken it down for me.

The surgery was quiet when we arrived, with only a small queue. Fatima helped me up the steps and we waited to be called by Doctor Ahlavi's new assistant. I sat facing the main door, willing it to open. Time passed. Fatima avoided my eyes. My turn came and we both made to stand, but I put my hand on her shoulder and said I would prefer to go in alone. I turned away before she could protest.

Doctor Ahlavi's door swung shut and I sat in one of the chairs as he finished his notes, the fan throwing its familiar shadows around the walls. I waited until he was ready. When he looked up, I was glad to see his kind eyes again. He smiled and said he was pleased to see me and asked how I felt. I said I was much better, but there was something I needed to ask him. He suggested we talk while he carried out a few tests. So I took a deep breath and began.

"I have a difficult problem with my family," I said, "especially my father." He shone a bright light in one ear, tilted my head to a different angle, and made a listening noise. "It's difficult for me to talk about." He shone the light in my other ear. "There's been a misunderstanding." He looked in one eye, then the other. I felt my pupils contract to pinpoints and could not go on.

He leaned back against his desk. "Yes, Maryam?" he encouraged, reaching for his stethoscope.

"Well, I think my father believes I spent the night with a man." The fan ticked in silence. "I didn't, Doctor, not in the way he believes."

Then I briefly told him about the day of the uprising, how Ali had given me shelter when the streets were dangerous. I did not tell him all about the caresses, which I knew had been wrong, but were still far from the sin my father suspected. As I talked, I tried to remain calm, but I could feel a chill sweat on the back of my neck and I noticed the doctor staring at my hands, which were clutched in my lap.

"Doctor, you have been good to me. My father respects you. Please talk to him and tell him my story. I'm afraid of what he will do. I haven't seen Ali since that night, and Fatima tells me he has been badly beaten. I know it's the work of my father's men." I tried to control my breath, which had grown quick and shallow. The doctor felt my pulse, and rested his other hand on my forehead. Its touch brought a kind of stillness that spilled tears down my cheeks.

"Maryam," he said in his gentle voice, "I have known your family all my life. I respect you all, and believe I can trust you to have told me the truth. I can speak to your father, but what then? You know the only peace you can bring him is through marriage. If I speak to him, will you be content to marry and put this trouble behind you?"

He put his stethoscope in his ears, made me lean forward, and tapped my back, listening to my breathing. I sat upright and he put the stethoscope beneath my shirt.

"What are these bandages?" he asked.

My head was bowed and curtained by hair. He lifted my chin so I had to look at him.

"I always wear them," I said, "to look like a girl." He continued to stare at me and I held his gaze. "I don't want to marry like my sister," I explained. "I still want to go to Tehran, to train as a nurse. I don't know if that will be possible now, if I should give up hope."

He walked to the window and stared outside for a little while. At last, he turned back. "Well, you are getting better," he said, "and I will speak to your father. But you must be sensible, Maryam. Be realistic."

I nodded, tidied myself, and stood to thank him. As I made to leave, with my hand on the door, I turned back to him. "Doctor, I have one other request. I believe Ali is coming to see you today. I had hoped to see him here. Please take good care of him, and give him my kind wishes." But he didn't look up and so I slipped from the room.

Fatima and I walked back down the steps to the road, and at last I saw Ali in the distance. He had a walking stick and pulled himself along, shuffling and slow, but as soon as he looked up, our eyes flew to each other. Fatima tightened her arm round my waist. "You shouldn't talk to him," she said, "not here in the street. Just walk by."

It seemed as if the world roared around us, and we walked through it, thunder in our blood and bones. His eyes were still swollen and his face badly bruised. I wanted to run to him, hold his head in my lap, kiss his eyes, and stroke him to sleep. We stopped in front of each other and he looked at the ground. I reached into Fatima's basket for the red book of poems, and gently placed it in one of his hands, which closed, bruised and bandaged, round the spine.

"I'm so sorry, Ali," I breathed as Fatima pulled me away. I looked over my shoulder as we turned the corner, and he was still standing there, looking at the ground. I felt as if the wind should tear me into the sky, as if I should breathe out and be no more. But I put one foot in front of the other and returned home through the dust.

The next morning I did not go to the kitchen for breakfast, or wait for Fatima, but joined Mairy and her children, Mara and my mother. They sat around the edges of a white cotton cloth in the center of the room, and Mairy made space for me beside herself. She handed me a glass of tea on a white saucer with pink roses painted round the edge. It had been one of her wedding presents. I reached for some bread and cheese. My hands felt unsteady, but they were still when I looked at them.

Mairy stroked my cheek with the back of her hand and told me she was glad I was getting better. Shirin, her smallest child, nearly two, sat nearby. I dipped my finger in honey and put it in her mouth. She smiled back, and rested her fingers lightly on my lips. I felt tears in my eyes. Her mouth moved trying to find its first words. When she had finished with me, she crawled on her mother's lap and pulled at her top. From the corner of my eye, I saw Mairy slip her chador and cotton top aside and Shirin became silent as she took the fat brown nipple, somehow so separate from Mairy, in her mouth. The warm glass of tea felt good in my hands, but a chill fever still lingered in my bones.

"What's in your tea leaves?" asked Mairy, with delicate creases round her eyes.

I smiled with her at the memory of times spent in the kitchen with Fatima, telling our fortunes. When I had finished my tea, I turned the glass upside down to drain onto the dish of pink roses.

Mairy picked it up and hummed softly as she gazed into the glass, looking for shapes and stories in the residue. "I see a horse leaping over a steep hill, and as it leaps into the air, many hopes and wishes and dreams are thrown into the sky as well. You will overcome, Maryam, and have what you desire."

"I need your good fortune, Mairy, more than you know."

"I know," she whispered back.

"Let me see." My mother reached for the glass. I watched her face, lined and sallow. "Mairy is telling you stories, Maryam. There is no horse. I see you faced by a person holding a heavy stick, and you have no protection but a speck of dirt, all that your hopes have become."

I held my sister's hand, and could hear Shirin panting and sucking at her breast again. I tried to ignore my mother's words and looked out through the window, where the sky was white and I could see seedpods on the tree beyond. The pods were translucent and pale, each encasing a black seed like the pupil of an eye or a tadpole.

"Mairy," I said, "shall we go to Haram tonight? I'd like to pray. I've been unwell for so long."

"Yes, of course."

So I thanked her for breakfast and left the room, without glancing at my mother.

Fatima was waiting outside. "Your father has sent for you," she said. Her face was full of anxiety and oily sweat. "Doctor Ahlavi is with him. You must go now."

I nodded and straightened myself, making sure my hair was covered, my chador held tight around me. Fatima breathed hard as we crossed the courtyard together.

"Don't worry," I said, managing to smile. "Mairy has read my tea leaves and all will be well."

Fatima looked sad and angry, but then she began to laugh, tears falling down her face. She sat on the wall and I took both her hands.

"I can go on my own. You stay here. Tonight, Mairy and I are going to Haram to pray. You must come too." She nodded. "All will be well." I freed my hands and walked briskly to my father's door.

I knocked and went in. My father had his back to me as I entered and did not turn round. Doctor Ahlavi was beside him and came forward with a gentle smile. The white marble stretched all around us. I felt still and small like a butterfly inside the shell of my body, wings shut in a sliver of black edges.

Doctor Ahlavi gestured for me to sit down. The room was so quiet. I picked up a small cushion and held it on my knee. It was white with animals and flowers embroidered in dark blue thread. Fatima had made it. I remembered her hands stitching during a picnic under the trees by the spring outside Mazareh, years ago. I wrapped my arms around it.

Doctor Ahlavi started to speak, and his voice filled the room. "Your father and I have spoken about the rumors," he said. "He knows you have explanations, Maryam, but you must realize damage has been done to your family's name and honor. Do you understand?"

I took a deep breath, the butterfly inside me slowly opening and closing its wings.

"Your father is deeply disappointed, Maryam,"

Doctor Ahlavi continued. "He cannot look on you as a daughter anymore. This can no longer be your home."

I stared at my father's back and beyond him to the flood of white light through the windows. It would snow soon.

Doctor Ahlavi said he had spoken to my father about how I could make a good nurse one day, and told him he could seek a training position for me at the new hospital in Tehran. "He has agreed, but with one condition: that you are examined to establish if you are still a virgin."

So it had come to this. I shivered and spoke quietly to my father's back. "And if I am a virgin, I can stay here?"

Doctor Ahlavi replied for him. "No, the damage is done. If you are a virgin, you must still go but you can do as you wish, train as a nurse."

"But if I'm a virgin, I'm innocent. You will tell him I am innocent." Blood rushed to my cheeks, and the butterfly fluttered its wings, hoping for space. But I couldn't move and my fingers grasped the cushion tight. Its tiny blue stitches caught under my nails.

"Maryam, I will not do the test. Your father will have you taken to the barracks, and the military doctor will see you later this morning."

"Why must it be a stranger? You wouldn't lie." I spoke to my father's turned back. "You would have the hands of a strange man, a soldier, touch me? It is forbidden." I walked across the floor and looked into his face, close enough to see each dark pore with its spot of stubble. "You don't mean this," I whispered. He refused to look at me. "You don't care if I'm a virgin. You do this to humiliate me."

"As you have humiliated me." His voice was calm and firm and full of anger. "I am a general in the Shah's army. My world will be as I decree. You will do as you are told."

I turned back to the doctor and touched the sleeve of his jacket. I saw my hands were pale, bloodless, as if they no longer belonged to me. "Help me. This isn't right."

He could not return my gaze and walked toward the window. "The hospital in Tehran is the finest in the country." He spoke in a strained voice, now with his back to me as well. "The courtyard has a square of tall, dark green African grasses, and the breeze whispers through them. A stream from the Alborz Mountains runs beneath the hospital entrance and the water is as cold as ice. The nurses wear white, like angels, as you will, Maryam, I promise." He turned and looked at me and I started to cry, frightened and alone. "Come, let's go," he said. "Your father has a car waiting outside."

"She can go by herself," my father snapped, almost a sneer.

"No. I will take her." The doctor met his stare.

"So be it," he replied. "She is no daughter of mine."

As we left, I hid my face in Doctor Ahlavi's coat like a small child who closes her eyes and believes herself invisible to the world. "Don't let Fatima see me," I pleaded. I could not bear to see her, or to be seen like this.

The jeep was waiting in the street and stank of cigarettes. I sat in the back with the doctor. The roads were rough and we shook against each other for the whole journey.

"Was this the only way?" I asked through my tears.

"Your father is a proud man, Maryam. There is no place in his life for compassion. His enemies would destroy him." He took my chin in his hand. "Today he wishes you hadn't been born to shame him, to betray his trust and his name. He must restore his dignity and show that he will brook no weakness—not even from his own blood. You know that." He raised his voice above the noise of the engine, the air full of diesel fumes. "This is how it has always been, for generations. But a part of him still prizes you and he won't discard you entirely." Somehow we shared a smile. "He will let you live a life, your life, even if it is far away from here. Do you understand?"

I gave a single nod as we drove into the compound. There were men everywhere, their boots crunching on the ground and their laughter loud like barking dogs. My hands were cold and greasy as we walked from the jeep and I was glad when we entered one of the buildings, then turned off an echoing corridor into a quiet white room. There were no windows and the fluorescent light whined. An examination bed stood in the center, covered with a paper sheet. The room smelled of linoleum and disinfectant, and a little of what had been cleaned away. There were footsteps outside and then three men in khaki uniform entered. One of them, a thin, tall man, changed into a white coat and washed his hands. The water in the basin sounded like nails on a blackboard, razor blades on metal.

"Come on, Maryam, let's get this over with." Doctor Ahlavi helped me to my feet. "Go behind that screen and remove your underclothes. Then lie on the bed."

"I can't," I said. "I can't move." I could taste blood inside my cheek.

"Can you send the soldiers away?" Doctor Ahlavi asked the man in white, who shook his head. "Maryam," said Doctor Ahlavi, turning my back to them and kneeling before me, "think of those African grasses and the white uniform waiting for you." I could smell his breath, his face was so close to mine. "Now hold my shoulders and I'll help you undress. I'm here. Send your mind to Tehran."

I closed my eyes and somehow knew that something in me was about to die. One of the soldiers pushed Doctor Ahlavi back aginst the wall, and I sent my mind somewhere else.

When I opened my eyes a little later, I found myself at home. Fatima was stroking my hair. "So you're going to Tehran." She smiled, although her eyes were red.

I looked at the dark gray strands of hair that had fallen from her scarf, her amber eyes, and her apple cheeks traced with thin red veins. I nodded, but didn't know what to say. She sighed and I imagined the air rushing between our bodies.

"Come." She patted my hand. "We must get ready for

Haram. Mairy will meet us by the gate." She went to prepare herself and left me alone.

I sat up and felt as if there had been an earthquake in my bones, just newly quiet, the dust settling over the torn cracks and crevices. I swung my feet to the floor and went to wash my face in the bowl of water Fatima had left by the door. I cleaned beneath my arms, my breasts, and at last between my legs. I was sore and bleeding, and retched as I leaned over the bowl. Afterwards, I looked at my reflection in the small mirror on the wall, at my straight black eyebrows and firm mouth, hazel brown eyes staring back. My horror was nowhere to be seen. I smiled, to see that I still could, although I was shaking inside. I pulled a dark chador over my head.

In the courtyard, I walked toward Mairy, and my feet seemed to push the earth away with each step. She was clutching her hands together, her eyes and face red and blotched with tears. I put my palm against her cheek and kissed her mouth. "You read the tea leaves well, my sister." She held me away from her and bowed her head. "No more of this," I said. "No more tears. Come, let's go and pray together while we can." Then I smiled, a numb smile.

Fatima joined us, and I walked ahead of her and Mairy into the street. The sky was a dusty blue and a full moon hung over the town, with Venus bright below it and Mars in the foreground. The air was full of the muezzin's echo. We passed Aunt Soraya's house and it seemed small; the dogs were asleep by the dry fountain. I thought of Ahmeneh somewhere inside, fingering the French silk she would never be brave enough to wear.

The branches in the orchard were quiet against the sky, the solitary gold apple still hanging fat and out of reach. "Wait," I called to Mairy and Fatima, hitching my chador over my knees. I pulled myself up to the lowest branch and shook the tree with my whole aching body. The apple fell to the ground. It was waxy in my hand, a mellow yellow and brown close up, smelling of summer.

"You should tie grass as well," Fatima said, "and make a wish."

"What for?" I asked. "Not for a husband."

"Why not for a safe journey, free from the evil eye?"

"That would be a good wish." I knelt by a clump of wiry brown grass and looped the stems in a knot where they grew. I felt empty inside and tried to think of the tall, lizard green African grasses that waited for me in Tehran.

Then I was gone.

In the taxi, decades later, Maryam looked at the backs of her hands, their thick veins and soft freckled liver spots, and closed her eyes. A day or so after she had tied grass and prayed with Fatima and Mairy, she left Mashhad behind. She had seen Ali one last time at Ehzat's home. They had sat quietly together, their fingers tracing the grain on the tabletop.

"We have one more verse," Maryam had said,

looking at his face, its healing cuts and bruises.

"That can wait for next time. You take care of the book until then." Ali had reached across and placed it in her hand.

Now, a lifetime later, she lifted the book to her face and breathed in its memories: Fatima, long dead and gone; Ali, when he was young; and the kitchen where she had grown up among saffron and coriander.

The taxi turned down the dirt track and the village lights grew bright in the blackness of the plains.

"Where will you go, Ali?" Maryam had asked all those years ago.

"To Mazareh, of course, and wait for you to come and find me again."

3. Ghosts

If only this long road had an end,
And in the track of a hundred thousand years, out
of the heart of dust
Hope sprang again like greenness.
                                        —Omar Khayyám

*T*he clouds lingered low, bruised and heavy over London. They seemed to suffocate the city, trapping the warm, polluted air above the streets. It sank through the open windows, leaving a trail of black grime and grit on the sills and curtains. It was November and the seasons had grown confused.

It was a week or so after Julian had left, and I had an

appointment with my doctor in Brook Green. I woke early and showered, the heat pummeling the back of my neck and down between my shoulder blades. I soaped myself, my father's broad feet and heavy bones, my mother's long, slim hands, soft skin, and dark hair. In the warm wetness, I closed my eyes and wondered who my baby would have looked like. I still had a scan tucked in my diary. I had watched the screen, the flickering black-and-white image, curved back like a comma with soft, swimming limbs, and a small black eye that gazed out like a creature from the deep, from inside me—a full stop.

Afterwards, I sat on the edge of the bath and combed my hair, long black strands crisscrossing my skin. Sunbeams shone low and intense beneath the purple clouds and the light picked up dust and dirt smeared everywhere. I bowed my head and felt again that I didn't know where to begin, my mother's words in my mind—*If I was weak, I was punished. It made me strong.* I reached for the same clothes I had worn the day before, piled on the floor where they had fallen.

Downstairs, Creswell nosed at the kitchen door. "Coming, coming." I spoke to the empty hall, going through to kneel on the cold tiles and stroke him good morning. I put on the kettle and opened the door to the garden. Sitting on the step, I pondered how Julian was doing in New York and imagined him asleep in his hotel room, overlooking Central Park. I ran my hands over the lavender and rosemary bushes by the door and breathed in their scent. "Like burying your face in dirt and pine needles," my mother had once said, teaching me to smoke a hookah in the garden. "No, like dirt and roses," I'd answered, balancing embers on the crumbling tobacco.

Storm clouds grew dark and humid over Hammersmith.

"Come on, rain," I whispered.

Creswell waited at the foot of the stairs as I got ready in slow false starts, nothing where it should be. At last I opened the front door and we walked out, one step at a time, into the midmorning where orange-brown leaves still clung to the plane trees. We passed the parade of shops with all its familiar faces, the Japanese girl smiling through the flower-shop window with her bright yellow broom and a quick, shy wave. We made our way beneath the railway arches as the Tube rattled overhead to Shepherd's Bush, Notting Hill, the City, and Creswell tugged me across Brook Green. The bag lady was alone for a change, sitting on the bench, a fag in one hand and the other twisting her hair. For a moment, our eyes met. "Spare some change, love?" she asked, but I shook my head and turned away.

In a few minutes I came to the surgery, in a ramshackle Victorian house set back from the road. I tied Creswell's lead to the railing and went inside. Dr. Wood's room was up winding stairs overhung with spider plants at the rear of the building. She was a small, wiry woman with short gray hair, and bright blue eyes that softened as I sat down. Not long ago, she had told me I was pregnant.

"Come now," she said in her gentle Scottish accent, "this won't take long. Go behind the screen and slip off your clothes."

She continued to talk as I undressed, saying she'd spoken to the doctor at the hospital. I eased onto the bed, rustling its sheet of white paper before she came round and gently laid her cool hands on me. *Empty.* I stared at the unfamiliar ceiling and ornate cornicing, and tried to think of nothing, feeling spoiled and hopeless. After a minute or so, she handed back my clothes and quietly patted one of my hands. "It will be all right, Sara."

"Will we be able to try again?" I asked. "For a baby?" My voice caught in my throat.

"In good time. Now dress yourself and come out when you're ready."

She left and I swung my legs from the bed. I hadn't eaten breakfast, and silvery stars flickered in my eyes.

"You need to give yourself time to recover," she said as I sat opposite her desk. "How are you coping?"

"A day at a time." I looked through the window. "I don't need to go back to work until I'm ready. My school's organized a supply teacher for the rest of term."

"Good, good." She nodded, her fingers pressed in a pyramid. "If you need advice, you know we're here. Come back in a week or so. You're doing fine."

I thanked her and with a deep breath pulled myself together, too weakly, and left. I struggled with the walk back, slipping round the edges of a bleak, barren pit inside. It wrung tears from my eyes. Home at last, I sank to the floor at the foot of the stairs and cried. I missed Julian. Time passed with Creswell curled at my feet, and the rasp of traffic outside.

I wiped my eyes and went into the kitchen. I sat and rested my cheek against the cool grain of the table, gazing at the wall, trying to stare my way through the savage pinpricks of pain and self-pity. I chewed the skin round my thumbnail and slowly slowed down. My eyes traced the mushroom-colored wall, the clock, the charm against the evil eye above the door, its scrapes and smudges. The wall was about ten feet high and twelve feet wide. I'll paint it; the thought came into my mind, somehow lightening me.

I rubbed my eyes and went to the phone. My father picked it up almost at once. "I could do with some company." I tried to sound less thin than I felt, relaxing at his voice and the promise of apple pie. "See you for tea, then."

The taxi driver had turned off the engine and Maryam sat still, looking at the yellow light beams tracing across the uneven earth to the outer mud walls of Mazareh. The silence was vast. She had forgotten such silence existed, broken only by the rub of animal flanks and the chains that tethered them, skimming the night like a flint over water. She held a hand against her cheek, her reflection half visible in the windshield. For a moment she wondered what Edward was doing, if he would remember to water her plants, but then she opened the door and pushed her journey-stiff body to stand and look around. An eternity of nothing, it seemed, a sinking, whispering peace like the bottom of the ocean. The sky domed above, black stretching for ever, and she turned where she stood in the flickering light of the car door. She wondered if she was really there, what she was doing. Should she not be with Sara? She climbed back inside. The taxi driver muttered under his breath, thinking of the many hours' drive back to Mashhad.

"What now?" Maryam whispered.

"*Khonoom,* madam," he sighed, looking ahead. "You've come a long way. You say this is your heart's home. What have you to decide?"

Maryam looked out at the yellow beams from the headlights again. In the summer, they would have been full of mosquitoes and moths battering against each other. A night for eating watermelon, juice running between her fingers, red and sweet on her hands. After all these years, she felt how old she had grown.

"Here, madam, let me help you with your bags."

The driver went round to the trunk and Maryam stood again, looking for constellations Edward had taught her: the Plough maybe. She could not quite recognize any of them. But I can see Mars and Venus, she thought, as the driver coughed, dropping her few bags on the dusty earth. They stood staring at each other until she shook herself and remembered to pay him.

"Should I arrange to collect you?" he asked, getting back in the car.

"No, not for now." She looked again at the sky. "I don't know how long I'll stay."

He watched her, standing there, head bent back to the night. "So long—*Khooda'hafez Khonoom,*" he called through the window, and she watched him go, lights lurching into the blackness.

She rubbed her face and sank down on one of the bags, closing her eyes to listen to the breeze and the tumble of dust on the plain. "Are you here, Fatima?" she whispered. "This would be a good place to haunt." As if in reply, a gust caught at her clothes and her cotton scarf, and Maryam lifted her face, half searching for Fatima's scent of figs on the air. "I've stood on pavements in London thinking you'd just passed," she said to the night, "only to find myself beneath a fig tree overhanging a garden wall." Her fingers skimmed the ground and the quiet hush of the plains welcomed her. "Forgive me," she whispered to any listening god. "I couldn't stay away my entire life." She lifted a handful of soil and let it blow through her fingers as the quiet settled again around the sweeping curve of Mazareh's outer wall, a soft light brimming within like a promise. She brushed the last of the dust from her hands and made to stand as two young boys stepped from the shadows.

"*Salaam,*" she called, wiping her face on her cuff.

They came carefully toward her. "*Khonoom,* are you well?"

"Better for seeing you young gentlemen," she said with a smile. "Please help me. I'm staying with the chief farmer here, Hassan Taymorey. Would you take me to his home? I am Maryam Mazar."

The drive to Richmond a few hours later was slow: the traffic crawled along the wide avenues of Chiswick and Kew, dust motes and sycamore seeds spinning from the trees and peppering the windscreen. It was good to wind up Richmond Hill at last, the dark river curling away on the flood meadows below. At my parents' house, Dad opened the door in a hallway filled with the scent of cinnamon and cloves.

"Come in. Keep us company." He hugged me. "Saeed's upstairs in his room if you want to go and fetch him. I'll put the kettle on."

I hung my coat on the banister and walked upstairs to the landing. The oak door to my mother's turquoise room was closed, and I went across to open it and look inside. It was cool in the half-light from the window. I felt the ache of her absence and entered, putting on the desk lamp. I sat there with her photos on the wall and tilted in frames: me growing up; her family in Iran, faces I had never met; and a small black-and-white passport photo of her as a young woman wearing a chador, porcelain skin and jet black eyebrows. She must have been twenty or so, about the age she first came to England.

My father always carried two of exactly the same photo in his wallet, side by side, as if she were keeping herself company. I used to think it had been taken in Iran, but it was a different story she'd tell, slightly embarrassed, of how it had been taken in the King's Road in the late fifties. She had needed a photo for her new Iranian passport, and had hurried through the autumn traffic, but forgotten her headscarf. The photographer had lent her one of his blackout sheets, wrapping it round her long hair like a shiny cloak. It gleamed in the picture. She was beautiful, but there was something sad in her eyes. "It's my trick photo," she used to say. "It makes me look somewhere I'm not."

I turned off the light and sat there for a moment in the dark, feeling the cut of a sharp edge behind my breastbone, my own loss. I wondered if that was what I had seen in her eyes: a longing for something broken or gone. I stood up and crossed the landing to Saeed's room and knocked gently. I hadn't seen him since the day on the bridge. He peered round the edge of the door.

"Hello," he said, a little shy. "I've been painting."

We went to stand by his desk beneath the window, and I looked at the still-glistening paint, the domes at Haram, gold and saffron in the night.

"It's good," I said, and he smiled. "I went there once, when I was about six. We used to go to Mashhad every summer before the Revolution. Fatima would look after me. Do you remember her?"

He shook his head. "She died before I was born. But I've heard about her."

"When I went to Haram, Fatima dressed me in a primrose yellow chador. It was light, like muslin or chiffon, with multicolored polka dots all over it, and I wore a pair of pomegranate red flip-flops. Can you imagine?"

We looked through the window, dusk falling. I had felt like a butterfly, chasing through the dust after my mother's swirl of black silks. It was one of my earliest memories. She had cried aloud in the mosque, tears that had left me feeling bewildered, not understanding, and wanting to go home. I still didn't understand.

"Sara," Saeed whispered. "I'm sorry I hurt you on the bridge. I feel very bad. Are you better now?" His voice trembled.

I was taken aback and sat on the chair by the desk. "Saeed, you mustn't think that was your fault." I took both his hands. "I've been better, but I'm all right. I'm sorry about what happened to you, that you were hurt too."

"My maman looked well at first, even when she wasn't."

"I know, but I'm not ill like that, I promise." He blinked back tears. "Anyway, tell me, how's school?"

He stared through the window again. "Uncle Edward says I don't need to go anymore. I'm starting somewhere new next term, so I've a long holiday now." A smile broke across his face. "I've been watching Laurel and Hardy videos." He rubbed the top of his head like Stan Laurel, raising his eyebrows and pulling a confused face.

I laughed. "Come on then, let's go and have some apple pie if you're hungry."

He nodded and tidied his paints away before we turned off the light and made our way across the dark landing.

"I'm going to paint a wall in my kitchen," I said as we started down the stairs. "I think saffron, the color in your painting. Would you like to help? You could do stencils."

He nodded as we entered the kitchen and my father put our tea on the table.

"Any news from Maman?" I asked as we sat down.

"Not directly." He shook his head. "I know she's gone to Mazareh, that village of hers. It's only got one phone, but I spoke to Shirin last night, you know her niece in Mashhad." I nodded. "You know Maryam's not been to Mazareh since she was a girl." We both looked into our teacups, trying to imagine it: the time, place, and distance. "But how are you, Sara?"

I shrugged. "All right."

"Surviving without Julian?"

"Just about." I watched him cut the apple pie into slices, carefully lifting them on to our plates. It was sharp and sweet. "Delicious."

He winked at Saeed, who grinned up through his fringe. "It's good to have an extra pair of hands in the garden. Your mother usually loves it out there at this time of year, stoking those bonfires of hers." We both smiled at the memory: ashes on her face and headscarf tied tight against the wind. "I was just thinking the other day how some of our best times have been in that garden. Remember when we caught the rabbit in the gooseberry bushes?" He laughed, a little too loud. "I flushed it out with the hosepipe and Maryam jumped on it with a blanket. What a sight! And those summers in the seventies when her sisters would visit: barbecues and dancing on the patio—like our own little slice of Iran in the back garden." He sighed, sipping his tea.

"She'll be back soon, Dad."

"Yes. And will you be ready to see her?"

I looked through the window, where the dried heads of hydrangeas nodded like waiting guests.

"I don't know yet."

He took off his glasses and rubbed his eyes. "I keep thinking how things got worse for Maryam after the Revolution, when her family couldn't come and go so freely. We stopped visiting Iran ourselves; it just didn't feel safe after all those hostage crises. It was as if she stopped getting the right mix of oxygen."

I remembered her tears in front of the nine o'clock news: lopsided bodies hanged, dangling and dead, from towering cranes in Mashhad. Her half brother, Shariar, had been one of them, dragged from his home. She would shudder in the quiet after we turned off the television, and my father would bring her a glass of brandy. I would watch them both, sitting side by side on the sofa, his head bowed and her face tipped back, looking into the light. "That's not my Iran," she would say, remembering the images of men beating themselves with chains, bloodied shirts on their backs.

"We know," my father would soothe.

"What do you know?" she'd say angrily, and search his

eyes. "It's my family back there. Thank God my father's dead. They'd rip him to shreds too, not just his son."

"Please don't be sad, Maman. Please don't be cross." I'd lean against the arm of her chair and she'd pull me on to her lap and bury her face in my hair.

"Poor Shariar," she'd whisper. She'd watched the news less and less, and would wander upstairs instead to her study and photos from the past.

Now I reached to squeeze my father's hand. "Anyway," I said, "tell me about Saeed's new school. What have you got planned?"

I listened to them talk, Saeed asking more questions. He wanted to learn how to pass a rugby ball, and my father promised to give him lessons in the park. Slowly we finished eating and the day caught up with us.

"I should be getting home," I said, feeling tired and pushing back my chair. "I'll come by again in a day or so. Saeed's going to help me paint my kitchen wall."

My father stood as well and ruffled Saeed's hair. "That sounds good."

He walked outside with me to the car. On the black-and-white path, we turned to look up at the dark window of Maman's room. I half expected the light to spring on across the turquoise walls and for her to gaze out and wave good-bye. This is what it would be like if she were dead and gone, I thought: just the two of us and her memory. We hugged good-bye as a gust of wind blew through the fir trees, lifting their lemon scent into the purple storm clouds overhead. I felt a drop of rain as I climbed in the car.

142

"Looks like it's going to break," I called as my father turned back to the house.

Maryam followed the two boys along the rutted track to Mazareh. Soft sounds carried through the cool air as they drew closer: the lilt of a voice through a half-open door, hidden from view; a child's laughter. The two boys carried her bags, lopsided with their weight, and Maryam reached out to trace the contours of the mud wall beside them, feeling the dirt trap beneath her nails. She knew tears ran from the corners of her eyes.

Ahead of her, a cobalt blue door opened in the dark wall, a slice of light in the night, filled by Hassan's silhouette, grown sturdy with the years. Maryam could see his face before he saw her, his thick jacket worn over layers of jumpers and heavy trousers patched and baggy at the knees. She remembered the young man who had teased her in the fields all those years ago, the same fields where Ali had once seen fireflies as a boy, stars growing from the earth.

"*Salaam,* Maryam Mazar," he said as the two boys tumbled through the door.

She held out her hand to him and thought how she would have liked to hear those words from her father, her mother, Fatima, one last time. He stepped back and she walked into the small courtyard of his home, turning where she stood on the scratched piece of ground. The two small boys stared up at them.

"*Dustam,*" she said, "my friend, it's been too long."

143

He nodded. "It's an honor, and I see you've met my grandchildren."

Maryam smiled at the boys. "I would have been lost without them."

"So," Hassan clapped gently, "please finish your work and take Maryam Mazar's bags inside." They chuckled as they struggled with the weight. "Come," Hassan beckoned, "my family is waiting for you."

She followed as he stepped into a narrow hallway, lined with shoes and a small sink to one side, before a heavy curtain to the next room. Maryam could smell the familiar scent of rose perfume mingled with cooking as she slipped off her own shoes. "May I wash my face before I join you?" she asked, and Hassan nodded, leaving her alone beside the cracked mirror above the sink. For a moment she leaned against the basin and looked at her reflection: no sign of the young woman she had once been behind her tired eyes and age. "Vanity," she whispered, thinking of all those hours in front of the dressing table, getting ready to go out for dinner or to the theater, Sara sitting at her side, watching her make up, Edward waiting at the foot of the stairs. She breathed in, the vast distances of her life tearing at her edges, as they always had. Pushing aside the curtain, she found herself in a large, square room with bright light gleaming off the uneven walls and several faces lifted toward her. She closed her eyes for a moment, and felt a hand rest on her own.

"This is my first wife, Noruz," said Hassan. "You remember her?"

Maryam looked at the old woman before her, stooped and gray beneath her black chador, eyes watering yet steely in her weathered face. "Yes, Noruz, we were young together." She leaned to kiss her.

"Still young inside." Noruz smiled. "We're glad the years have given you the peace to return. Please, my children would like to welcome you."

They turned toward her three grown-up, sturdy sons and two daughters, standing side by side.

"And this is my second wife, Nahir." Hassan beckoned to a younger woman, at least thirty years his junior, who stepped from the doorway to the kitchen, hiding her mouth with an emerald chador.

Maryam looked from her to Noruz and reached for both their hands, thinking of her mother, alone with her Russian cigarettes as her father took a new wife to his bed. "Thank you for welcoming me into your home," she said as the Ayatollah's picture watched over them.

"Maryam Mazar must be tired," Noruz said to her husband. "Let's eat and then she can rest. Come, Maryam, sit beside me."

They sat with their backs against the wall as Noruz's daughters and Nahir brought food from the kitchen, laying it on the white cloth before them: steaming basmati with a mutton stew.

"You will share my room to sleep." Noruz patted the back of Maryam's hand.

"Thank you." Maryam nodded before turning to Hassan, sitting proudly with his sons on either side. She asked him how things were in the village.

"There's much to see," he answered. "We'll show you tomorrow."

"I long to see Mazareh in the daylight again." Maryam remembered the thin midday shadows, when she would sit on her heels and watch the men play backgammon, the rattle of bone dice in the summer months.

"We all now have running water and electricity." Hassan tucked his thumbs into his belt. "You can see the granary and Farnoosh will take you to her clinic." Maryam looked across at his eldest daughter, bent over her food. "She's a good girl. She has the whole village for her child. You look after us when we're sick and old, eh?" Farnoosh glanced up, something drowning in her eyes, the one never to be married.

"I'd like that, Farnoosh." Maryam smiled warmly. "I worked in a clinic once in Mashhad, long ago. It was one of my happiest times."

"Why did you leave?" Farnoosh asked, but her father spoke over her.

"That was the clinic with Doctor Ahlavi?" he asked, and Maryam nodded, looking at Farnoosh's knuckles gripped in her lap, wanting to talk to her but not knowing how to begin. "He's a good man, Doctor Ahlavi," Hassan continued. "After you left, he came here for some time with Ali Kolahin. He set up the clinic and helped Ali establish our school. We have ninety children here now, and four teachers. Ali takes care of them. He's a good man too."

Time washed round the room as Maryam had known

146

it would, flooding in from the mountains, pulling at her hair and clothes. Ali had spent his entire life here, she thought, all the years since that night in their room of creeping shadows and candlelight. *Go to Mazareh, and wait for you to come and find me again.* She heard his voice in her mind, moving beneath her skin like a trace of fingers. She rested her head in her hand and took another mouthful of food.

"Your father was kind to us before his death," Hassan went on. "He could have sold this land to another, taken the money, whatever he liked, but no. He gave us absolute ownership of the produce of Mazareh. All the profits from the sugar beet, meat, everything we grow these days, we keep."

Maryam listened, trying to think of her father, trying to remember a glance that held no judgment. As she ate, she thought of how she had once sat on his shoulders when she was small, by the shores of the Caspian. They had walked on white sand, every now and again turning to see his footprints wash away in the surf. On their way home in the afternoon, they had stood beneath a peach tree and from his shoulders she had reached to pick one, soft and warm in her hand. They had sat in the short grass and shared it then, looking back at the sea in the sinking sun. She was no longer sure if that was a memory or a dream, and had no one left to ask.

Later, as the family cleared away the dishes, not letting Maryam help, Hassan turned to the corner where a grainy newsreader flickered on the screen in her black chador. He shook his head. "What do English people think of us, Maryam Mazar?"

She turned to watch the news as well—Fallujah, Tikrit, Baghdad. "I don't know," she replied. "I'm not sure they have time to think, to know how they feel about Iran. Most of them would wish you well. They didn't want the war with Iraq."

"And your English family, what do they think?"

Maryam watched the purple flame flicker in the kerosene heater. "They do their best," she replied. "We tried to bridge our two worlds as well as we could." She covered her eyes for a moment, black with pinpricks of light. She was no longer sure if she had tried as hard as she might have done; if a part of her hadn't rather rocked the bridge, and kicked it hard to crumble beneath her.

"You must rest now, Maryam," Noruz said as she came back from the kitchen, and Hassan nodded. The rest of the family stood along with him, bidding each other goodnight before leaving through the heavy curtain, across the courtyard to the honeycomb of rooms beyond.

Hassan bent to turn off the kerosene heater and cold crept quickly into the room. "Winter's drawing in," he sighed. "Soon we'll be shoveling snow from the roof again."

Maryam rubbed her calves, not used to sitting on the floor, and not quite recognizing the thick ankles as her own. "I remember sleeping on the roof here in the summers of my childhood. I'd pray to the fat yellow moon, and I remember you singing of the mountains." Hassan nodded. "Maybe you'll sing for us again?"

"Inshallah." He looked at her, as if he had just realized she was really there, this pale-skinned woman, the landowner's daughter from his youth.

"Goodnight, Hassan Taymorey." Maryam bowed. "Your family is very kind."

"You're welcome. I hope we will be able to sacrifice a sheep to bless your visit. And we must go to the school. Ali Kolahin is expecting you."

"Yes," Maryam breathed and turned to the night.

That evening, as I drove home, the sky broke, slowly at first, lonely darts of rain on the windshield. It was almost eight o'clock as I went down Richmond Hill, trying to concentrate on the road, my head numb with the day. The valley and night fell away to the left, filled to the horizon with the city's orange glow and a distant spiral of planes queuing to land at Heathrow, their blinking lights small but urgent beneath the dark storm clouds overhead. The windshield wipers scraped across the glass, smudging the dust and grime so I couldn't see. The road was quiet and I pulled to the curb and stepped out, rubbing my eyes. The wind picked up and heaved the trees, branches grabbing at the air.

There was a gravel promenade halfway up the hill. It was deserted, and I walked to the balustrade and leaned against it, closing my eyes. The air was full of the smell of mulch and bark and the rot of the river. The rain fell more insistently, and I lifted my face to it, splashing from the branches, as the currents puckered and mur-mured below and the lightning glimmered. "Shhh," I whispered, wrapping my arms round myself as the earth turned to mud. "At least you have no earthquakes here," my mother would say when we complained about the weather. "No black holes and fissures that will tear open the earth and swallow you whole." Thunder rumbled in the distance and I thought of Creswell, alone in the house, and hurried back along the slippery path to the car.

By the time I reached Hammersmith, the rain was pooling in the road, the drains clogged with leaves and rubbish. Lights from the shop windows reflected on the pavements and cars crawled past each other, faces peering out through desperate windshield wipers. At home, the wind tugged the car door open and then slammed it shut. I was drenched, and dropped my things at the foot of the stairs before hurrying into the kitchen. Creswell whimpered under the table and I crawled next to him, rubbing his muzzle as the win-dows shook. "Sorry you've been alone." I pulled a cushion from one of the chairs and rested my head as he nervously licked my chin. I patted his flanks, my eyes heavy, and we listened to the rain. Half awake on the hard floor, I started to hum an old Beatles tune: "I Wanna Hold Your Hand," one of my father's favorites. Years ago, he would croon and spin my mother round the kitchen with her feet off the floor. "Stop," she would laugh, a little anxious, pushing him away with a hand over her mouth. "What would my father say?"

She had a beautiful accent, full of long, soft vowels which strangers sometimes mistook for French.

Lying there, I thought of her turquoise room and her photos, her father, the grandfather I'd never known, and her words by the river. *When I humiliated him, he humiliated me. It made me strong.* I didn't know what had happened to her to make her say those words, the reason she had given for slapping Saeed and all that had followed. She had looked so tired, and must have been struggling more than I knew with Mara's death and Saeed's arrival. I traced the unvarnished knots of wood on the underside of the table, where smooth beads of resin still bled from the oak planks.

When the worst of the storm had passed, I got up from the floor. "Come on, Creswell, you can sleep on the bed tonight." I fetched the phone and went upstairs. There was a large mirror on the middle landing where I stopped to look at my face, and for the first time saw the old woman I would become peer back from beneath my weary eyes and dry skin. She seemed to recognize me, as if she had been waiting. I was too tired to wash, and so just wrapped my rain-wet hair in a towel and crept beneath the duvet. I phoned Julian's mobile in the lamplight and imagined the call clicking through exchanges and satellites between London and New York.

"Hi there." He had recognized the number.

I curled round myself to hear him. "Hi there," I echoed. "Can you talk?"

"Yes, I finished early. Just out for a stroll."

I heard noise in the background. "Where are you?"

"Guess," he said. It was a game we'd played before. I imagined him holding the phone out to the air, and heard children's voices and the sing-song of Christmas music. "Where do you think?"

"Sounds like Santa's grotto." I stroked Creswell's nose, nuzzling into me.

"Central Park skating rink."

"Skiver," I teased, my limbs sinking into the mattress.

"Don't worry, I'm staying on firm ground." There was a pause, half the world between us. "How's everything at home?"

"Oh, so-so. There was a big storm tonight. I had to get under the kitchen table with Creswell." He laughed and I wished he was near. "I went to the doctor this morning." I listened to his silence and the tinny fairground music. "It was all right. She said we could try again, in a while."

"Sara," he said, full of care and hope.

"I know," I replied, "all in good time."

"All in good time."

"I sort of said a prayer on Richmond Hill tonight, in the storm."

"How pagan of you," he answered, his voice tender.

"Yes, I suppose so. It felt right."

We listened to each other, quietly keeping our heads above water.

"You go to sleep now."

We whispered our goodnights and I put down the

receiver. I had forgotten to tell him about my plans for the saffron kitchen.

Later that week, I drove to Richmond to fetch Saeed and go for the paint. He was sitting on the doorstep when I arrived and stood politely to shake hands. The front door was open and I went inside to let my father know we were going. I saw him before he heard me, in his study with his head in his hands. He looked up and for a moment I think hoped to see his wife, eyes expectant then gently resolute above his smile.

"You all right, Dad?" I asked.

"Yes, fine." But he looked puffy-faced and his hair was disheveled.

"Heard from Maman?"

"No, she's still in her village, but don't fuss. It will be fine. Are you off?"

"Yes. It's lovely outside."

We looked through the window at the blustery garden.

"Some branches came down the night of the storm," he said. "I might go out and tidy up a bit this afternoon. Get some air." He looked at the backs of his hands.

"All right, see you soon. I thought I'd take Saeed to see Doctor Ahlavi as well."

"Good idea."

An hour later, Saeed and I were standing in the car park, loading cans of paint into the boot of my car. "There's someone I'd like you to meet," I said, unlocking the passenger door. "He's Iranian; quite old now. He knew our mothers when they were young." Saeed's eyes rested on mine, a nod and a flicker of dimples.

It was a short journey, just beyond Teddington and Hampton Court. Saeed pressed his forehead against the window, gazing at a thin mist of rain in the late afternoon as the schools spilled on to the road. We watched the bus stops, crowded with customized uniforms, short skirts and headscarves, turbans, dreadlocks, and blazers jostling together.

"In Iran, boys sit at the front of the class and girls at the back. When we go home, we watch MTV on satellite. Britney Spears."

"What's that like?" I asked.

"Like going to the Zoo." He grinned as the thought occurred to him.

Away from the high street, we turned through the gate to Bushy Park, a narrow gap in the high wall. It opened up before us like a secret garden, deep and dark green in the early dusk. We drove slowly along the central avenue, winding down the windows to watch the deer beneath the trees, and then we were beside Hampton Court Palace with its long lawns and twirling brick chimneys. My mother had lived nearby when she first came to London, and I tried to imagine her in her early twenties, halfway between Saeed's age and my own, wandering along the cobbled yards and river walks.

"What is that place?" Saeed asked.

"It's where our kings and queens lived hundreds of years ago."

We watched it pass.

"Did you ever go to Persepolis?" he asked.

"No, but I'd like to . . . one day."

"There's a carving that my mother loved. The lion of winter fights with the gazelle of spring. She said they fought to hold back time." He looked out into the gleam of streetlights.

In a little while we turned on to an estate of cheaper housing where weeds pushed up through the pavements. Old council flats squatted beside pebble-dash two-up, two-downs, caravans, and rusty cars squeezed into the tiny gardens. I parked and we walked over to one of the narrow houses, its garden overgrown with nettles and cluttered with rubbish. I rang the bell, and at a grimy window by the door a creamy lace curtain twitched and a watery old eye peered out from beneath a black woolen hat.

In Mazareh, the ewe bucked in the gray-pink light of morning and Maryam shivered, a blanket round her shoulders and the pillow's creases still etched on her cheek. The cobalt blue door was open to the curve of dirt track outside, and children peered in on their way to school as Hassan pulled the ewe's head back with a firm jerk and sliced the knife across its throat so its body collapsed to the ground. Maryam could taste blood in her mouth. The ewe lay where it fell with its neck flipped back, the wound like a new mouth steaming blood into a puddle on the brown earth, hard with frost. Hassan's elder son, Reza, threw a bucket of water to wash it away, and it ran in pink rivulets to the children's feet. They watched quietly, wrapped in thick scarves and gloves on their way to school, eyes wide at Maryam. She smiled at them and Noruz clapped her hands, stepping over the carcass to wave them away.

While Hassan and Reza hung the sheep to bleed, Maryam went inside with Noruz to get warm. The room was quiet and they sat together on the carpet, their backs against the wall, listening to the hiss of the heater. Noruz poured glasses of tea and they watched the morning brighten, white light flooding through the window, as they sucked sugar crystals in their cheeks.

"How did you sleep?" Noruz asked. Their beds had been unrolled side by side.

Maryam thought of the cardboard-hard cushion and narrow mattress on the floor, the soft red nightlight above the window and an eternity of blackness beyond, the peace of the place. "Like a baby," she said.

Noruz nodded and gave a single, slow blink of her eyes.

When they went outside again, the ewe had been stretched on its back on the ground, with its head on a stump by the door. Maryam looked at the neat row of teeth and the half-shut eyes, whites just visible. Reza had slit open the fleece along its belly and in the pits of its legs, showing creamy-white skin beneath the coarse, dirty wool, which he hacked and scraped back with a knife. Slowly the fleece peeled away, and a smell of raw scalped meat filled the air. "We will eat well tonight." Hassan looked up at Maryam from where he squatted on the ground, his hands smeared with fat, wool, and blood.

"Yes." Maryam breathed in the fresh mountain coldness and the straw-dirt smell of animals. She looked at Noruz, her watering, knowing eyes, and reached for her hand. "I wish Fatima would walk round the corner now, and Mairy and Mara. Then I would never leave again. I would walk into the hills with them, and nothing would take me from this place." She laughed, tears on her face from the cold and her memory, rolling down the hillside with Mairy, earth and sky spinning, biting into her flesh, letting her know she was alive.

"And your family in England?" Noruz asked.

"I would bring them here." She smiled, knowing it was impossible.

"Would they come?"

Maryam thought of Edward, his patient blue eyes and his kindness, the polite knock on the door to her turquoise room, cups of tea as she stirred the bonfire, peering at each other from a great distance. She squatted on the ground beside Hassan, holding the fleece back as he scraped it from the carcass. "Maybe Sara would come."

Later, she watched Noruz move slowly round her kitchen, preparing *kofta* for the evening meal. She remembered Fatima sitting on the doorstep in Mashhad, making large meatballs in the long shadows at the end of the day, egg yolk and mince sticky on her fingers, a dark, sweet prune pressed at the center of each one. "Tinker, tailor, soldier, sailor, rich man, poor man, beggar man, thief." It was an echo of Sara's fluting little-girl voice, stones round the edge of her dinner plate.

"So you will see Ali Kolahin soon." Noruz glanced up. "How long has it been?"

Maryam stood to get more tea from the samovar on the hob. She looked through the window and felt the bright sun on her skin. "A lifetime; over forty years." She sat back at the table. "Long enough to have a grown-up daughter, a new language."

"Less beauty and more knowledge," Noruz mused, eyes still on her work.

"I hope so." Maryam watched the tea leaves float and swirl in her glass. "I feel I've been between places for so long. I needed to come back. There were too many unfinished conversations, too many people I wanted to see before I die."

Noruz nodded. "It's the way as we grow older: the struggle to make sense of our days."

"It's shattered me over the last few months." Maryam looked at the gold band on her finger. "Saeed, my nephew, came to London after Mara's death. He meant no harm, I know, but somehow he pulled back a veil I'd tried to forget or ignore, just by his presence, his chatter, and his green eyes. I suppose he was the son I could have had in another life, and I—stupid old woman—felt mocked for it."

"You've been lonely. Perhaps he reminded you of that."

Maryam pictured Edward and how he would read to her from the Sunday papers as she stared through the window, watching the clouds and changing leaves.

Noruz pushed her headscarf back with the side of her hand. "You know, when Ali Kolahin first returned here from Mashhad, it was terrible to see him. His feet dragged up and down the yard of his dead mother's home. I don't know what would have become of him without Doctor Ahlavi. It was as if all the light had been beaten from him."

Maryam thought of all the times she had cried for Ali, more than anyone would ever know. Eventually the loneliness where he should have been was drowned out by the clatter of others, the space of days, months, years. "Sometimes it can be almost unbearable to remember the past," she admitted.

"But now you'll see each other again," Noruz replied. "The past is past."

"Yes, now we're old and our story is tittletattle for my niece in Mashhad."

"And then what will you do? Turn round and return to England?"

"I don't know how long I will stay."

"And what of your husband?" Noruz raised her eyebrows.

"He's the father of my daughter."

"Is he a good man who will wait for you?"

"Yes, he *is* good." But Maryam wasn't sure if he would wait, or even if that was what she wanted anymore. She lifted her wedding ring to her mouth. It was cool against the small scar left by her father's blow all those years ago.

Noruz shook her head and turned away.

The following morning, Farnoosh walked with Maryam through the village, the path as potholed and uneven as a riverbed. They soon came to the mud-packed square at its center, fringed by the outer walls of family compounds, a lane at every corner leading to the plains beyond. Her clinic was on one side, brick-built with a gray concrete step. Farnoosh took the keys from beneath her chador and they stepped inside, blue linoleum on the floor and rabies and HIV/AIDS posters on the walls.

"We only have medicine for coughs and stomach upsets." Farnoosh pointed to a high shelf. "The doctor visits every month; otherwise, people must travel if they're sick."

Maryam remembered Doctor Ahlavi and his gentle presence. He had tried to do his best for her. She looked around before Farnoosh beckoned her outside again and locked the door. The village was empty, with the farmers at work in the fields and the children in class. Maryam could see the path to the school, and to Ali. It tugged at her. Later, she thought. After a lifetime apart, she could wait a little longer. She and Farnoosh walked to the edge of the village, only a few minutes away, where Farnoosh pointed to a pile of red clay bricks for a new building beside the prayer house. "It will be for women and girls who bleed and aren't clean to pray with others." Maryam looked out to the hills. Fatima had helped her hide her bleeding for years. "Don't let me be treated as an outcast and dirty," she had pleaded. It had happened anyway.

160

Beyond the village walls, thin sheets of plastic fluttered in the wind, torn and crumpled amid the rocks, weighed down with discarded debris from the fields. Sheepdogs like wolves lay tethered to the earth, blinking flies from their eyes as the two women walked by in silence. Maryam looked at the ground, the shuffle of their feet, and bent to pick up a red stone with sharp, pointed edges. A fox head, she thought, turning it in her hand. She would wish on a fox in London, its silhouette gone as soon as glimpsed, dustbins turned over and feathers on the tidy lawns.

"Why have you come here, Maryam Mazar?" Farnoosh asked, watching from the corner of her eye, her chador clutched at her chin as the hillside grew ahead of them.

"You tried to ask me that the other night." Maryam slipped the stone in her pocket. "I suppose it's become harder to be so far away from where I grew up. The older I am, the more shallow my roots have felt in England. There I have no one to share stories with, or to remember. In London, I'm surrounded by people who know this country only through their news, a cartoon of Iran. It can be lonely."

"I'll be dead and maybe never have seen Isfahan, let alone Mecca or London," Farnoosh replied. "I could die here and have no stories."

"But here you have your family," Maryam replied.

"You think that's enough? When you leave yours behind? Please don't patronize me." She turned away, and Maryam stopped and sat on the stony ground with her arms around her knees. She thought of Edward, his tidy care, and of this young woman, a bird longing to escape that had never learned to fly.

"I don't mean to patronize you, Farnoosh. I know my life's been comfortable, with freedom to travel. But every time I sleep, I hope to dream of this place."

"And do you dream?"

"Sometimes. But there are many types of freedom and each has its price: freedom to love, to travel, to belong. For each freedom we choose, we must give up another."

"Your family was rich. They could afford your freedom."

"I'm not so sure. Some freedoms can be a gift of hate as much as love." Maryam felt the blood rise in her cheeks and remembered her father's last words to her: *She can go by herself . . . She is no daughter of mine.*

"I've upset you." Farnoosh looked down at her hands. "I'm sorry."

Maryam shook her head. "You're entitled to ask questions. After all, I'm staying in your home. Maybe one day you and I will go to Isfahan together, or even further." A smile flickered across Farnoosh's serious face, almost childlike, and she held out her hand to help Maryam stand. They started on the path back toward the village.

"My mother says you have a daughter," said Farnoosh.

"Yes, Sara." Maryam felt warmed just by the name. "She's about your age."

"What's she like?"

"She's a teacher; an English girl, but with my eyes and something that tugs at her." She remembered Sara's laugh, how she would cover her mouth with her hand.

"Does she speak Farsi?"

"Enough to get by. It's hard to have a child so far from everything you know, to know what's right or wrong. Sometimes I've been terrified by all the freedom at her feet, and how ill equipped I've been to help her choose."

"But you have a husband you love." Farnoosh moved closer, linking arms as they walked. "Your daughter's life will be good enough and she won't regret being born."

Maryam stopped at her words, recalling the day on the bridge and the unborn child. She put her hands in her hair, her scarf falling back as she turned on the hillside, red dust in her eyes.

Farnoosh reached for her hands. "Maryam, custom says I must be childless, that I will have my old parents for children." Tears ran down her face. "Maybe you will help me find another way. You have seen the world. I hope you find some peace here now."

Maryam shook her head and opened her arms to hug Farnoosh, longing for her own daughter. They walked on as dark snow clouds gathered above.

The door swung open and Doctor Ahlavi beamed, a hand held out in welcome. *"Salaam, salaam."* In his other hand he held a walking stick with a silver and turquoise handle. I ushered Saeed toward him and they shook hands formally, eyes taking each other in. Doctor Ahlavi's mustache twitched, thick and lead gray above his kind smile, as he shepherded us into the next room. It was small, with layers of Persian carpets, three or four, piled on the floor. Saeed knelt and ran his hand across the coarse wool weave, and Doctor Ahlavi chuckled. "In Mashhad, I could spread them all out on marble and have a maid beat them. Here, there's no space, but they keep the draught from the floor. Sit, sit, please." Hard cushions covered in thick fabric were propped around the edge of the room and we sat near the window, the orange streetlight finding its way through the falling night and the thin curtains that he tugged across. "Some privacy," he said with a smile. "Please be comfortable. I will bring tea." He shuffled from the room in his black jogging pants and thick jumper, bare brown ankles and wiry black hairs showing above his slippers.

A gas fire hissed in the corner and we looked at the fading wallpaper, hung with black-and-white photographs and a picture of the old Shah, Mohammed Reza Pahlavi. There was a clatter of drawers from the kitchen. "I'll just go and help," I said to Saeed, and he turned to watch me before his eyes fell on a bookcase behind the door, faded spines inscribed in Farsi. "He won't mind you reading," I suggested, and left him looking at the titles.

Next door was a pale blue kitchen. A large ceramic

samovar painted with red roses sat on the hob. Doctor Ahlavi leaned on his walking stick, looking out to the narrow back garden, a few yards wide and fenced in on all sides. Through the dusk I could see a small bird table and at the far end a wooden bench, both overgrown with weeds. I thought that Julian and I should come and help tidy it one weekend.

"Not much of a castle, my wife would say." He smiled weakly. "But I don't go out there much these days. A good book and my memories are world enough." The water grew noisier in the samovar as he reached up to a small cupboard, bringing down a round silver tray and glasses with matching filigree holders. "Your mother likes proper Iranian tea, like we had in the old days. Tell me, how is Maryam?"

"She went to Mashhad and Mazareh, about a fortnight ago."

He looked back through the window into an indigo sky. "It's been a long time," he said, mostly to himself. "I wondered if she'd ever return to Mazareh."

"Why's that?"

"You should ask Maryam. Mazareh is *her* past."

"Yes, of course." We smiled at each other. "Can I help with anything?"

He pointed to a high shelf, where I reached for a box of *gaz*, sweet nougat with pistachios, and dark amber, crystalline sugar. "Please take the tray through to Saeed and I'll bring the tea."

In the other room, Saeed had a small pile of books by his side. Doctor Ahlavi followed me in, resting the teapot on a narrow side table. Then he reached into a chest of drawers and pulled out a white square of linen which he handed to Saeed, who unfolded it on the carpet, placing the tray in the center. From another drawer, Doctor Ahlavi took a small bottle. He unscrewed the lid and sprinkled some drops of fragrance on the carpet. "Just how Maryam likes it." Rosewater filled the air as he sat carefully beside us, inviting Saeed to pour. "I'm sorry about your mother and for your family's loss," he said with his head bowed. "Mara was a lovely woman."

"Thank you from my family," Saeed replied. His voice was calm, and I felt thankful for Doctor Ahlavi's gentle sympathy and the comfort his presence bestowed.

"How long have you been here, Saeed?" he asked.

"Since September."

"And how do you find it?"

"Cold, but Sara and her father are kind."

"And what news do you bring of Iran?"

Saeed looked at him. "No news. It's the same as always."

Doctor Ahlavi's eyes narrowed and he sipped his tea before repeating, "the same as always." He looked up at the light and his skin was grainy and lined. "Saeed, my young friend, you know little of Iran and its place in the world before the Revolution. You weren't born. Maryam will tell you of Iran in those days. We were welcomed around the world for our oil, yes, but also for our culture, our civilization. In 1978, the whole world, presidents, royalty came to Persepolis. Did you know that?"

Saeed nodded.

"And yet one year later, it was gone. The Shah left with his bag of earth for Egypt and Khomeini covered us in black." He breathed in, muscles taut beneath his skin. "Now, a quarter of a century later, if you have an Iranian passport, people here, the authorities, think you're a terrorist, someone who may have a bomb strapped to their belly. We're in 'the axis of evil,' they say, the scourge of the earth." He stared at us. "I'm treated like a refugee, as if it is a thing of pity, of scorn to call myself Iranian. I tell people, 'I am proud of my country.'"

I rested my hand on his arm. "Things will change."

"Not in my lifetime," he replied with an old man's fatigue at the world.

Saeed's eyes moved between us. "Doctor, do you have children of your own?"

Doctor Ahlavi wiped his eyes, reaching for the nougat. "Two daughters, about ten years younger than Sara's mother. They live here now. They followed Maryam. She was the first to come to England from Mashhad. It was unheard of in those days, and in a way she opened the gates for other young women to follow. The thing is, we always believed our daughters would come home. Even Maryam's father, I think, hoped that day would come." He pointed to the edge of a photograph tucked between some books. Saeed reached across and handed it to him, placing it on the white linen cloth. "It was taken in my old surgery in Mashhad, many years ago."

We looked at the grainy black-and-white image and, even though it had faded with time, we could still see the different light, clear and bright as it struck the marble. Two small girls held hands and gazed out from beneath their headscarves.

"Is that their mother?" Saeed asked of a young woman standing behind them.

"No, it's Sara's." He smiled at me and I lifted the picture, her still, serious face staring back. "Maryam helped in my clinic for a while."

"She looks so assured. And who's that?" I asked of a young man kneeling to one side, dark and lean, glancing back over his shoulder at her.

"I think you'll find that is Ali." Doctor Ahlavi spoke slowly, carefully. "He worked for your grandfather. He would escort your mother and her sisters in town."

"Is he still alive?" I asked.

"Yes, he was from Mazareh. He teaches the village children there now. His English was good. He taught himself, and Maryam."

"They were friends," said Saeed. "My mother told me."

"Really?" I looked at their faces, youth glowing in their skin. "I wonder if she'll recognize him."

"I wonder." Doctor Ahlavi took the picture from my hand and placed it back beneath the book cover.

"Where are your daughters now?" Saeed asked.

"They married Englishmen, like Maryam did. One

lives in York and the other in Norwich. They're good girls. They come to see me when they can. But they broke my wife's heart, if only they knew it. She wanted to be with them, to see her grandchildren, but the little ones couldn't even speak her language. She grew ill." He held his hands, palms outstretched, to the small, faded room. "In Mashhad, Saeed, we all lived in one street: brothers, sisters, uncles, aunts, husbands, and wives, families all together. Here we are strangers to each other, to ourselves."

We sat quietly with his words, nothing to offer but silence.

"Do you have any pictures of my mother when she was young?" asked Saeed.

The doctor looked at his hands in his lap, legs stretched before him. "Yes . . . Mairy, Maryam, and Mara," he sighed. "Three sisters, but all so different. They might as well have come from different centuries."

"How do you mean?" I asked.

His hand skimmed over the carpet's twists of color. "Well, I suppose Mairy was old Iran. She was traditional and obedient, full of quiet care. Maybe she had the easiest life, accepting tradition. She was your grandfather's balm. Then there was Maryam. She was born before her time, as they say; trapped by it. She had her father's spirit, you know—good for a warrior, but not for a girl born into a world of kitchens and children." He rested his hand on mine. "Maryam would have none of it. She wanted her own destiny and no one could stop her. You tell her that, Sara. She slipped straight through her father's fingers. He could not clip her wings."

His eyes were wet and I didn't know what to say, thinking of the mother I knew, her rose garden and bonfires, her turquoise room and the smell of cooking, an echo of her words on the bridge: *He humiliated me.*

"Did she anger her father?" I asked.

"You must ask her that yourself." He looked away. "It's her history."

I watched him, feeling confused as my sad tides lapped inside. "Mara, she was the jewel." The doctor's voice lifted again as he looked at Saeed. "If Mairy was obedient, and Maryam was defiant, Mara was full of cheekiness and teasing. She swam the middle stream."

The room fell quiet and I listened to the voices of people walking along the pavement outside, a few yards away on the other side of the wall.

The doctor took a white handkerchief from his sleeve and wiped his face. "Please forgive an old man's rambling." He gazed into his empty glass.

"Let me take that." I eased the glass from his hand. "I'll just put the tray in the sink." I left them opposite each other and turned on the overhead light in the kitchen. I ran the hot tap and scrubbed the plates and glasses until my fingers were red. How much of my mother's past was a secret from me, locked and hidden away? I stared through the window at the scrap of garden and heard their voices next door.

When I came back, Doctor Ahlavi had a small chest

in front of him. Its inlaid metals shone in the lamplight.

"We should go soon," I said, as Saeed fiddled with the lock.

He persisted and opened the latch. Inside was a folded cloth of faded red velvet. It smelled of the Persian carpets stacked in our loft, a trace of naphthalene. The doctor lifted it out and handed it to me. It was heavy and I put it on the carpet, unfolding the cloth like a large envelope, stitched on three sides and fastened with leather straps on the fourth.

"Untie them," said the doctor, hurrying me along.

Saeed watched, his eyes wide.

"You do it," I said, pushing the parcel toward him.

He took it in his lap and slowly loosened the knots, reaching inside to pull out a dark leather folder, ornately tooled with flowers and crescent moons.

"It will show you a little of where your mothers grew up. And here, Saeed, let me find the picture of your mother." Doctor Ahlavi pulled the book toward him on the carpet and turned the pages. The mounts had aged, and photographs, notes, and newspaper clippings, browned and thin as tissue, slid and tore over each other. He laughed as they started to fall out. "They've been locked up for too long. That's the mosque at Haram; and here's Mara, and that one's of her wedding day."

The two photographs were mounted side by side. The image of a schoolgirl gazed out over the head of the photographer, dimples identical to Saeed's at the corners of her mouth. He reached out and traced the

171

crimped side of the picture. The wedding photograph had been taken just a few years later. Mara was sitting before a large mirror with her husband, the white cloth between them filled with small dishes of spices, sweets, and cakes.

"The tradition is for the bride and her new husband first to see each other in the mirror," Doctor Ahlavi explained. "The cakes are to sweeten the marriage. Here it's a kiss for the bride. In Iran, they feed each other honey from their fingers."

"Where's Sara's mother?" asked Saeed.

"She wasn't there," Doctor Ahlavi replied. "Maryam had already left Iran. Her father was dead. She'd married Edward. It was difficult for her to return for a while."

I remembered fragments of conversations, crumpled photos and airmail letters arriving on our kitchen table, often months after births, deaths, and marriages had taken place. The scent of rose perfume in the room was sweet and strong and I wanted some fresh air. "We should go, Saeed," I repeated. "We can come again."

He looked up, disappointment in his eyes.

Doctor Ahlavi reached across and patted his hand, pushing the folder toward him. "Please, take it," he offered. "It is for you. I'll be offended if you leave it. I won't be here for ever." Saeed held the gift to his chest, and I leaned across to kiss the doctor's cheek.

"We'll come again soon, when Maman's back," I said.

The doctor shook his head. "That may be some time."

The light in the hallway flickered as we put on our coats before stepping outside over the takeaway pizza and curry leaflets. The orange-black London sky was clear and we both shivered in the cold as the bolts scratched shut again and locked Doctor Ahlavi back inside.

"Let's go to the school now and see Ali Kolahin," Hassan said to Maryam.

"Yes, it's time." She stood. "Just give me a moment." She left the room, went across the courtyard, and through an arch into a smaller square brimming with daylight. She pulled back a red rug hung over an opening in the wall and stepped through to where she had slept beside Noruz. She knelt down by her bags. Through the window, she saw her own faint reflection and, for a moment, felt as if she was stretched as thin, as if light should pass through her. She bent to unzip the bag and shuffled around inside, slipping free the faded cherry red book. She held it to her face, and breathed in the familiar scent of the brown-edged pages. She had kept it close for so long, through so many years and in so many places. She thought of going to the white-yellow cliffs of Dover with Sara as a child, and before that of St. James's Park and her Sunday trysts with Edward, when he had taught her the last verse of the poem. She had never expected him to fall in love with her, but he had. All those times when she had found herself looking for a splinter of Ali in his eyes. She had not wanted to hurt him.

Hassan was waiting for her by the cobalt blue door when she came out of the room. As they walked, she didn't really hear him telling her about the new machine they had purchased for milling grain, how she must see it later. She felt herself passing through time, like drapes hung between one room and the next. Voices from the past whispered around her, echoes of Fatima, Ahmeneh, Soraya, her father: *The fire burns you . . . sickness makes you weak.* They could hold her back no longer as she passed the clinic and the sound of children rose from the playground. She eased through a gap in the wall and there it was, space unfenced to the horizon. Seeing her, girls in white scarves and boys in wool hats ran to her, laughing, shouting, reaching out their hands. *"Salaam Khonoom,"* they called.

"You seem to be expected." Hassan chuckled as they swarmed round Maryam, and she sank to the steps of the school's unadorned flagpole. She stretched out her arms, it seemed for all of them. The girls touched her face and clothes and the cheekier boys pretended to kiss her hand. She saw them through a blur of tears and heard them laugh at her for that. Then she laughed too, lowering her head, before in a falling hush she felt a firmer hand take hers and another beneath her elbow, helping her stand. At last, she lifted her face to Ali's and saw the lines of his years. It was the same air she had breathed a moment before, but now Maryam felt life in her veins. She handed him their book, the pages falling open where they always had—*the world, which*

174

seems to lie before us like a land of dreams—and Ali looked at her, his eyes finding hers so quickly, with no need to speak. There, beneath the surface of reflections, was their lost world. He would reach out and touch it if he could.

"You've come far, Maryam Mazar. And you've met my family." He opened his arms to the schoolchildren as they played.

"Yes." Maryam held out her hands as well, as if rain were about to fall from the sky.

Ali stared down at the book, remembering when he had first given it to her, their last time in Mazareh, when his mother had been alive and he had told the story of the fireflies. Side by side, they faced the horizon together. He turned to see her face again, and she turned to him as well. Her smile was the same as he remembered. She wiped the tears from her face.

"So, you will feast with us tonight, Ali Kolahin?" interrupted Hassan.

"Yes, I'd like that, thank you, Hassan Taymorey."

"Good. I'll tell Noruz."

Ali looked again at Maryam. Where to begin? He thought of the young girl who had run across the dark courtyard in Mashhad, her chador flying behind her like wings in the night and dark hair falling over her face. It had been another lifetime.

"So, until this evening." Hassan clapped him on the back.

"Yes, until this evening." Ali bowed to them both and turned back to the school.

"Your hejab," Hassan said to Maryam with a nod as Ali walked away.

She smiled at his care, reaching to pull her scarf forward from where it had slipped to the back of her head. "Let me stay here a while, if that's all right, Hassan. I'll make my own way back."

He nodded again, walking away, and she sat on her own once more, listening to the children's laughter and the sigh of the plains, until a young woman in black came to the top of the school steps and rang a brass bell. The children lined up neatly, rows of boys and girls gazing over at Maryam. She smiled and stood to go, when she glimpsed Ali looking through a nearby window. He was watching over her, as tall and straight as in his youth, his hair thick but white now, and his eyes even darker for it. She returned his gaze as she always had, unblinking, each in their own stillness, as the children filed in. At that moment, the butterfly caged inside her, the one she had thought long dead, opened its wings and would have flown out through her mouth and into the sky if it could.

Back in her room, Maryam knelt by her bag on the floor again. She took out her small photo album, pictures of Sara and Edward, confetti and scuffed knees. The night fell quickly as she gazed through the window, a blanket round her shoulders. Noruz brought tea and rested her palm on Maryam's brow. "I'm just tired," she said with a faint smile, "time catching up with me." Noruz saw the album and sat beside her, turning the pictures quietly on the floor as the light left the day, shadows disappearing in the moonlight. She left after a couple of minutes and returned with more tea, some paper, and a pen. "Write to your daughter." She pushed the paper into Maryam's lap. "Tell her to come here and see your home."

Maryam looked at the sheets torn from a notebook, pale brown and thin as tracing paper. She leaned back against the wall.

"Write," Noruz insisted. "I must cook." She left her alone.

Maryam picked up the pen. Where to begin? *Dear Sara. Dearest daughter of mine. I deserve to ask nothing of you.* The page stayed empty. She looked at her reflection in the window and reached up to touch the pane of glass. "Everyone's gone now," she whispered: Fatima, Mairy, Mara. She saw her father in a corner of her mind, his back turned, and her mother slowly rocking on the floor. Then she looked out at the night sky and in the glass reflection all she saw was herself, tired and alone.

"Maryam."

She was startled by his voice, and focused on his reflection beside hers in the glass as the drape fell closed behind him. "I'm not sure you're really here, Ali," she whispered. "I've been imagining you for so long."

"I'm here."

She heard the smile in his voice. "I've been speaking with you my entire life, in my head."

"I know. You've been with me, too."

She turned to look at him, and he saw the young woman he'd known peer from behind her bloodshot eyes. She held out her hand and he took it, helping her stand and she stepped toward him, his arms around her again at last. She shut her eyes in the peace of it, rest, a moment. "Stay, stay, stay," she whispered, struggling before seeing Edward in her mind. "I won't leave again."

"Shh," Ali breathed, her head on his shoulder and the walls of Mazareh around them. "All you need do now, Maryam, is come to dinner." He felt the warmth of her skin and wished he could take her somewhere quiet, where they could sit and say nothing, after a lifetime of nothing. "Noruz sent me to call you, and Hassan will sing. All else can wait." In their minds, the shadows of another room crept round them, candlelight from long ago when the rain had poured all through the night.

"All right," Maryam said, and they stepped apart. "You go, and I'll follow." Ali let go of her hand and left through the drape and into the dark.

After he had gone, Maryam tidied her hair. She searched through her bag for the rose pink chador she'd bought with Mairy in the bazaar years ago, and shook it open, holding it to her face; a scent of English lavender in its folds. She wrapped it round her head and shoulders and knelt to look in the fragment of mirror that Noruz had propped on the windowsill. She looked tired, she knew that, and rubbed cream on her face, its fragrance reminding her of the marble bathroom back in London. She took a deep breath, trying to hold together the torn edges of her world, treading carefully from one place to the next.

When she walked across the courtyard into the bright main room, Noruz beckoned her to sit by her side again and Ali nodded from the opposite corner. She returned his smile, feeling their slow restitching of time begin as the room fell quiet. Hassan knelt a little apart on one knee near the door and his voice filled the room. Maryam looked at her wedding ring as she listened. It was a song of seasons and pastures, crops and harvests, a song she'd grown up with: Ehzat and Fatima humming over the stove, onion skins on the floor. She glanced at Ali again. He was still there. Afterwards, the men clapped and Hassan stood, his cheeks flushed. "Welcome, our guests." He bowed and the meal began.

Maryam sat quietly. She smiled at Farnoosh and listened to the men, savoring Ali's delight as he talked of the schoolchildren and their mischief. The television flickered silently in the corner and plates of saffron rice and lamb were served. "Delicious again," she whispered to Noruz. "You'll make me fat."

"It's not so bad to be a little plump," Noruz replied. "But these men," she continued, rolling her eyes. "Let's have some fun now." She rearranged her chador before clapping her hands twice, so that Hassan raised his eyebrows at her. "Excuse me, but we can hear this village talk any night. This is a celebration. Who will tell us a story or recite a poem?" Her grown children stared into their food. "How about our schoolteacher?" Noruz suggested. "Will you give us a poem?"

Hassan coughed, about to protest, but Ali rested a hand on his sleeve. "It's my pleasure, Noruz *Khonoom,* since you ask. This is a fine feast. It's the least I can do in thanks and to welcome back dear friends." He cleared his throat and stood in his loose clothes the color of earth, and Maryam saw the spirit of her young lover again. She could call him that now. "I hope you like our friend Omar Khayyám?" Taking in each face in the room, Ali began:

> *What is the gain of our coming and going?*
> *Where is the weft of our life's warp?*
> *The lives of so many good men*
> *Burn and become dust, but where is the smoke?*

Verse after verse, he stretched out his arms to the room:

> *Though you may have lain with a mistress all your life,*
> *Tasted the sweetness of the world all your life,*
> *Still the end of the affair will be your departure—*
> *It was a dream that you dreamed all your life.*

He finished with a bow and Noruz clapped her hands. "Many thanks. You have earned your dinner, my friend," said Hassan, and patted Ali on the back as he sat by his side again.

Later, as Hassan's family cleared away the plates, the news broadcast played quietly on the television in the corner and Ali glanced from the screen to Maryam. "So tell me," he asked, "do you think America will leave us

180

to live this quiet life?" She looked from the screen and its images of war to face him, and thought how his whole world had been this village: days, months, years within these walls, beneath this sky.

"I hope so," she said.

"Sometimes it seems that America will not be content until it has pulled out all our teeth and nails and we are weak as a beggar." Ali shook his head.

"I think that maybe they're a terrified people," Maryam replied.

"Terrified and powerful at the same time, like a street bully."

"I know. They just want to keep their homes safe."

"Well, we are no different surely, and they go about it in an odd way."

Maryam nodded as Hassan interrupted, rubbing his hands together. He offered to fetch the hookah. "Ali, will you join me?" he asked before leaving the room.

They were alone.

"You know I always hoped you might return after your father's death," said Ali.

They both thought of the dark eyes that neither of them had seen grow old and die.

"I couldn't. Even now my nieces in Mashhad look askance at me."

"Too afraid or too proud?" he asked, and saw her downcast eyes.

"Perhaps. I was young, far away. I didn't feel I had a choice. I had a small daughter, a different life; not perfect, but a life. It took me a long time to find a home after those dark days, and to feel safe again. Please don't judge me for that. And the Revolution was terrifying. After Shariar was killed, it was hard to imagine coming back for a while."

Ali looked at Maryam's hands in her lap. "I heard he was executed. They said it was for your father's deeds under the Shah, and that Shariar's mother died soon after."

Maryam thought of Leila. She had scarcely known her half brother, but he hadn't deserved that death. Her father hadn't known his actions would be cast as crimes that his son would pay for. "I'm just grateful my sisters were left in peace," she said.

"We've lived in brutal times," he replied, and saw Maryam look at the scar on his face, left by her father. "I know people who were seized off the streets in Mashhad by the religious police, the *pastars*. Sometimes they seemed little better than *Savak,* the Shah's secret force."

She shivered.

"But the streets aren't dangerous anymore?" Ali shrugged. She went on, "My friend Parvin in Tehran told me how one day she was able to walk through the city in her heels and headscarf, and the next day—after the Revolution—she was sent home from work and told only to come back if she wore full hejab over her hair, a manteau down to the ground, and shoes that didn't click as she walked. She never returned to her job. Her family was wealthy enough, and they sent their daughters to school in America. Now she can wear her heels in the street again, but her children will never come home."

"The cities are far away from here," Ali said. "In the villages, here in Mazareh, I think life has gone on more or less as always, for good or bad, with more feast than famine."

"Didn't you ever want to marry here and start your own family?"

"Yes, of course, but as you say, you were far away. The school has been my family and filled my days, although I have thought often of you. And now here you are: the same woman who walked through the orchard with me as a girl."

Maryam reached out her hand. "That girl in the orchard has been starving for this place. Have you been content here, Ali?"

"Content? I hope I've made a difference to some of these children's lives. That would be enough . . . And I'm glad you're here again, for a time at least." He lifted his hand to touch her face and she rested her cheek against his palm.

"I'm sorry it's been so long," she whispered, as Hassan returned with the hookah.

Ali turned away and they moved apart.

Noruz came back from the kitchen and rested a hand on Maryam's shoulder. The evening had come to an end. "We should leave these men to their talk," she said, as the sweet wood scent of their tobacco filled the air.

Maryam brushed the crumbs from her clothes and

stood up. "It was a perfect meal." She thanked Noruz and Hassan as he smoked his pipe.

"Sleep well." Ali wished her goodnight as she wrapped a shawl round her shoulders. "We'll go to the mountains soon. Hassan will lend us his truck, and I hope Noruz will do the same with her company."

"As long as it's before the snows come," Noruz replied, turning to go outside.

Maryam followed Noruz across the dark courtyard and the wind tugged at her scarf.

"God help me," she whispered to herself as she lay back on her thin mattress and closed her eyes.

My parents' house was dark except for the light in Maman's study, the curtains open. Saeed left the car with Doctor Ahlavi's parcel still hugged tight to his chest. The air had a numbing coldness to it, as if the morning would bring the first frost of the season, and I rubbed my hands together after ringing the doorbell and waiting to hear my father's tread on the stairs. Saeed rang the bell again. Still there was no answer. "Maybe he's fallen asleep," I said. "Come on, I know where the spare key's hidden."

We lifted the latch to the gate at the side of the house. The passage was charcoal black on the other side and the air smelled metallic and newly of winter. Saeed reached for my hand and we stood still, waiting for our eyes to recognize the dark shapes. Then we walked carefully along the path, down the side of the house covered in ivy and cobwebs, which brushed against my face and clothes. As we left its shadows, the garden grew clearer, gleaming in the light of a thin crescent moon. It was quiet except for the city's distant rumble, hardly a murmur in the trees.

"You can't see the stars," Saeed said quietly.

"They're there," I promised. "Just hard to see through the dirt in the air."

We walked round the edge of the patio. The greenhouse was on the far side, overgrown with moss and behind a tall yew hedge. I stepped inside. It was empty for the winter except for a tray of garden tools, and an upturned flowerpot in the corner. I lifted it and found the brown envelope with the keys inside. As we turned back to the house, I saw the light in the attic, a small square of white, and my father's face staring through the leaded panes, cutting him into small squares. Even from that distance he looked different, strained and bloodless.

"Dad," I whispered, my hand on Saeed's shoulder.

My father pushed at the window and it creaked open in the still air. I saw him lean out, his hands gripping the outside sill so half his body strained into the night. He craned his neck and scanned the treetops. I watched, unable to move or make a sound. Then, in a voice I didn't recognize, he shouted: *"Maryam!"*

It echoed off the roof tiles and along the bricks and paving stones, whispering down the passageways between silent houses, beneath their loggias and over the surfaces of still ponds, koi carp fat and hidden below. A dog barked back rough and urgent from behind a closed door and blood rushed to my face. Then my father disappeared again from view.

"Dad," I gasped again, and my legs came to life. We ran along the side of the house, Saeed stumbling in the dark, back to the front door. I fumbled with the keys and then we were in. "You wait in the kitchen," I said, trying to sound calm, and ran upstairs.

The lamp in my mother's study cut an oblong of light across the dark landing and I glanced inside. The middle drawer of her dressing table was open and her scarves tumbled across the floor, dusky pinks and rose reds. Everything else looked tidy enough, but the drawers of her desk were all pulled out as well. My eyes ran over the photographs and my mother's face— forty years younger—stared back.

On the landing, the door to the loft was closed but I heard the floorboards creak overhead. I eased open the door and started up the bare wood steps, already well trodden when we had first moved there thirty years before. "Dad," I called softly, as I reached the top step and felt a chill draught through the window. The strip-light whined.

"Hello, darling," he said before I saw him, his voice low and spent. He looked up from the old leather couch where he sat, squeezed between a lifetime of storage boxes and crates, discarded furniture, chipped vases and old lampshades. There was a half-drunk bottle of red wine on the floor and a glass in one hand. His face was beaded with sweat, pale blue eyes red-rimmed and swollen as a tide of despair rolled from him across the room. He reached out his other hand to me from amid the sea of junk, his fingers outstretched, and I went to him, tears breaking.

"Oh, Sara," he said. "I don't think your mother's coming back this time."

His words washed around the room and flooded over me and the attic, full of memories, board games, Christmas decorations, second-best books and least-favorite paintings propped against each other. "No, Dad," I whispered, and we both leaned forward so our foreheads touched, motes of dust and spores spinning from the timbers overhead. "What's happened?"

He sat back, lifting the glass of wine to his lips.

I started to speak again, but he shook his head, and so I waited as the temperature fell and our breath smoked gray-white in the air. I pulled some old picnic blankets from a bin liner behind the couch and tucked them over his shoulders before standing to close the window. Outside, the mossy tiles stretched away, with the dark space of Richmond Park in the distance. I turned back to take a blanket for myself and sat beside him. In his hands he held a piece of paper I hadn't seen before.

"Have you spoken to her?" I asked quietly.

He pursed his lips. "I couldn't reach her. So I called Iran Air, and she's not been in touch with them to arrange any flights. Then I phoned Shirin in Mashhad, and they haven't heard a thing since she left. They don't know when to expect her back."

"That's not so bad," I said. "She's probably just got caught up."

"It's different this time, Sara. I don't know why. She would have called."

I frowned, trying to understand, as my eyes cast round the room, falling on the spines of stacked books that I recognized without trying: *Heidi, Alice in Wonderland, What Katy Did.*

He turned the piece of paper in his hands.

"What's that?" I asked, and when he didn't reply, I pulled it free from his fingers. It was as thin as rice paper, brown and ragged on one edge where it had been ripped from a notebook. "Is this Maman's?" I asked, knowing it was. She'd drawn her family tree for me once on the same paper from the back of an old diary, carefully ruled lines between brothers and sisters, husbands and wives. Their names were written in Farsi and English, but they were faceless and voiceless to me: Hashemieh, Soraya, Khadijeh, Ehzat. I loved their sound, like a sea breeze across sand dunes. "Is this from Maman's room?" I asked again, but he turned away, gazing up as a moth fluttered and battered itself against the light. I unfolded the paper carefully. It was poetry. There was a small envelope attached to one corner of the page with an old paper clip. I unclipped it so I could see the lines properly, written in sky blue ink in my mother's careful, round hand. I read them aloud. *"Ah, love, let us be true / To one another! For the world, which seems / To lie before us like a land of dreams, / So various, so beautiful, so new . . ."*

My father broke in: *"Hath really neither joy, nor love, nor light, / Nor certitude, nor peace, nor help for pain . . ."* His voice trailed away. "You know, I taught her that, when we first met. I used to think it was one of the reasons she married me." His face was gray and he rested his head in his hand. "We used to meet in St. James's Park, to watch the pelicans. She had this wonderful scarlet coat, and I'd see her coming through the crowd, hair down to her waist." He paused. It was a story he'd told many times before. "One day she took a book from her bag. It was as red as her coat. She'd already learned the first few verses and didn't want me even to look at them, just the last one. But she wouldn't let me watch her practice. I had to turn away. I'd listen to her and look up at the roofs of Horse Guards, and think I was the luckiest man in the world." His voice was flat.

"You didn't stand a chance," I whispered. It was the same line I always delivered at the same point in the story I'd grown up with.

"I didn't stand a chance," he repeated quietly. "The thing is, she didn't learn that poem for me, Sara. I know that now." He looked at the floor, at its knots and scratches. "Once upon a time, I used to think of your mother and me as two blind people, trying to reach each other across a crowded room. Now I wonder if she was even there, or if it was just me stumbling in the dark."

"Don't say that."

"Oh, Sara, it's always been like that. She's never been fully here, although I've spent a lifetime trying to pretend otherwise. I just wanted to cherish the moments we've had." He stared through the dark window. "I've been thinking of that time after we got engaged and I took her to meet my ma in Whitby. I thought it might help her feel more settled. We planned to meet in a restaurant on the harbor and have fish and chips. Ma lived in rented rooms after my father's death, and I guess she didn't feel up to us visiting."

I thought of the sepia wartime photos of my grandma, short puff sleeves and sensible skirts, curly brown hair and a wide mouth. She had died before I was born.

"We traveled over from Pickering and there was the crashing North Sea. Ma was so neat. She hardly said a word all lunch. She'd never been out of England. I don't think she knew what to say. All I remember is the sound of cutlery and the smell of batter." He shook his head. "Maryam scarcely touched her food, just pushed it round her plate, and I suddenly felt so ashamed to have taken her there, with its cheap Formica tables and plastic cutlery. And I felt ashamed of my mother too, in her cheap pink lipstick. Maryam was so polite, but she must have felt so, well, out of place. She excused herself, saying she'd been unsettled by the journey or something, and went to get some air."

I pictured the door swinging shut and her walking away, my father sitting alone with his ma, everything and nothing to say.

"I watched her through the window, going down the cobbled lane toward the sea. Ma didn't want to stay long after that. She just tidied herself up, asked me to say good-bye for her, and went home. I remember her shoes clicking on the floor. It made me feel sad because she must have bought them specially. Anyway, I paid up and walked down to the wharf to look for Maryam, and there she was in her red coat. She'd walked out way beyond the fishermen and stood at the end of the jetty, holding on to the rail as if she might blow away. I ran up to her against the wind, and she was whispering in Farsi. When I took her hand and she turned round, her face was wet with tears and sea-spray, and for a moment I don't think she knew who I was." He stopped, his breath rasping in his throat. "I asked what she was saying, and she said her poem, telling it to the wind. *Her* poem, she called it, not ours, *hers*. She smiled that smile she hides behind. She was sending it to Mashhad, she said, *her* poem. I put my arm round her and walked her back to the car, and, you know, I thought at that moment that maybe she'd wanted to blow away; that somehow I'd caught her by mistake."

We sat quietly then, and I hoped Saeed was all right downstairs. "She'll come home, Dad, I know it," I said. "Mum does love you."

He shook his head. "Yes, of course she does, but I think we've passed through each other in a way." He turned to me, his jowls soft and unshaven. "I don't think she's going to end her days here. I've had all that Maryam has to give me, and I'm grateful for it." His voice was a whisper. I shifted so I could look him in the eye, and he seemed to age as I watched him, his flesh shrinking back beneath his skin.

"Christ, Dad, is that all you can say after a bloody lifetime? That you're grateful?"

He reached down and picked up the small envelope that had been attached to the page of poetry. It had slipped from the couch on to the floor. He handed it to me. *"A bloody lifetime?"* He raised his eyebrows and laughed. "You don't need to tell me that. It's *my* bloody life."

He rested his head in his hands as I turned over the envelope. It was small, the kind charities put through the door to collect money, green and faded as if it had been left in the sun. It wasn't sealed and at first I thought it was empty. I frowned, but then ran my finger along the inside and found a sliver of stiff paper, smaller than a passport photo and unevenly cut on one side, browned at the edges. It had been cut from a larger photograph and showed the side of a man's face looking over his shoulder. I recognized it at once from the photo Doctor Ahlavi had shown Saeed and me.

"Ali," I said.

My father looked up as I held out the photo in the palm of my hand and I saw him wince inside. He took it from me and raised it to the light. "Her father's servant?" he asked. His voice was thin and strained.

"Yes, I think he did work for her family. Doctor Ahlavi has the whole photo. What's this about?"

"I think she learned the poem for him. She never let me look at her when she said the words. Now I know it's because she was saying them for someone else."

"You don't know that, Dad."

"She used to call out in her sleep, but turned away if I asked. 'The past I've left behind,' she'd say. 'Be true to one another.'" He spat the words out, his face contorting.

"Don't. It will be all right." He reached for the bottle of wine. "No, it's late." I put my hand on his arm. "Have a rest. It will make more sense in the morning."

"Maybe," he replied. "So come on. Help your old man to bed."

His eyes were hooded as I stood to pull him up from the sofa and we made our way downstairs. His feet fell heavy on each step. We crossed the dark landing to his bedroom, and he sank back at last, the side of his face crushing the pillow.

"I'll take Saeed home with me tonight," I told him as his breathing grew steady.

I closed the door and leaned back against it. How I wanted to rest, a long, black sleep, with Julian curled around me. I returned to the loft and turned out the light.

Noruz woke early as usual, when the morning was still dark, and watched the day lighten from the courtyard step. There would be no snow, she decided. She turned back through the drapes and nudged Maryam awake. Her eyes flickered over the room before settling on Noruz with a smile. She had slept well, dark and deep, the sheets not damp and twisted as they could be in London. She changed under the blankets into layers of her warmest clothes; not enough time for the heater to take the night chill from the air.

Outside, Ali waited with the engine running while

Noruz fetched a basket of food. When they were all squeezed onto the front seat, Maryam smiled to Ali over Noruz's head, still blinking sleep from her eyes. She pulled the blanket round her shoulders and leaned her forehead against the cool window, while the heater blew warm at their feet. They drove quietly out of Mazareh, just awakening, and the brown plain opened up before them, with mist in the dips and curves of the earth. The sky lightened slowly as they rolled in and out of iced potholes, crunching beneath the tires. They watched the sun rise from behind the mountains. It touched the white peaks and glinted off the windshield and in their eyes, casting long shadows where small birds swooped, flashes of white tail feathers and brown wings amid the thistles and dust.

Noruz rocked back to sleep, hunched over the basket in her lap. Her breath grew heavy and Ali glanced past her at Maryam's silhouette against the dawn, the lines on her face. He lifted his hand from the wheel and reached across to stroke her scarf behind her ear. She turned to him, her eyes soft in the peace and warmth, as if just waking, and they watched the mountains grow before them, as Noruz snored. She woke with a cough when Ali shifted down a gear and the truck started to climb into the first foothills. They had been driving for over an hour and the plain behind was now bathed in daylight.

Noruz rubbed her eyes in the warm air. "Let's stop and have some breakfast, Ali," she said, patting Maryam's hand.

They pulled in at a low ledge that looked back toward Mazareh and climbed out of the truck, searching for the village, lost in the haze of the morning. The air blew fresh from the snowy peaks and Maryam breathed it in, as sweet and chill as her memory. She turned to where Ali had laid a rug on the ground as Noruz poured from a thermos of sugary black tea. They took it in turns to cup the warm plastic mug in their hands, while the others broke bread and cheese from the basket. Maryam looked back across the distance they'd come, there at the foot of the Masjed Mountains, with Turkmenistan and Afghanistan beyond.

"I wish Sara was here." She looked from Noruz to Ali. "My daughter," she said, and he nodded. "She's a teacher. You'd like each other." She felt hopeful and then looked away, thinking of Edward. It made her feel ashamed.

"So, tell her to come." Noruz raised her eyebrows, reaching for more bread.

"But for now, just enjoy the day, Maryam, with no more battles in your mind," Ali replied. "It is *you* who are here." He looked from her to the clouds shredding high on the mountain peaks. "My father taught me the names of these mountains once. Noruz, do you remember them?"

"Of course, and Doctor Ahlavi told a story about them when he brought you back here all those years ago." Noruz remembered Ali from those days when his cuts and bruises were still raw. She had helped nurse him soon after she had married, which was just as well, she thought, or she would have fallen for him herself.

Ali nodded up at the sky. " 'The Story of Gossemar-bart.' "

"I don't know that," said Maryam.

"You weren't here," he said gently.

She rested her face in her hands. "I remember the name, Gossemarbart, but I don't know which mountain it is."

"We're on it." Ali crouched to run his fingers across the ground.

"So, *salaam,* Gossemarbart." Maryam dug her own fingers into the chill earth so it wedged beneath her nails. "What are the others called?"

"Come, I'll show you."

He led her beyond an outcrop of rocks to where they could see the peaks stretching away on both sides into the pale morning. Maryam's feet slipped on the shale as she followed him, and when she looked back over her shoulder, they were out of sight of Noruz. Ali brought her to his side. She stood close and followed his hand as he pointed from one jutting and jagged lonely peak to the next, smoky gray and lavender blue; snow blowing from their ledges to blur with the clouds. "Mazar. Allahgar. Doshargh." Ali spoke each name and Maryam repeated after him. "Koosorg. Khomari. Sarhang." She turned to watch his face as he spoke. His collar was turned up against the breeze, gray stubble on his brown skin. "Salbarla. Nesar. Solehmoneh. Are you paying attention, Maryam Mazar?" She smiled at his teacher's voice. "Araqehmah. Sardasht. Barrahkar."

She whispered the words beside him, like learning to breathe again. "Zeerat. Tomor. Gossemarbart." They reached for each other's hands.

"So much time," she said, her eyes full.

They stood alone in the cold.

When they returned, Noruz was sitting in the truck cabin and they squeezed in on either side of her. She rubbed Maryam's cheek with the back of her hand as Ali started the engine. It coughed into life and they pulled away, slowly winding up the mountainside in the weak sun. By midmorning they were high above the plain.

"We have a few hours before it grows dark." Noruz looked at the sky. "It slips away quickly at this time of year. You two walk, make a fire. I'll stay in the warm."

As Maryam stepped from the car, the cold wind gusted into her lungs and she gasped, her eyes watering. It felt good, clean, and she pulled her coat tight. Ali tucked a blanket around her shoulders, his fingers gentle against her neck. They had stopped on a narrow plateau and it was easy enough to walk once they turned out of the wind. Maryam craned her neck to look at the sheer face of gray-brown rock above them, deep, dark fissures with snow and ice on the ledges. There wasn't much firewood, just twigs from the shrubs and dried leaves, crisp with the cold. They walked between the boulders as the mountain whispered.

"I brought some logs in the truck," said Ali. "We have enough."

"You've thought of everything." She smiled, and he shrugged, his turn not quite to know what was real. "We're here," she said quietly, and he looked down at his hands held before him. The winter light glanced off his cheeks. "Come, let's wander." She held out her hand.

Ali looked at her outstretched fingers and she followed his eyes to the gold band and all it stood for, her other winters and another life. He cradled her hand in his palm. "Maryam," he said, "let us make this one day ours." A kind frown played across his eyes, as he gently slid the ring over her knuckle and nail, smudged with earth. He placed it in her palm. "It wasn't a Muslim marriage." Maryam shook her head, as much to herself as at his words. "So come."

She stared at her palm, not moving, remembering black rain on a London pavement and her white bridal veil billowing in the wind. She closed her hand into a fist. Just one day. It had existed in her mind for ever, it seemed: its prospect, loss and promise, stretching back and forth through the years. "No, Ali," she said at last. "Not like this. Of all people, you must accept me as I am." She took the ring and slid it back on her finger, her chest tight, angry and sad.

Ali tipped his head back to gaze at the sky and cleared his throat. "You are the same as you ever were." He saw the anguish in her eyes.

"Don't cheapen me or yourself." She turned to the plains. "We have more than this one day, you know that, we always have. We speak more to each other in our minds in a moment than others share in an entire lifetime."

He closed his eyes. "Do we? More than you share with your husband?"

"What do you think?" she replied. "He's a good man, but we don't even share the same language, the same memories. When I talk to him of my love for Mazareh, it means little to him. When I talk to him of my childhood, it's a land beyond his imagining. But he gave me respect and a home that I thought I would never have again. He's the father of my child."

Ali breathed out, seconds passing. "I'm sorry, Maryam, for this moment, for that one night, for its damage, and for every night since."

She shook her head. It had been the start and end of everything. They had paid the price. She did not want to think of it. "No need, Ali. No need."

They stood apart from each other, looking at the ground, until Maryam stepped forward and again held out her hand. Ali bowed his head and this time gently closed his fingers around hers and the cold gold. They walked slowly along the edge of the plateau, saying nothing, watching the sheets of sand twist and billow across the plain below and the ragged clouds tear overhead. They eventually came to a large saffron slab of rock that jutted from the mountain edge, hanging far above the plain, and Ali stepped up ahead of her before reaching back to help. They clambered up and sat side by side in the sky. Space dropped away all around and they breathed it in, the plain far below, full of emptiness. This was always here, Maryam thought, all this time, and it would be here for ever.

She looked at the back of Ali's hand, the dark hairs and thick veins. "We have grown old," she said, her hair blowing free from her scarf.

"I'm older when you're not here, *joon-am*."

She smiled and rested her head back. *"Joon-am,"* she echoed. "I never thought to hear those words."

"Shh, see," Ali whispered, and just beyond the ledge, gliding up on a slipstream, a falcon stretched its wings, rising high from the valley.

"Hah." Maryam threw her arms open to the sky and Ali laughed into the wind.

Later, as Maryam warmed her hands by the fire, Noruz brought out cold lamb and rice from the night before. Ali wrapped the meat in bread and held it to warm on a stick over the smoldering wood and ash. The sky was already dropping to a deeper blue and the shadows lengthened again on the plain below. They had moved the truck to provide some shelter, to protect the fire, and Noruz climbed back inside to eat.

"I'd forgotten days could be like this," Maryam whispered, and Ali nodded, turning the stick above the glowing embers, flickering in his eyes.

They ate hungrily, in silence, looking into the distance. After they'd finished, Ali kicked over the gray ashes into the dusk, leaving a charred black circle on the ground. Maryam stood apart from him and watched the sun start its decline over the mountains on the far side of the plain, Mazareh and the trace of a pale moon in between. Ali came and stood before her, and she leaned to rest her forehead on his shoulder and the thick weave of cloth. "You know I've left a life behind, a home," she said. "I can't undo the life I've lived."

"I won't ask you to do that, Maryam."

The wind wrapped around them and so they rejoined Noruz in the truck and started their winding journey down the mountain. The headlights dipped and lurched around the curves and bends until they slowly returned to the valley floor.

We arrived home from my father's late and Saeed fell asleep on the sofa. I tucked a duvet over him and crawled upstairs to my own bed.

In the morning, I heard him downstairs as I opened the blind, cold air squeezing round the window's edges. I shivered, the previous night fresh in my mind as I dressed, looking at the tumble of our belongings and the mantelpiece full of pictures. Julian would be home at the weekend, at last. I padded downstairs, my feet bare on the floorboards, as Saeed came through the front door, carrying tins of paint from the car. "Sleep all right?" I asked and he nodded, young eyes bright again with the day. He'd let Creswell out into the garden, nosing at the leaves in the fence's shadow, and took the bowl out to feed him. I watched them through the window, trees glistening as the frost melted in the morning sunlight. *Help your old man to bed.* I thought of my father and went into the sitting room to call him, their black-and-white wedding photo beside me.

"How are you?" I asked.

His voice was tired. "I don't know anymore, Sara." He paused. "I'm sorry about last night." I tried to protest, but he wouldn't let me. "I've decided to go home myself for a while, if you're all right with Saeed."

I was surprised. "Of course, yes. To Whitby?"

"Clear the cobwebs." His voice lightened as he spoke.

"Well, it sounds like the right thing. You'll be okay?"

"Yes. *You* take care . . . I'll call."

I went back into the kitchen and leaned against the table. *It's* my *bloody life*. I looked at the wall, its familiar stains and smudges, and decided to move the clock first. It was heavy, balanced on my hip, dust coming off on my fingers. I rested it behind the sofa, leaving a large keyhole shape behind on the wall. When Saeed came back from the garden, I set about making breakfast and he fetched Doctor Ahlavi's parcel. He sat at the table and his fingers ran over the leather binding and turned the thick pages.

"Sara, look, there's a fairytale inside the back cover." He held up a booklet of beige parchment, Farsi script uncurling across it. " 'The Story of Gossemarbart.' "

I pulled up a chair and thought of Doctor Ahlavi, wondering if he knew it was there. We turned the pages and a fine red sand fell from their folds, dusting the table. Saeed touched it with the tips of his fingers. "It's the same color as the earth at Torbat, my family's villa outside Mashhad."

"Can you read the first line?" I asked, remembering how my father would read stories in the summer evenings or winter lamplight.

Saeed traced the page from right to left. *Once upon a time, long ago, a girl child was born to the family of a shepherd living on the saffron slopes of Gossemarbart, and so the mountain gave the small girl her name . . .* He smiled and lifted the booklet to his face. "It smells of home."

"Let's read more later," I promised. "Shall we do the painting first?"

He nodded and carefully put the booklet away.

After we'd finished breakfast, I hunted for the card Saeed would need to make stencils, finding it along with a sharp knife and dust sheet beneath the stairs. He pulled a cushion on to the floor and sat with his back to the radiator, concentrating as a gazelle sprang from beneath his fingers. I kicked the dust sheet open beneath the kitchen wall. It was flecked with paint, pale blue from our bedroom, yellow from the hall, the days of decorating after we'd first married and moved home. I remembered massaging Julian's neck, sore from craning back, and how he'd turned and pulled me under him, making love on the floorboards. I taped round the door and skirting board, ivy tapping at the window in the breeze. Only Fatima's charm was left on the wall, hanging from a silver chain. It was a flat, circular stone with a single black spot in the middle, like a pupil, ringed with turquoise and dark blue—a single eye to protect against evil. I unhooked it, smooth and heavy, and rested it on the table, giving it a nudge with my finger. It spun and winked.

"Saeed, help me with this," I called as I opened the first can of paint and poured it into the tray like cream. He came and stood beside me as the roller soaked it up. "How would you describe the color saffron?" I asked, and he put his head to one side, looking through the window, hearing a rattle and wheeze of traffic from the road.

"Fiery like the sunset," he suggested.

"Or like blood when you cut yourself, as it breaks the wound?"

He pulled a face and I thought of the scan of my baby, translucent skin and pulsing red life, a life that had gone. I struggled for another image.

"Henna on my mother's fingers," I said.

"The earth at Torbat or the dust from Gossemarbart," he replied.

We lifted the roller together and gave the dirty, dull wall its first fiery stripe. Creswell barked from beneath the table. I put my hand in the paint and made a print on the wall. Saeed reached up as well, his hand smaller beside mine, our fleshy mounds and lifelines.

"Again?" I asked, as we lowered the roller back into the paint.

"Like lava," Saeed almost shouted, "burning out of the ground."

"Hookah embers, hubble bubble."

"Poppies and pomegranates."

I felt tears in my eyes and started to laugh. We lifted

the roller and swiped another flame across the wall. "Yaa," I breathed, and Saeed echoed, chuckling as he held out his hands. About time, I thought, leaning back against the table as the day stretched ahead. "Let's have some music."

We cleaned up with some rags before returning to our work as soft jazz played, reminding me of Julian.

As I painted, I remembered the early summer, a Sunday, when I'd wandered upstairs and forgotten why, gazing through the window, where a soft breeze blew full of nodding honeysuckle, jasmine, and foxgloves. I'd leaned back on the white duvet and fallen asleep. Julian had woken me, his hands stroking my hair behind my ears, and I'd arched up to kiss him, half awake, his mouth on my neck, opening my blouse, and slowly, softly we'd made love. And I'd felt it happen, there and then, something anchor inside. I'd curled round and whispered it to him as he kissed my eyelids. The soaring joy of that time seemed so far away.

I thought of another summer, years before. I had been twenty-four and just finished teacher-training. A group of us, old college friends, had rented a cottage on the north Norfolk coast, an old fisherman's house, full of twisting corridors and a maze of sagging rooms, none of the doors fitting anymore. It was tucked at the end of a cobbled lane near to sand dunes and the sea. We'd booked it for a month and life had slowed right down, the air full of salt and seagulls.

Julian had arrived one weekend from London. The first time we'd met had been in Oxford; or hadn't met, as he would later remind me. It had been the end of our first year, and Julian had come to take his brother, a friend of mine, for a drink at the Turl Tavern. We'd been punting, a group of us, and had been late, a summer storm puckering the Cherwell and shining the leaves and snake's-head fritillaries. "They don't grow anywhere else, only on this flood meadow," I'd been told, and I'd knelt to stare at them, purple-spotted leaves and orange stamens. We'd clattered into the pub and Julian had looked up from a table in the window, with gray-blue eyes and a book in front of him, his hand round a half-drunk pint of Guinness. And he'd frowned at us, *all* there for a drink, before his eyes had rested on me, taking me in, and I'd looked down at myself, bare legs striped with mud, wet hair roping over my shoulders, and returned his gaze, "like a star-tled creature," he told me years later. And I'd turned and left just like that, my feet slipping over the wet cobbles on the way home. "Don't run away this time," he'd said, ducking under a low beam into the garden at the fisherman's cottage. I'd frowned and looked away. He'd come the next weekend as well, and the others had teased me. My mother had rung every Sunday to make sure I was okay, but more for her sake than mine.

On our last weekend in Norfolk, Julian drove me to Holkham Bay. I sat silently during the journey, watching the hedgerows and the light in a sky full of the sea's reflections. A kestrel hovered and swooped overhead as the corn fields turned to straw. We parked and I carried my flip-flops through the dunes, enjoying the roughness between my toes, as I reached my hands up high, breathing in the scent of pine needles from the trees behind. The beach stretched before us for ever, beneath an enormous sky, blue and towering with gray-white clouds. "An English sky," Julian said as he took my hand. We walked quietly and I looked at our fingers from the corner of my eye, treading carefully around the jellyfish washed up on the beach, translucent and pink.

Storm clouds caught up with us on the way back, blowing the sand like a river round our ankles, and we ran into the shelter of trees. Then Julian turned and bent his sun-browned face to me, and I stared at him. "Who are you?" I said, and lifted my mouth to his.

And so it had begun.

I started teaching in London and cooked him Persian meals, taking him to the parade of Iranian shops near Olympia, fairy grottos full of the music I'd grown up with, and we bought pomegranates, *gaz,* and dried figs, and got drunk on red wine, dancing to his Mills Brothers tapes.

I put down the roller and went to get a glass of water, rattling in the sink, and filled a glass for Saeed as well before stepping out to the garden to stretch. The sky was already growing lilac-gray in midafternoon, and I heard schoolchildren going home, playing in the garden next door.

The autumn after that Norfolk summer, a decade ago, Julian had taken me to meet his grandmother at the Lanesborough, overlooking Hyde Park. She'd been a flapper, and still had it in her eighty years later: pink cheeks and laughing eyes, fat veins in the back of her hand that shook as she lifted her teacup, and two heavy oak walking sticks propped by her chair. I'd loved listening to her, but had suddenly felt so far away from it all: her, Julian, the mint green and flamingo pink decor and silver-service waitresses in white aprons. Julian must have seen it in my eyes; he'd seen it when we'd first met, after all. I'd smiled and gone to the bathroom—"To powder your nose," his grandmother had said with a wink—and leaned my head against the cool marble tiles.

When I returned, Julian was waiting on a sofa.

"Don't run away again." He held out his hand.

"No. You know your family's different to mine," I said. "It's like they've always been here, and they know everything's just so, as it's always been."

He frowned and I closed my eyes, concentrating to explain.

"My parents had to start from scratch—no routines, no extended family, no customs or ways of doing things that make you feel like you belong to something that's been going on for ever. No easy habits. My father had his English way and Maman had her Iranian way, and it was all mixed up. Sometimes it was wonderful, but sometimes it was horrid—people who were nasty or rude because they couldn't understand what she said or meant, her own frustration."

He put his arm round me. "I think I know what you mean. It's what makes you different. You never assume or take anything for granted. You listen to what I say, and even if I have trouble saying it, you sort of work out what I'm feeling, sometimes better than I do." He laughed then. "I think that's because you grew up as your mother's eyes and ears in a way. It's made you alert, tender."

Later that afternoon, back from the Lanesborough, we'd slept together for the first time; *my* first time. "That's your foreign bit," he'd said, "saving yourself."

I shook my head. If only he knew the tales my mother had told, her dark foreboding: "In Iran, women are cast out just for the *suspicion* of dishonor. Always prize yourself, Sara."

Looking out at the garden, I thought of her and Ali, and of my father's words: *She learned the poem for him.*

"Did you have boyfriends before you met Dad?" I asked her once as a girl.

"No, of course not. Iran's not like that." She'd turned away.

"Why not?" I'd persisted.

"It just wasn't done, Sara. People got married. No boyfriends."

"But what would happen if you did have a boyfriend?"

"I don't know." Her eyes had burned. "You'd be punished."

Later, as dusk was falling, we finished the wall. It glowed red-orange and Saeed smiled up at me. I washed my hands and made tea and toast before sitting beside him as he drew the outline of a rose. "Tell me something about Iran, about Torbat and your villa outside Mashhad," I said. "Is it like Mazareh?"

He put down his drawing and called Creswell over, patting his knee. "I've never been to Mazareh," he replied. "My mother said it was cold and dirty. The villa isn't so far from Mashhad. You turn off the motorway and the road's a dirt track. The villa is on a slope above some apple trees, where we'd kick leaves in the autumn." He grinned. "You have to climb a steep path to the door. It has a big room with a fire, and a porch where we would sleep if it was warm. Some weekends I went there with my mother, just us two. We'd light a fire and sit on the porch in the dark. She told me stories about the trees. She said they turned into spirits in the moonlight with white branches like angels' wings."

"I'd like to go there one day," I said, wishing my mother had talked more of her home and family in that way.

"Me too." He took a deep breath and wiped his shirt sleeve across his face. " 'Hold me with your eyes,' she'd say, if I got scared of a noise in the trees. She said it when she was dying too. 'Hold on to my eyes.' " He looked round the room and I reached for his hand. "I hold on to them in my sleep. She's still there."

"She's always there," I answered, realizing my mother was, too. Maybe that's just the way of it, I thought. And my baby, thumb-sucking, unblinking. What had we given each other to hold on to in the dark? "I'm glad you're here, Saeed." We watched night fall through the window. "Let's have a rest while the paint dries."

After we'd finished our toast, I went upstairs and left Saeed to himself.

The house was cool so I slipped under the duvet. I tried to call Julian but just got his voicemail. I imagined the grid of streets below his Manhattan office block, the rush of people and shuttling lifts, Fifth Avenue sparkling and glutted with Christmas. I fell asleep and dreamed of rollerblading round Central Park, my lungs full of oxygen as sunlight shone through the trees, warm on my skin, round and round. I flew through the branches into a blood red sky.

When I woke, it was black outside. I'd slept for hours. I stretched and rolled out of bed and tiptoed downstairs, as quiet as I could. The television flickered silently in the dark sitting room. Behind the kitchen door, I could hear the hiss of spray paint, smelling of pear drops. I knocked gently.

"Come in." Saeed's voice was full of anticipation.

I looked round the door frame, and there it was. His shapes danced and tumbled in burnt ochre, soft cinnamon, and burnished gold. The storm light glowed on the table. It was wonderful, like a cave painting, or something stolen from an Inca or Maya temple. "Persepolis," Saeed said, standing on the chair, adding the last few stars to a small galaxy he'd painted high in the corner. Creswell nudged the back of my legs and we both went in. He growled and then barked, loud and crisp, at Saeed sparkling with paint.

That evening we sat together, eating bread and cheese. I poured a glass of wine and thought of my father by the northern night sea, my mother in Mazareh, and Julian flying home into the sunrise. I looked at the tumble of shapes, still in the center of it all, and Saeed yawned and took his plate to the sink. "Sleepy?" I asked, and he nodded, eyes half shut. "Thanks for today." I hugged him goodnight and listened to him pad upstairs to bed.

In the cold morning, Ali led Maryam and Farnoosh across an unswept courtyard of dark weeds to a low brick building where unmarried schoolteachers, women from other villages, lived together. One had fallen ill, and Ali waited outside as the two women went through an unlocked door and down a dark, narrow corridor. Steps led off on one side, through a heavy curtain and into a single small room. There was a camping stove on the floor beneath a large window, opaque with dust and scarcely covered by a thin cotton sheet which let the light through.

On a pile of rugs in the corner, a woman lay on her side beneath a carefully darned sheet. The room was too warm, and Maryam lifted her scarf across her mouth, as Fatima had shown her years ago in the poor, fetid quarters of Mashhad on the fringes of the bazaar. Farnoosh knelt beside the woman, wiping her face with the edge of the sheet.

"What's wrong?" asked Maryam.

"She's had a bad stomach for a week now, but she didn't want to cause any trouble. You've been foolish for a teacher." Farnoosh shook her head at the pale woman.

"How old are you?" Maryam asked.

"Thirty-three." The woman looked up through tired eyes.

"Can I get anything for you?"

"Some tea, please."

Maryam turned away. The woman was the same age as Sara, but Maryam knew her daughter would never be so worn or weary, however many years passed. There was a small kettle in the corner and she knelt to light the heater.

"I can fetch water." A voice sounded from beneath the nearby table, startling her.

Maryam lifted the cloth and found a small boy underneath, about ten years old, younger than Saeed, with dried tears around his large brown eyes. "Hello. Who are you?" she asked.

"Bijan Ku'cheek," he whispered.

"Little Bijan, hello," she said again, reaching out her hand. "It's nice to meet you. I'm Maryam Mazar."

He crawled out and turned round in the center of the room, just once, before bending for the kettle and pushing back the drapes to go outside, where the water pipe stuck up from the earth. Maryam heard his thin, fluting voice talking to Ali beneath the window as she handed a stethoscope to Farnoosh. She thought how she had not felt useful for so long, just tending the garden, cooking, waiting. The boy returned, his thin arms stretched with the weight of the full kettle.

"So, who are you?" she asked, as he rested it on the heater.

"My son," the ill woman replied.

"We have our own blackboard next door," Bijan said. "I can write my name in English."

"How clever." Maryam gently pinched his cheek. "Come, let's make your mother some tea to help her get well." She watched him move round on his haunches, reaching beneath the table for tea leaves and cups, and sweets flavored with cardamom.

"For guests," he said with a smile, and she put one in the corner of her mouth.

"Where's your father?" asked Maryam.

"He left when I was pregnant," the woman replied. "We've been fine without him, haven't we, Bijan?"

"I look after my maman," he said, standing carefully and slowly carrying the cup of tea across the room. "Will she be better soon?" he asked Farnoosh.

"Yes." She nodded. "It isn't serious. You should go to school. I'll stay here this morning. Please take Maryam Mazar outside and tell Ali Kolahin all is well."

"Are you sure?" asked Maryam.

Farnoosh blinked her consent, waving them away with her hands. "This room's too small for all of us, please go."

Bijan took Maryam's hand. "This lady will take my mother's class," he declared, standing before Ali outside, with a chill white sky above them.

"Is that so? Well, come along then." He smiled at Maryam. "You can tell us a story or fairy tale, perhaps?" They each took one of the boy's hands, and he walked between them.

"We've cared for a child before," Maryam said as she remembered the small boy she'd picked screaming from the dirt all those years earlier. Ali nodded, and Maryam thought of Saeed and all that had happened, as sand blew up from the plains into her mouth and eyes. She watched their feet move together, up the steps and into a classroom of about thirty children.

Ali cleared his throat in the doorway and they all looked up from where they sat cross-legged on the floor, boys at the front and girls at the back. "You've a guest today. Maryam Mazar will tell us a fairy tale."

She looked round, Ehzat's story of Zohreh in her mind, the firelight and the smell of Fatima's cooking, followed by a memory of Edward's voice. Sara would sit on his lap of an autumn evening as he read her favorite story. "Yes, but on one condition." Maryam smiled. "That I sit in the middle; no front or back to this classroom."

"As you wish," Ali agreed.

She walked carefully between them and eased herself to the floor with Bijan by her side. She looked at the faces turned toward her and their expectant eyes.

"Please tell us your story," said Bijan, pulling at her hand.

Maryam looked over the children's heads to Ali in the doorway. He nodded his encouragement, moved to

215

see her there at last, as he had always hoped. And so she began. She heard Edward's voice again in her mind, and in a way welcomed him too. "It's called 'Hansel and Gretel.' It was my daughter's favorite story when she was your age."

Ali looked through the window as he listened, nothing but the empty brown plains between their gathering and the mountains. When he closed his eyes, he could almost imagine Maryam beside Fatima's fireside again, but he realized how little he knew of the world from where her story came. She didn't seem to want to peer far back into that other life with him, as if it would make her slip and tumble away. He wondered if that was how she'd been with her husband in England: everything separate, past, present, here, there. It was a way to survive. When she did talk of that life, as they sat drinking tea with Noruz, something about Maryam seemed blank to him, lacking the spirit that he'd known in her as a girl, as if she wasn't fully alive. He had no idea how quiet that spirited part of her had learned to become.

Ali turned to look at her in the classroom, telling her story to the children, who laughed with delight at the wicked witch's demise, burned in the oven's flames by clever Gretel. "And so a dove flew ahead through the forest, guiding the two children away from the gingerbread cottage and back to their home, where their father waited." Maryam recalled how Edward would close the book with a flourish then. "And they all lived happily ever after." She looked up at the satisfied smiles around her.

Ali clasped his hands together. "So, let's thank Maryam Mazar and hope she will come again."

The boys and girls stood and clapped as Bijan tugged Maryam to her feet. She hugged him, longing for Saeed and to be able to say sorry. She wished she had told him stories as Mara would have hoped. The children rushed around her and Ali to go outside to the playground for their break.

"Thank you," she said to him in the bustle.

"Please make it a habit," he replied.

Later that afternoon, Maryam listened to Noruz move about in the kitchen. She sat close to the heater, a bright white square of sunlight slanting through the window. She stared at the blank page on her lap and thought of her daughter, various birthdays, Sara's large, hopeful eyes, and the last time she'd seen her, fallen on the bridge, people peering through their car windows as the ambulance siren shouted for space. She tried to picture Sara at that moment, in her home, gazing through the window, her hair tied back, with a pile of exercise books before her. She picked up the pen.

My dear daughter,

How do I write to you now? As I walk these plains and mountains where I grew up, you are always in my heart and mind. I have thought of the first time you were placed in my arms, bloody and beautiful, the most precious thing, and how I have hurt you.

Maryam looked at her writing, the careful English, so opposite to how she felt, the flood of Farsi that should be spilling across the page.

I wish I had the words to tell you how I feel about so many things, about how thankful I am to have seen you grow to be the woman you are. I do not expect or ask you to forgive me, Sara. I am beyond forgiveness.

She put the pen down and moved the paper to the floor. *Beyond forgiveness,* she thought, closing her eyes, a negative image of the room on her eyelids, fading away in black and white. It's where I have lived my life. She imagined her father turning toward her, his silhouette in the shifting dark, the smell of cigarette smoke on his clothes. "I was little more than a child," she whispered. "Didn't I deserve pity?"

She felt her bones and fiber soak it up, life as it had always been, that look on her mother's face and in Saeed's frightened eyes. If it were a sound, how she felt, it would shatter glass, the tremor beneath her skin, always there since that day in the barracks. The soldiers' footsteps in her mind turned into the drum of Saeed's and Sara's running toward the bridge. The sound of a child's laughter replaced by the rush of their breath, eyes that rolled like frightened animals in her dreams. She pressed her head back against the wall. "You taught me well, Father, to be ruthless." She held her hands against her temples. "Noruz," she called, the voice dry in her throat.

Noruz hurried in from the kitchen. "What is it?"

Maryam looked up, her face blotched and taut. "Noruz, what happened to me?" Her hands were fists in her lap. She turned to stare into the bright daylight and Noruz moved to untie the cotton curtain, white with red poppies, to cut the glare from her eyes.

"What do you mean?" She knelt and took Maryam's hand.

"Sometimes I feel hunted by the past." Maryam lowered her head.

"Shush," Noruz whispered, peering into Maryam's eyes. "Come, let me tell you a lesson Doctor Ahlavi taught me once, about the brown square of earth outside. It's a story of the world and of time. He told me it one day when I was sad."

Maryam closed her eyes and listened as Noruz began. "You know that every spring, crocuses grow in the courtyard outside. They come from the dirt, green shoots from nothing. One day the flowers come purple as night, the nights when we were young. And inside the petals, saffron grows the color of blood. Then they die, and the ground is dirt again where chickens shit. That's the way of things: saffron, shit; saffron, shit." Maryam smiled at the word in Noruz's mouth. "I was sad and Doctor Ahlavi told me this: to remember that saffron comes from the dirt."

Maryam thought of the doctor and looked at the wrinkles fanning from the moist corners of Noruz's eyes. "He is the father I would have wished for." He had tried to protect her. She tilted her head to one side and tried to shake her own father from her mind. "Say it again, Noruz."

"What? Saffron, shit; saffron, shit?"

Maryam frowned, trying to keep a straight face, her eyes dry and red. She felt her cheeks flush as Noruz gave in to her own smile, covering her mouth with her chador. It was a relief. Their laughter broke round the room, and a dog barked in reply from the courtyard outside.

"Shush." Noruz held a finger to her lips. "Hassan will think we have been smoking his opium."

They started to laugh again, tears running down their cheeks.

"Oh, Noruz." Maryam sat back. "I will ask Sara to come, to see you, this place."

"Yes, you've said that, of course." Noruz nodded. "Your father will have died wishing he had asked you to come. Believe it." She raised her eyebrows. "Perhaps you have something good to learn from him." Maryam took a deep breath. "So, I'll bring some tea now." Noruz pushed herself up, reaching for a tissue in her sleeve. She blew her nose, still chuckling, and Maryam picked up the letter again.

I know I have no right, Sara, but if I have anything left to give you in this life, or to ask of you, it is that you come and see me here, where I have spent some of my happiest times. My dear Sara, you are the flower of my days. If you come, maybe we will better understand each other and in time that may be something. I will stay here and wait for you. Tell your father to take care and send Saeed my love, my regret. I pray that one day you may each be able to forgive me.

She put down the pen. She would take Sara to her father's tomb at Haram, she thought. Let the past and its fruit meet. That might bring a peace of sorts.

Noruz returned. "You've finished?" she asked, and Maryam nodded. "Hassan will post it." Noruz glanced at the page in Maryam's lap. "Have you told her how to get here?" Maryam looked down at the letter again and shook her head. "So, have some tea and write some more. It's no small journey. You know that better than me."

"Will it be all right if I stay here longer?" Maryam asked.

"You are Hassan's guest and a friend to me. This land bears the name of your family. You are always welcome." Noruz put a lump of sugar in her cheek. "You could help teach English to the schoolchildren."

"I'd like that." Maryam smiled.

"So be it. I will speak to Hassan. He can arrange everything. All will be well. Now finish your letter."

Maryam turned to start another page. She headed it *Travel to Mazareh*, and began a list of advice and directions for Sara to come to her.

The weekend Julian came home, I woke early to bake croissants. Saeed was asleep in the spare room. Downstairs, his shapes still cartwheeled through the warm saffron in the cool day. It was Saturday, quiet, and Creswell turned in his basket as I sprinkled flour on the table and broke chunks of bitter dark chocolate. It would smell good. I wanted to pick ivy for the table, and pulled Julian's coat over my nightshirt.

Outside, a winter chill rose from the earth. On a morning like this, the dew would be lying in a white cloud at the end of my parents' garden. I couldn't believe I would never see my mother there again, that there would be no more tombok music, no more almond-eyed dancing. The ivy came away from the fence in long strands, smelling of sap. Back inside, I piled it into a tall turquoise vase and set the table. Then I pulled up a chair and rested my head on my hands. I didn't hear the taxi pull up outside or the click of the front door.

"Sara."

I heard his voice first, a whisper in my ear, and felt my hair being lifted, warm breath on the nape of my neck. I blinked awake then, lifting my head. "Hello." I put my arms round his neck, and he bent to kiss me. "I've missed you." We rocked against each other, and then the landing creaked upstairs and Julian stood upright, quickly alert, with his hands on my shoulders. I smiled and put a finger to my lips. "It's all right. Saeed's staying with us." Julian shook his head, confused, jet-lagged, but kind. "You'll like him. He's been wonderful. I'll explain." I stood and he pulled me to him, his face against my neck. Then he saw the wall over my shoulder and laughed. "It's Saeed's inspiration, really," I said, before he kissed me again.

We heard Saeed's tread reach the bottom of the stairs and stood apart as I turned to put the kettle on and Julian sat down. Saeed came and stood in the doorway, rubbing his nose and wearing one of Julian's T-shirts down to his knees.

"Good morning," I said, smiling broadly.

Julian patted the chair beside him and Saeed perched there, still half asleep but more awake than he showed. He looked over his shoulder at the cascade of color and blinked at me, then looked out through the window.

I took the croissants from the oven. As we ate, Julian talked of New York and Christmas, the crush and glitter of Tiffany's and Bloomingdale's, carol singers and houses lit from lawn to chimney. Saeed's eyes opened wide at it all, far from Torbat's orchard of fallen leaves and red earth.

Julian found the letter later. After breakfast, he wanted to sleep and I crept under the duvet with him. He liked the window open wide and the blind billowed like a sail. I lifted my nose to the cool breeze, full of oceans and ages, whispering with the slipstream far above, tugging at the angry green waves on Whitby's shore, at the deep blue Caspian. Late morning, the post rattled through the door. It had piled up for days on the sideboard. I woke with pins and needles and stretched to go downstairs, to Saeed in the kitchen with the fairy tale I'd forgotten. Julian padded down after me, stubbled and sheepish, come-to-bed eyes above Saeed's head. "In a while, crocodile," I said, and he picked up the post, the letter opener cutting and slicing the envelopes.

"One for you." He stroked the back of my leg.

I looked at it, white, creased, and unopened, my mother's writing in smudged blue Biro. "Later." I looked through the window. "Let's go for a walk." I propped the letter on the sill. "I know you're tired, but it would be good to get some air, don't you think, down by the river?"

"Okay." He pulled me onto his lap and kissed me in spite of Saeed.

I put my arm round his shoulder and rested my head against his. "I want to talk. So much has happened."

"What's been going on, Saeed? Apart from this magic." He nodded at the wall.

Saeed looked at him. "It's all been a bit topsy-turvy," he said, practicing Edward's expression, new in his mouth. Julian and I laughed, and Saeed grinned too.

"So how can I make my mark?" Julian asked.

Saeed went to the corner, where the spray paints and rags were piled. He came and sat on the chair beside Julian and took his hand, laying it against a dust cloth. He shook the spray can and coated Julian's palm. "Above the door." He pointed, pushing his chair into place.

Julian, smiling, stepped up, and left his handprint on the wall. "What about you two?" he asked, but Saeed was already spraying my hand and then his own. Soon our prints were next to Julian's, fanned above the door with space still left for Fatima's charm. Julian lifted me down from the chair, in spite of the gold paint, and I felt our bodies press for each other. "Okay, walk in half an hour, Saeed," he said, and led me back upstairs to the bathroom. "Looks like you could do with a shower." He stroked the hair from my face.

The water ran hot and we stretched into it, my arms round his neck as he lifted me up, leaning back into the cascade and warm peace. Our mouths and fingers on each other's skin. Afterwards, we changed like guilty teenagers before hurrying downstairs and quickly out toward the river. Saeed walked ahead, with Creswell tugging at his lead.

Julian put his arm round my shoulders and I told him in a rush all that had happened: about my dad and Whitby; our visit to Doctor Ahlavi; the poem and Ali. We crossed over the Broadway, through the throng of people, and then, without quite realizing it, we were on the bridge for the first time since that day. Part of me wanted to turn back, but Julian led me on to where it had happened. I knelt on the pavement and touched the tarmac, spreading my fingers wide, rubbing and looking for blood that had long since been washed away. Julian pulled me up and held me. Saeed was already safely on the other side. He waved to us, a single sweep of his arm from the bank, and we turned to follow him down the unmade river path.

The letter was still waiting on the windowsill when we got home. Saeed and Julian kindled a fire next door and I sat at the kitchen table, turning the envelope in my hand and looking at the saffron wall. I turned another letter in my mind, one left on another windowsill, in my mother's kitchen, a winter long gone, months after Fatima had left. It had been the news of her death, propped up waiting for us. I'd been late for school that morning, and my mother had smiled as she'd straightened my tie and smoothed my hair. "We can read it tonight." It had been a ritual I loved: sitting in the corner of the sofa with her, a cup of hot chocolate each, and she'd trace each word with her finger, reading aloud, first in Farsi, then English.

"Let me open it," I'd asked that evening, careful not to tear the Ayatollah's stamp. I handed it to her and our eyes bent to read together, the first line. I waited and turned to see her take a sharp breath. She made a sound I'd never heard before or since, like something dying, a cry, moan, gasp. She threw her hands to her face, knocking the hot chocolate from the arm of the chair and splashing the carpet and curtains. "Oh dear," I whispered as she bent double, her head on her knees. She pushed me away, slipping to the ground, and I sat on the edge of the sofa and cried, not knowing why, waiting for my father to come home, hours later. I grew tired and she grew quiet lying there. Eventually, I knelt and stroked her hair, fanned out on the carpet's deep Mashhad red weave of flowers.

I heard Julian and Saeed next door and reached for the letter opener. The tissue-thin sheets lay on the table in front of me. I unfolded them. "Julian," I called, my eyes fighting through her words: requests, instructions, hopes.

226

He came and I held out the pages.

"I have to go to her," I said as he sat beside me.

"What does she say?"

"Too many things. Everything. She says she's waiting for me."

"But you're only just getting better, Sara. I've only just got back," he protested.

"I know, but I don't feel I really have a choice. I have to go and bring her home."

That evening we sat and ate quietly. "I suppose I can get my mother to come and stay while you're gone," Julian suggested. "She could teach Saeed a thing or two." They mock-grinned at each other, learning to get along.

"I don't want to think about it." I felt I was losing my moorings.

Later, in the sitting room, we watched the fire's embers spark and shoot up the chimney. "Shall we read some more of Doctor Ahlavi's fairy tale?" I asked Saeed, sipping a glass of red wine. He nodded and went to fetch it.

His voice was slow and careful as we listened: *The land of Gossemarbart's birth was ruled by a ruthless khan, who each year demanded the villagers pay him a tenth of their wealth. But in the year of her birth, there was a terrible drought and her father had nothing to give . . .* It was just the start.

We didn't finish "Gossemarbart" that weekend or the next. My father had decided to rent a holiday cottage in

Robin Hood's Bay, near Whitby, so Julian phoned his mother and she traveled up from Bath, full of care and efficiency, and thinly veiled delight at my own parents' troubles. Still, it would be good to have her around. She dusted and tidied where I'd spent the previous days dusting and tidying in anticipation of her arrival. Julian hurried back to work, away from her raised eyebrows and pink rouge; and I packed my bags, not feeling I'd made any decision, just that I had to go, and wondered if my mother felt that way, too.

Her letter told me how to get a visa through a small outfit next to the Iranian Embassy near Hyde Park. She told me how to fill in the forms, the right names and numbers. I visited them one Monday, through an anonymous doorway, up dark steps, and had my passport back in a fortnight. Saeed came on the Tube with me to buy tickets from Iran Air, opposite the Ritz, everywhere bright with Christmas, just a few weeks to go. I was served by a gentle, bald man, who reassured me traveling was safe. I tried not to think of Julian's mother and her clipped asides. The flight would leave the following Sunday and return ten days later. "I suppose the sooner you go, the sooner you'll be back," Julian had said that morning.

Saeed and I walked along Bond Street, windows full of glitter and holly. We linked arms in the bustle. "Would you like me to bring anything back for you?"

He shook his head, then changed his mind: "Maybe some saffron-red earth?"

We stood together beneath the gray London sky,

amid its towers and parks, as the river twisted out to the sea, and autumn leaves caught in the breeze and swirled up and away.

4. Mazareh

Time will say nothing but I told you so,
Time only knows the price we have to pay;
If I could tell you I would let you know.
                                        —W. H. Auden

*S*ara was sick, squatting by the roadside between Mashhad and Mazareh, the taxi pulled up on a scruff of earth behind her. She retched, hands holding her head, clutching the dark scarf in place as dust and grit blew up from the road. She slumped on the ground, waiting for the clammy sweat on her back and neck to dry. A donkey ran with a cart along the inside lane, eyes bulging and frothing at the mouth as horns blared and trucks, cars, and lorries swerved to overtake it. Sara stood again and tried to breathe slowly, smelling the sulphur billowing from a factory they'd passed earlier. She looked back to the nicotine sky over Mashhad, then forward to the horizon, the mountains she'd flown over the day before, as the taxi driver punched his horn. She wiped her mouth on her sleeve and climbed back inside.

It was the policeman at the fuel stop who had upset her, his sharp knock on the window, peering in. His skin was pockmarked, with a sheen of grease. "He must see your papers," the taxi driver explained, and she'd passed them to him, with some money folded inside as she'd been told. He made her step from the car and turn round as he watched her, close enough to smell him. She took a drink of water and swallowed as the taxi pulled away again, remembering her mother's letter, its list of instructions: what to wear, how to look, who to meet, names and addresses. *My niece, Shirin, will look after you when you arrive in Mashhad. She will make sure you have a safe taxi and the right documents to travel to Mazareh. Bring warm clothes and strong shoes. The nights may be freezing.* Sara held on to the door handle, gritting her teeth as the car swerved round another hole in the road. Some prayer beads and a picture of Aya-tollah Khomeini rattled on the dashboard.

She had stayed with Shirin in Mashhad for a couple of days after her flight from Tehran, and remembered stepping from the plane, an old Aeroflot jet, into the cold turquoise morning. *"Salaam,"* she'd heard across the tarmac as a petite woman bustled toward her, dressed all in black, bug-eye sunglasses, and peach gladioli bouncing in her arms. "Sara Mazar, you are your mother's daughter," the woman proclaimed with a smile.

"Shirin?" Sara asked, her voice hoarse from a night's traveling, as the woman took her arm and led her across to the terminal.

"My husband Hameed is somewhere." She looked around, clicking her tongue, until they found him, a sturdy, red-faced man waiting by the baggage reclaim—a single creaking conveyor belt in an arrivals hall of marble and bright white sunlight. They'd shaken hands as Shirin chatted to Sara about her journey, whether she was happy, sad, hungry, tired.

"Enough, woman." Hameed pinched his wife's cheek. "Of course she's hungry and tired and needs a bath and none of your nonsense gossip." He winked and Shirin chewed her lip as Sara followed them to the car park, apricot leaves tumbling along the ground. "You like Madonna?" Hameed turned to ask from the front of his silvery four-by-four, the only one in the car park. She shrugged, and so they drove through the outskirts of Mashhad to "Like a Prayer."

The taxi driver reached forward to turn on his radio, wires trailing round their feet, and this time Persian music crackled through the speakers, reminding her of the garden in Richmond, the smell of blackberry bushes in autumn and the rasp of her cassette player. Lightly, she lifted the driver's prayer beads from the dashboard and saw his gruff nod as she let them slip cool through her fingers. She rested her head against the window, and thought of seeing the dawn break over Tehran in the hours before her connecting flight to Mashhad. The customs officer had peered at her from behind a white picket gate that had made her smile, and she had looked down at her hands, remembering her mother's instructions: *Be demure, Sara.* Past the shoving elbows and crush of reunions, she stood outside the terminal, not knowing quite what to do. She walked by a lopsided barrow of fruit near the exit, laden with cellophaned watermelons. An old man was sleeping by its side with sores on his legs like small open mouths. Families pushing for taxis jostled her out of the way, and she worked out how to get one herself, sinking into a battered front seat as the driver loaded her luggage in the trunk. She had three hours until the flight, and when he asked her where she wanted to go, she had said the only name she could remember: "Alborz," the mountains, and they sped away.

Tall, slim buildings slipped past, painted with murals of the ayatollahs and warrior martyrs, twenty stories high and bedecked with roses and lines from the Koran. The city had clambered with the road up the mountainside, amid low-rise buildings, gray and shuttered. Icy streams tumbled down channels on either side, with a smell of dust, metal, and snow in the air. At last the taxi pulled into an empty car park and Sara stepped out. "Fifteen minutes," she gestured to the driver, and walked to a bench overlooking the city, the light already changing to a gentle, brown dawn. She watched the bare shadows of trees, leaves trodden into the soil, as tenement windows slowly lit up in squares of white and yellow.

Driving back to the airport a little later, she watched the streets come to life: shopkeepers sweeping their pavements before brightly lit windows, filled with swathes of herbs and piled-up fruit. Her eyes followed a young girl in jeans and black headscarf who sauntered, yawning, from a bakery, with sheets of bread carried beneath her arm.

That was just a couple of days ago.

In the taxi to Mazareh, she wiped her mouth, the taste of bile still there. They watched the mountains approach, where her mother waited. Looking down from the airplane, she had imagined landlocked faces in the dry, stony ground, where even the twisting scars of riverbeds had seemed empty, the water running as dark as earth. As they approached now, the foothills were gently domed, rising smooth, ochre and burnt sienna from the dusty plains.

The previous day she had sat on the steps at the rear of Shirin's home, as the sun sank in the afternoon sky. She had woken after lunch while the rest of the house was still asleep. *It will be the holiday after Ramadan,* her mother had written. She wandered through quiet, cool marble rooms, and between places in her mind, imagining Creswell in a corner and missing Julian's warmth when she awoke alone. Long shadows fell beneath the half-open curtains of the drawing room, where she saw a photo of her grandfather tilted on a walnut sideboard. He met her eye-to-eye, with his dark chiseled sockets and cheekbones. She stared at him, then turned away.

She had gone through the kitchen and down the steps to the back door, walking round a crate of clementines on the floor. Taking one, she walked outside and sat on the steps beside the half-empty pool, full of dead leaves. She stuck her nail in the rind and heard the door open again, as Hameed appeared with cups of tea for them both. Their conversation played again in her memory as the taxi turned off the motorway on to the potholed, empty road. It stretched ahead in a chalky-white line to the horizon.

"So, Sara, tell me, how do you find us?" Hameed asked.

"I don't know," she replied. "I feel a bit like a child; everything's new."

He chuckled at the ground. "You'll be fine. But you must prepare yourself for Mazareh. It's not like here. It's just mud and straw buildings, a dirt track, stinking of animals, sheep and cows. The toilet is a hole in the ground. My wife doesn't know why Maryam stays there so long."

Sara shrugged. "It's her past." Doctor Ahlavi's words echoed in her mind.

"Well, tomorrow you'll be there. Perhaps you can bring her back to us."

"I hope so."

They sat and watched the sparrows swoop, their chatter broken only by the ricochet of a broadcast call to prayer.

"You must be cold." Hameed went inside to fetch a sheepskin rug. He came back with Shirin, looking younger, rested, her face clean of makeup. She carried a large platter of raw lamb shish kebab for that evening, and Hameed wheeled out a barbecue from beside the pool.

Shirin sat on the step then and took Sara's hand. "You look so like your mother when she was younger," she said. Sara asked how she remembered her, and Shirin looked away then. "I was a small child when Maryam left. I really know her only from pictures, stories from my mother, Fatima, and Mara."

"What stories?" Sara asked, the soft breeze flaring the charcoal alight.

"Sad stories, I suppose, about the price of looking for another world, of not being satisfied with what your family wishes."

"Maybe she found a good world," Sara replied. "I'm here because of it."

"I know." Shirin squeezed her hand. "They're just the stories people tell to fill the gaps. Tomorrow, you'll see for yourself."

"Maryam and Ali," Sara replied.

"You know?"

"I know there seems to be some mystery, but no more." Sara had thought of her father then, and the letter she carried from him to her mother in Mazareh. It had arrived from Whitby the day before her departure. She longed to bring her mother home to him. "I would like to hear your story, if I may, to fill the gaps," she said.

Hameed shook his head. "Take care, Shirin. It isn't your story to tell."

"Husband of mine," she replied, "this girl has come from London and tomorrow she'll be in the middle of nowhere. She should know what to expect."

He turned away as Shirin settled down, the sheepskin round their shoulders.

She began. "Well, the story is that Ali worked for our

grandfather, a man of position, prestige, a soldier in the Shah's army. You know this?" Sara nodded, thinking that it wasn't the first time Shirin had told this tale. "When Ali was a boy, our grandfather brought him to Mashhad from the village to run errands, be useful, that sort of thing. It was a good chance for a village boy. They say he was talented and learned quickly, and that our grandfather grew to rely on him, writing his letters, attending meetings. He became a young confidant of sorts, a surrogate son, maybe, until our grandfather had one of his own." She paused then. "Although now my uncle Shariar is dead." She shook her head at the ground.

"Anyway," she continued, "Ali worked hard and grew up within our family's walls. He earned our grandfather's respect, his trust. He taught himself English from the radio—can you believe it?—and taught Maryam as well. They would read together, and in time became friends. They say he was handsome." Shirin looked up at Sara and smiled, a woman's smile. "But in the end, this didn't please our grandfather. There was a night of riots when they disappeared together. No one knew where they were, what had happened. The rumors weren't good for our family's honor. Ali was a servant, after all, a peasant, for all his learning. They were men like him who killed my uncle."

Sara watched the charcoal ash blow across the pool. "Was Ali a revolutionary?" she asked, surprised.

"He's nothing," Shirin replied. "His life has been nothing."

Sara frowned at Shirin's judgment of Ali; taken aback at the scorn in her tone even though Shirin had never known him.

"When my mother told this story," Shirin continued, "she'd say that our grandfather, in his temper, couldn't forgive Maryam her waywardness. He had to protect our family name. He had tried to marry her to someone of her own class, but she refused, and so in the end he sent her away to Tehran and then England, out of sight. And he banished Ali, without books, to the village he'd come from." She looked at Sara. "In those days, this wasn't so bad. It was merciful. At least they were alive."

"Well, I suppose it's been my mother's life to live." Sara turned to face Shirin, who raised her eyebrows in return.

"But, you see, it's not just *her* life," Shirin replied. "It's the life of her family here as well, and now her family in England. The story is, she broke her father's heart, and she hurts you now, too, does she not, with this life of hers?"

The taxi made its way between the hills, a breeze blowing through the window, cool and smelling of snow, as the sky darkened in the late afternoon. "We'll be there soon." The driver coughed, gesturing to Sara's scarf, which had slipped to the back of her head.

She pulled it forward again, tightening the knot beneath her chin. Her mother was close, and the prayer beads slipped through her fingers. She had returned home from Oxford once, at the end of her first term,

237

driven back from the sinking river fogs, longing for the sweep of Richmond Hill and Christmas with her family. "I thought you might not come back," her mother had said, waiting on the doorstep, cheeks mottled with the cold.

"Where did you think I'd go?" Sara asked, while Edward shook his head.

"The other side of the world." Maryam had laughed and hugged her too hard.

Now she had brought her here.

The taxi driver pointed to a gray dust cloud growing in the distance. "See, they come to meet you."

Sara watched the cloud approach and come into focus.

Four old Russian motorbikes emerged from the dips in the road, two young men on each, in thick jerseys and heavy clothes. They circled the car as it moved over the bumps and ruts, peering in, unshaven and lean. They drove two behind and two ahead, escorting Sara to the village.

Nearly an hour later, they came to a scratched old sign: MAZAREH. Sara looked through her fingers. She could hardly see for quiet tears. It was the place she had always wanted to know, even as a little girl wearing her mother's scarves in the empty house. The motorcyclists whooped, pulling pistols from their back pockets and shooting into the sky above the mud walls ahead. Her arrival had been announced.

Maryam heard the gunshots empty into the air. She sat on the flagpole steps in the school playground, with a book on her lap and a small girl on either side. They had all looked up as the shots rang across the mud walls, and Maryam's finger stopped at the line they had been reading. In the middle distance, light splintered off the mountains and she listened to her breath, the playground emptying, feet chasing and drumming toward the square, to Sara.

"*Khonoom* Mazar, it's your daughter!"

Maryam looked at the face turned toward her. The child's words floated white in the air.

"Go, Maryam," shouted Ali as he walked from the school, and the two girls tugged her to stand.

She looked over her shoulder at him, the book fallen to the ground.

"I'm here," he said, and bent to lift the book from the dust as the little girls tried to run, pulling Maryam through the gap in the wall and the short distance to the square.

Sara stared through the windshield into the sun. Its rays were low and rose pink through the motorbike's dust. Doors opened like mouths in the smooth curve of walls ahead of her and people as brown as earth stepped out as the gunshots whispered away. Children jostled forward as she sat in the car and wiped her face on her sleeve.

"A long journey," the driver said, clearing his throat, and she nodded, holding out the prayer beads. "Please, keep them. I have others."

She held them in her palm, lime green as the first

leaves of spring on the acer in her garden. She looked at the children's faces through the window, and they stepped back as she opened the door.

"*Salaam,* Sara Mazar," they whispered in a familiar rhythm, just like the chant of her junior classes at school when she started a lesson: *Good morning, Mrs. Johnson.* Other villagers had gathered as well, dark-eyed women passing words behind their hands, breaking into a slow handclap. Then they parted.

Sara and Maryam faced each other in the dust.

"Welcome, Sara," Maryam said. Her voice carried a weight of hope and sorrow.

Sara looked at her large eyes beneath her black scarf and her weathered skin.

Why? was all she wanted to shout, beg, plead.

Maryam walked forward and her chador dragged over the cold earth. "Welcome," she said again, so quiet, and reached out for her daughter's hand. "You must be tired." There was a gray weariness in Sara's face that she hadn't seen before.

They leaned toward each other, foreheads touching, tears in their eyes, before a small girl tugged at Maryam's elbow, pulling her away.

"They all want to meet you," Maryam explained.

Sara's hand fell by her side as her mother turned and knelt to introduce each child, familiar with every name. Sara shook each of their hands at least once, up and down, soft and warm, smudged with dirt. For a moment she shut her eyes, dry and heavy with the journey and the lull of strange voices. She felt far away, the prayer beads still in her hand and another flicker of lime green in her mind: the tail feathers of an escaped canary high in a pine tree looking out to sea. She welcomed the sliver of memory: Holkham Bay, lying with Julian in the sand dunes. It had made them sad, that small lost bird, waiting in the sea breeze.

"Sara Mazar, Sara Mazar," a single voice echoed, and she looked across the square. A small old lady hurried toward them from a cobalt blue door, a bursting grin of wrinkles across her face.

"This is Noruz." Maryam stood, again taking Sara's hand.

They looked at each other, searching for something, as Noruz bustled forward, stretching to kiss Sara on each cheek.

"Night's falling. Please come to my home now," Noruz pleaded in Farsi.

"My bag," Sara remembered, turning round.

"Hassan, Noruz's husband, will bring it," said Maryam. She pointed him out as he crossed the square, and Sara reached to shake his hand, but Hassan flinched and turned away. He went to speak with the taxi driver instead. "He's been praying," Maryam tried to explain. "He thinks touching you will make him unclean."

Sara looked from her to Noruz. She felt as if Hassan had slapped her or seen her naked. Maryam used to bind her breasts, she had told Sara that once, hiding herself away to look like a young girl.

"I'm sorry," said Maryam. "It's just his way."

"It's all right." Sara's voice was threadbare. "Would

it be okay for me to be alone out here for a little while, just to get my bearings? It's been a long journey."

"Of course," Maryam replied. "We'll make tea, just through the blue door. Little Bijan will keep you company."

The small boy had been waiting in the nearby shadow of the clinic, and came forward now with his fingers in his mouth. He took them out and held his hand open to Sara, damp and warm. "Clever Gretel," he said, and Sara burst into a smile then for a moment, understood only by her mother.

"I told them our fairy tale, in the school," Maryam explained, and Sara nodded, remembering her childhood evenings in front of the fire. "Come in soon. Noruz is a wonderful cook."

Sara watched them go through the cobalt blue door and wandered to the concrete step of the clinic to sit down. She waved as the taxi lurched away, children and families disappearing back into their homes. Bijan sat by her side, quietly drawing shapes with his finger in the earth, and Sara let herself settle, watching him. He put his hand in his pocket and held out a sweet to her, and she took it, smiling, a taste of cardamom. She felt tired beyond words, longing for sleep.

Inside, Maryam placed Sara's bag beside her own in the room she shared with Noruz. The three of them would sleep side by side. She folded a towel ready for Sara to wash, remembering the tall airing cupboard on the landing in Richmond, full of soft sheets and fresh laundry. She sat on the floor with her reflection in the black window. So, it had happened. She had brought Sara to Mazareh; and now Sara would meet Ali. "Could we have read this in our tea leaves, Fatima?" she whispered. "As if all lost things could be washed up and made whole again." She looked at Sara's bag and glimpsed Edward's handwriting on an envelope: *Maryam Dean*. She reached for it, his ivory writing paper from the bottom drawer of his oak desk, pale blue ink. She lifted it to her face, the smell of her other home, and recalled the lamplight in Edward's study and the scratch of his fountain pen. He would blink up from his work when she brought him cocoa in the evening. *Till death us do part*. She placed the letter back in Sara's bag. It wasn't yet hers to open. Sara should give it to her, as Edward would have asked. Maryam returned outside, to where Sara was sitting on the step of the clinic. A glow of light from the surrounding compounds kept the pitch-black night at bay. "Your mother will be waiting for you, Bijan," she called, and he stood up from his drawing in the dust.

"Goodnight, then." He held out his hand to Sara, before ambling back across the square, to his room on the village edge.

Maryam sat beside Sara on the step, alone at last. They both looked at Bijan's scrawl on the earth, the outline of a house.

"I'm glad you're here." Maryam held out her hand and Sara rested her fingers in her mother's palm. "I don't know if you can forgive me."

Sara shook her head, not knowing the answer. "I don't know what to think."

"I'd do anything to make it all right."

"I know." Sara looked into her eyes. "All I really want to know is why."

"Yes." Maryam bowed her head. "We can talk. But first tell me, how is Saeed?"

"With Julian, and his mother. She's keeping them both shipshape."

As they had often done before, they both smiled at the thought of Sara's big, bossy mother-in-law with her pink rinse. It didn't last.

"And Edward?" Maryam asked.

Sara looked away. "He's been trying to get in touch; waiting for you to call." She felt a leaden sadness and tiredness in her belly where life should be. "He's written a letter to you. It's in my bag." She turned back to her mother and wanted to shake her, but her arms felt heavy and numb. "He's locked up the house and gone to Whitby. He knows about Ali." She waited. "Shirin told me, Doctor Ahlavi, Saeed. It all fitted together. So where is he—this Ali?"

Maryam looked at her daughter with her chin in the air and recognized the challenge as a far gentler version of her own, long ago. "Maybe you'll meet him tomorrow."

"You don't deny it?"

"I don't know anymore," Maryam said. "Should I deny a friendship in my old age?"

"But he is why we're both here, isn't he? Why you've stayed so long?"

"In a way. Ali is all that's left of my past. Everyone else is dead and gone, even Mara now. He's the only person who knew me then, who can help me remember."

"But what about Dad? What about me, and Saeed?"

"I don't know." Maryam's voice was quiet. "Please don't be angry."

"Don't I have a right to be?" Sara's head was in her hands, her voice taut.

"Yes, yes, you do, and we have time to talk, but please don't be like me or my father. Look at me." Sara lifted her face. "Anger has no going back. A slap cannot be undone. Some insults can never be unsaid. They worm away inside, however much you regret, hope, pray, until something terrible happens—like the day on the bridge. I don't want you to suffer like that."

"But you've made us suffer. Why did you do those things?"

Maryam put her hand to her lip, the scar made by her father's ring.

"Because, in a way, it was done to me."

"But what happened to you? *Why* did this happen?"

"Sara, that will live and die with me."

"Why?"

"Because I would not have you hear it."

"Not even if it helps me understand this mess?"

"I don't know." Maryam bowed her head.

"But I've come all this way."

"I know. But not now, please." It hurt her to swallow. "I'm sorry."

Sara felt exhausted, clambering with bruised bones toward some understanding that seemed so far out of reach. She didn't want to fight, and waited for her blood to calm before reaching for her mother's hand. "So, it's cold. Let's go inside."

They stood, and Maryam gently tidied Sara's scarf.

Side by side, they walked across the square and into the quiet compound, passing through the drapes to where they would sleep. Sara took it in, her home for the coming days. She washed the grime from her face in a sink where the water ran like darts of ice, before Maryam took her across to the main room to eat.

Sara smiled, polite but tired, as the faces turned to greet her. She noticed Farnoosh eating quietly and slightly apart, how she smiled up at Maryam, a little nervous, and then at her. Noruz patted Sara's hand. "Welcome," she said, as she helped to fill her plate, and the chatter washed over them.

"Tomorrow we could visit the school, if you'd like," suggested Maryam.

"Doctor Ahlavi said Ali teaches there," Sara replied.

"Yes, he does."

"Fine." Sara didn't know what to think anymore. "And we'll call Dad as well?"

"Yes." Maryam looked at her hands, and felt her worlds blurring, as she must have wanted when she brought Sara to Mazareh. "It's best to call in the afternoon, because of the time difference. We may need to queue. There's just one phone."

"All right." Sara nodded, pushing her food round the

plate. It would be midafternoon in London now, she thought, time for tea and toast, Saeed swinging his legs beneath the kitchen table. She looked at Maryam again. "I don't feel like I really know you anymore."

"There's so much for me to show you here," Maryam continued, her voice faltering. "There's a spring about a mile away, in the foothills. I used to go there with Fatima as a child. We can see the stone woman, and the old shrine."

Sara listened, trying to picture her mother in the places of which she spoke. "Okay, but I need to sleep now, if it isn't rude. I'm so tired."

Maryam saw the shadows beneath her daughter's eyes. "They'll understand."

Noruz smiled as they stood and Sara murmured her apologies. They returned to the small room beyond the courtyard and the red drapes, where Sara took off her jeans and slipped beneath the coarse blankets still wearing the rest of her clothes. She was too tired and cold to undress completely. She handed Maryam the letter, then leaned back on the pillow, hard as board, and shut her eyes. She thought of the vast spaces and shadows beyond the window and walls, where there was nothing for hours and miles except the whispering dark.

Maryam listened to Sara's breathing deepen. It had been years since she had watched her sleep, dark eyelashes on her pale skin. She rested against the wall and turned the letter in her hand. It had been so long since Edward had written to her, the love letters of her youth.

Slowly she slid her finger to open the envelope and unfolded the heavy vellum pages. She started to read, his voice in her mind.

My dear Mari,

I hope this letter finds you well. I write it looking out to sea from my sitting-room window. By now Sara will have told you of my retreat to Robin Hood's Bay. It's mid-morning and I sit before a rolling North Sea with a sky full of storm light. I have your photos for company as well. I hope you don't mind that I took them from your room, to help me think. I took that paperweight, too, the trapped red rose. It was such an ugly, dead thing. I went to the end of the jetty in Whitby the other day, remembering you in your red coat all those years ago, and threw it as far into the waves as I could. I am sorry I ever gave it to you.

I have been walking on the moors most days, and doing my best to remember our good times, the quiet moments. I think we had a gentle under-standing, did we not, over time. It felt like happi-ness to me, just that quick smile over your knitting, looking up from the flower bed, your bonfires or the washing-up. We have had a life, Mari, and our own little girl. Take good care of her and send her home when she is ready.

I know you will not come home for a while, which is why I write. I suppose I have always known from the earliest days that you would need to complete this journey of yours, although I hoped it might be some other way. I have been thinking of your bad dreams when we first married. You would call out. I wasn't sure if it was a name or just a sound, but Sara will tell you we have deduced there is someone real enough to whom you have returned. I will not write his name. Still, I find I cannot absolutely hate him, whoever he is. We have shared the summer and autumn of our lives, and I have a feeling winter will bring you back to me, to the walls we made our home. But please don't think me magnanimous. I fear I am weak in this acquiescence of mine, some sort of English packing up of feelings as efficient as the way I will pack up and let our home of thirty years. The mirror above your dressing table has been smashed, one terrible afternoon. It's mended now. Our wedding pictures as well, burned on the fire; not all, just enough for me to see where the venom of loss might take me. That's why I'm here, with the sea again.

So I think I will let the house after Christmas and put everything into storage. In the night here, I find myself imagining the other lives that will tread the corners where we lived for three decades. Will they have a family and a hallway full of shoes, boots and bicycles? Or will they be old, as we have become, taking the stairs a step at a time, polished tables and books by lamp-

*light? This is the life we have lived. I will write
again. Please get word to me on how you are,
that you are well.*

Yours only,
Edward

Maryam lay on her bed, the pages crumpled on her
breast. She thought of the last time they had been
together, when Edward had driven her to Heathrow, sitting in silence. She had rested back in the plush leather
seat, watching the gray outer suburbs of London pass
by, as the sky grew loud with the screech and scream of
jet engines. She'd turned to watch the side of Edward's
face and leaned to kiss his cheek as they queued in
traffic. He'd turned to her, eyes brimful of tears, and
then looked away again, parking the car and taking her
luggage to check-in. They had hugged at the departure
gate, and he'd kissed her forehead.

"You have been the most beautiful thing in my life."

She hadn't been able to talk as he let go of her hands
and walked away. She wished she had said, "And you
have been the most patient and gentle of husbands. Part
of me never expected to feel safe again."

Sara woke early, her stomach unsettled and her neck
stiff from the hard floor. She listened to her mother
breathing and Noruz whistling gently. From where
she lay, she could reach the edge of the thin curtain
and look out, up at a mackerel sky, lilac and gray in
the dawn. The sour odor of a day's travel and the

dark night made her feel nauseous as she had the day before. It grew worse as she tried to sit up. Clammy and giddy, she tugged on her jeans and stumbled out through the drapes. Noruz turned on her mattress as she passed, looking through the thin slits of her half-open eyes.

Sara hurried across the courtyard in her socks, her hand over her mouth as she reached the toilet. She retched, kneeling there by the hole in the ground, her eyes closed and hands chill as ice. She wanted Julian and waited for her breath to slow, with dirt beneath her nails. Afterwards, she sat outside on the step, preferring the cold breeze to the kerosene fug inside. She pulled a rug round her shoulders and listened to the day begin.

In a while, Noruz padded out as well, sucking her gums and sniffing the air. She beckoned Sara across the courtyard and through to the main room, where she gestured for her to sit on the carpet. Noruz brought tea, bread, and honey from the kitchen and watched Sara eat with small, careful bites.

A little later, Farnoosh joined them and sat quietly apart in the corner. She rocked gently on her haunches, chewing slowly, focused on the middle distance. Something about her made Sara sad, reminding her of one of those shy, troubled girls back at school, who hung back and mixed with no one. She was never sure if they needed to be hugged or left alone. Farnoosh glanced at her from the corner of her eye before gathering up her chador and crossing the square to the clinic for the day to begin.

• • •

Maryam wandered round the room where they had slept, kneeling to fold Sara's blanket, which was still crumpled on the floor. She thought of Edward's letter. It was as he had always been, making the space she needed. She buried her face in the blanket where she stood and felt the streets of London slipping, sinking, drowning beneath the quiet plains, her mountains, and their expectation of nothing. Would a part of her have that old life gasp for breath again? She didn't know. She would share the letter with Sara, she thought. It might create an understanding of sorts. She crossed the courtyard and found her daughter sitting in the main room on the floor, with a scarf tied round her head like a gypsy. Maryam thought how young she looked, just awake.

"Did you sleep well?"

"So-so," Sara replied.

"Noruz has looked after you?"

"Yes." She turned away and tore some more bread.

"I read the letter from your father last night. I thought you might like to see it." Maryam held the envelope out and Sara reached for it.

Just as her mother had, she turned it in her hand and tried to picture him writing, with his shoulders bent and sea mist through the window.

"Can I take it outside?" she asked.

Maryam nodded, and Sara stood and thanked Noruz before stepping out into the courtyard. After she'd gone, Noruz sat beside Maryam and they sipped their tea.

"Sara looks better this morning," Noruz said, reaching to put cheese and quince jam into a fold of bread. She chewed slowly.

"Yes," agreed Maryam. "She's still tired, but she has a shine in her cheeks."

"An hour ago she was sick in the toilet. I smelled her breath."

"Oh, Noruz, I hope she's not ill."

"But her appetite is good." Noruz shrugged. "Maybe she's eating for two." Maryam looked away then, through the window, as Noruz raised her eyebrows and put a sugar cube in her mouth. "Time will tell. Take her to the old shrine."

"You and your old wives' tales." Maryam shook her head. She thought of Sara, and of the dark building in the foothills, with a brown dome like a lidless eye.

Sara sat on the step outside, hunched over in the cold as she read her father's words: *I know you will not come home.* She rested her head in her hands and looked at the ground. They both seemed to be giving up, falling away from each other. She folded the pages back in the envelope, not knowing what to do, when she heard footsteps beyond the compound wall. The blue door scraped open and Bijan stood there, his winter coat hanging from his shoulders. He reminded her of Saeed.

"Maman," he called, almost a whine, his hands tight like fists by his side. His eyes stared into her face, but she couldn't understand, he spoke too fast, and so she led him through the drapes back into the main room. His voice grew louder as Maryam and Noruz looked up from their tea, and he pulled at Maryam's hand.

"His mother's been ill, and now she won't wake up," Maryam explained.

Noruz pushed herself to stand as well, leaning against the wall. "Go with him to Farnoosh at the clinic. She'll know what to do. I'll get word to Ali."

Sara looked lost. "What can I do?" she asked, as Edward's letter fell to the floor.

"Come with me," Maryam answered, and they crossed the square with Bijan.

He broke into sobs and clung to Maryam as she knocked on the clinic door. Farnoosh hurried to open it, fetching her bag as they spoke. They soon crossed the village to the courtyard of dark weeds, where the leaves had been frosted by the night.

"You wait here with Sara," Maryam told Bijan. "We won't be long."

Sara watched her mother and Farnoosh hurry away with firm footsteps, down a dark passage. She sat on a low mud wall with the little boy. As they waited, a stray mongrel stretched up from the shadows. *"Fez'oul,"* Bijan whispered as the dog loped toward them, flies circling. "I've no food for you today, my friend." He knelt to stroke the dog's rough flanks, the sharp rise and fall of its ribs, before letting it go, slinking down the path out of Mazareh. He wiped his face on his sleeve and leaned against Sara with a tired sigh.

She hugged him and thought again of Saeed, dusted

gold with spray paint in the candlelight. Beside her memory, the village seemed so desolate in the harsh light of morning, the mud houses and the stink of animals, a bone-biting cold. No wonder people got sick, she thought, stroking the back of her hand against Bijan's tear-streaked face. She wondered what life he would have here in the middle of nowhere. What life would her mother have? Surely she would come home eventually. She looked up as a man with white hair approached.

Bijan slid from the wall and ran to him, crying again with his arms outstretched. The man picked him up and continued to walk toward her. It was the face from Doctor Ahlavi's photograph, much older, but with the same silhouette and dark eyes. *I cannot absolutely hate him, whoever he is.* Sara recalled her father's words and, at the same time, realized she no longer had his letter. She heard her mother's echo as well: *Ali is all that's left of my past.* Her face flushed. It felt like a betrayal, but there was nowhere for her to hide. He held out his hand and she stood to meet his gaze.

"Welcome, Sara Mazar. I am Ali Kolahin." He spoke in careful English.

"Yes. Hello," she replied, as Bijan slipped to the ground and reached to hold her hand as well as Ali's. Bijan tugged at Sara's fingers and, distracted, she smiled down at him, and in that moment, in her smile, Ali felt as if he saw Maryam standing before him again, as he had never known her, in the prime of her life. It passed like a shadow as Sara looked up and Bijan tugged at Ali's hand so that he knelt to speak with him.

"Tell me what's happened," he said.

As they talked, Sara watched Ali's face, the lines around his eyes and the jagged scar on his jaw—here was the stranger her mother had hidden away all her life. He made her feel sad and cheated, as if all the memories of her childhood might now prove to be just figments of her imagination, half-truths or lies.

Ali listened intently to Bijan before standing again. "Let me go and see. Wait here." He left them on the wall and walked toward the house, calling into the dark.

Maryam came to meet him, her eyes narrowing against the sun as it slipped over the flat roofs, bright on her face. "She died in the night," she said. "We thought she was getting better." She felt hopeless, the waste, and looked at Bijan sitting beside Sara, who returned her gaze. "You've seen my daughter." She frowned at Ali, feeling at once anxious and hopeful at their meeting.

"Yes. She reminds me of you." He touched her arm.

Sara saw them together, Ali's hand on her mother, and felt a flood of bitterness. Her grip tightened on the little boy's hand, but she let go at his whimper and looked down at his tear-stained face turned to her, questioning and accusing at the same time. It was how Saeed had looked on the bridge, his panic. She stood and walked toward her mother, half hidden by Ali. Sara thought of her father and the letter she had mislaid. She imagined again how he must have bent over the pages, trying to understand Maryam, to explain their life together, and now to let her go. "No," Sara whispered to herself. "No, Maman." She raised her voice as she drew closer. "Dad doesn't deserve this."

Bijan ran past her and clung to Ali's leg.

"What do you think you're doing?" Sara asked beneath her breath. She stood in front of them, her hands gripped in fists by her sides. Maryam saw anger and tears in her daughter's eyes. "What are you playing at?" Sara asked, looking from one to the other. "Is it bloody Happy Families in the middle of nowhere?"

"Don't say that," Maryam pleaded. "It's not like that. You don't understand. You're wrong." She tried to soothe, defend, and explain all at once, all much too late.

Sara bowed her head. She couldn't think clearly, and just remembered the pain in her belly when she'd awoken in the hospital with her baby gone. Then she remembered all the mornings she'd woken up as a small girl when her mother had disappeared to Iran, and made cups of tea for her dad as he sat in the study with his head in his hands. "Maman will be home soon," she used to chirp.

"How dare you?" Sara said in a whisper. "How dare you begin to tell me what's right or wrong? You have no idea how much hurt you've caused. Look at you. Does our home in England mean nothing?"

"Of course it does." Maryam stepped forward to try and take Sara's hand.

Sara pushed her away. "Don't touch me! What did

you expect, that we'd all greet each other with open arms?" Her anger uncoiled, and she drew back her hand. For a moment she wanted to hit her mother as hard as Maryam had hit Saeed, and to make her crumple up as she had seen her father bent double in the loft. But Ali took hold of her wrist and firmly lowered it to her side, Maryam reaching for Ali's arm as well.

Sara stared at them, feeling a shot of shame. She tugged her arm free and turned away. The village spun in front of her eyes and she crouched on the ground with her head in her hands. Bijan came to sit beside her and she looked at him through her fingers. Part of Sara felt like a small child too, swept up in this strange place, with nothing as it should be.

Maryam shook her head. "I'm so sorry, Sara. I'll explain." Her voice was shaking.

"Hush," said Ali. "You two must talk, but not now. Now, we must look after Bijan. Maryam, please go into the house."

Maryam rubbed her face on her sleeve, and bent to touch Sara's shoulder and to kiss the top of her head before going inside.

"I'm sorry for your anguish," Ali said to Sara. He knelt before her, Bijan by his side. "There is sad business for us to do in Bijan's house this morning. You must let Maryam attend to that, and then you can both do as you will."

Sara didn't look at his face, and so Ali stood and left to follow Maryam, with the little boy by his side. Sara let her fingers run over the dry, sandy earth. She felt weak and ashamed of her anger as it dissipated. "Oh, Dad." She spoke to the image of him in her head. "I don't know what to do." In her mind he shrugged, with no advice to give. She stood then, dusting off her hands, and looked around.

The villagers were starting their day, and some watched her as they crossed the square. She returned the nod of a wizened old man as he went by on the back of a slow gray donkey. Sara knew she must look strange to them, with her pale skin and odd mix of clothes. She didn't know whether to meet their glances or look away. The headscarf rubbed against her skin and irritated her, muffling her ears. She decided to follow Ali and Bijan inside.

Maryam and Farnoosh had already laid the body straight on its mattress on the floor and tidied her short black hair. The dead skin was cool and waxy beneath their fingers, and Farnoosh folded the woman's hands across her torso, muttering that she had failed. "No." Maryam shook her head. "You did all you could." She thought of all those who had died with no farewell from her, those she had loved and had had no chance to mourn.

They stepped back as Bijan came in and knelt beside his mother's body, looking at her face. Sara stood quietly behind them in the doorway. "See me, Maman," Bijan whispered, and lifted one of his mother's hands before dropping it heavy by her side. He reached out to touch her closed eyes, pushing back an eyelid. "See me, Maman," he said again, his voice breaking, as the whites of her eyes looked back.

"Enough." Ali carried Bijan from the room.

Maryam watched them go and saw her daughter standing there.

"Sorry. I'll wait outside," Sara said, her own tears spilling. She turned to leave as Farnoosh pulled a sheet over the dead woman's face.

Maryam followed Sara back down the passageway and into the bright winter light. Heavy snow clouds rolled across the mountaintops toward them as she joined Sara and they leaned together against the crumbling wall.

"She was your age, the dead woman," Maryam said, "but she looked older than you ever will; worn out. There's so little medicine here, but she shouldn't have died."

"What will happen to the little boy?" Sara asked.

"I don't know. He has no father, but someone will take him in. Most families are large enough to add one more." Maryam thought of Saeed and his green eyes. She had grabbed him by both his arms and shaken him, just once or twice, and his face had gone bloodless and numb, as if he wasn't there. She didn't want to remember it, her actions and his hurt. "Shall we go? Farnoosh can take care of things now."

They both stood and made their way back across the village.

"I wish I hadn't got angry," Sara said quietly.

"You have a right."

"I don't know what to make of it all." Sara thought of Ali's face and his tenderness with Bijan as she walked beside her mother. Both watched the ground and its clutter of hoofprints as they thought of the dead woman and her child's grief.

"We can talk properly this afternoon," said Maryam. "If you like, we can walk to the spring outside the village and then to the shrine. It's not far. We can take a flask and wrap up warm." Gently she reached to slip her arm through Sara's, who didn't pull away. Maryam glanced across at her bloodshot eyes and drained color. "Noruz said you were sick this morning. You don't feel ill?" she asked.

They came to the blue door.

"I'm fine," Sara replied. "Just a bit at sea."

"I'm glad you're here, that you came—in spite of everything."

"*Because* of everything," Sara answered, and leaned forward so that their foreheads rested against each other for a moment. "I don't want to lose you, Maman."

Maryam closed her eyes. "I will explain myself, I promise."

Back in the main room, to Sara's relief, Noruz pointed to Edward's letter propped on the windowsill and Maryam tucked it away in her sleeve. They sat together again and talked of the morning. "Ali Kolahin would be a good father for the boy," Noruz said, in between sucking tea through her teeth. "But we must bury his mother first, before the ground freezes." She patted Sara's arm. "If we have a heavy snowfall, you will be here until spring."

"I'll make sure you're not stranded," Maryam said swiftly.

A little later, Maryam and Sara set off into the foothills with a flask of cardamom tea as light snowflakes fell through the air. They walked slowly, wearing the thick Afghan coats Noruz had pressed on them, tight over their European fleeces and scarves. "What will happen to the dead woman?" asked Sara.

"She's from another village." Maryam breathed harder as they climbed. "Her relatives will come and collect her. The tradition is to wash and bless the body, wrap it in a clean sheet, and put it in the ground."

Sara watched the stones beneath their feet, sharp shards of shale slipping as they labored up the steep incline, where only thistles grew from between the cracks and crevices in the earth. "It's a lonely place to be buried."

"It's her home." Maryam turned to look back at the village, disappearing behind the curve of hillside and below the massing snow clouds, like another land of mountains overhead. "I think it would be a good place to die, to be buried. It's more peaceful than London."

They made their way to the top of the incline and stopped. A gentle valley of pink rock sloped away ahead of them, like a cupped palm in the foothills. The spring lay dark green at its heart, part shaded by silver birch trees, bone white trunks and crimson branches reaching into the sky. The wind scudded the water.

"Mairy and I would have rolled down this hillside once." Maryam smiled, her steps widening as she started down the slipping scree surface.

Sara sat back on her haunches and watched. It was beautiful, timeless. She closed her eyes and felt the chill on her skin, breathing in the salty earth smell of rocks. For a moment she pictured her father descending through the clouds on the battered old sofa from the loft, a glass of red wine in his hand, and smiled, wistful and sad at the thought of him, so far away. Her mother reached the spring and waved up to her, and Sara stood to follow as the veil of snow fell more steadily, dusting the boulders and branches. The pool glinted darkly, and it was quiet but for the clear sound of running water where the spring emerged tumbling from under the rocks beneath their feet.

"Would you like some tea?" Maryam asked when Sara reached her. They perched side by side on a root that rose up from the earth and gripped the water's edge, each with a plastic mug in her hand. "We'd come here with Fatima sometimes for summer picnics." Maryam remembered the cold lap of water against the backs of her knees, even in August, splashing Fatima as she tried to call her in at the end of the day: *Come here, child, mischiefmaker.*

"You know, you're different here," Sara said. "Less like you might blow away. In London, sometimes, you seem at one remove."

Maryam watched the snow dimple the water. "Looking to see how things are done, how to fit in," she said. "We never really escape. All I ever wanted as a child, a young woman, was to be free of etiquette and tradition, arranged marriages and everything just so. All I found was another world where I had to work out the new traditions, habits, how to appear just so. Isn't it silly?"

Sara shook her head. "No. But are you going to tell me what's going on now?"

Maryam looked at the clouds, growing dark. "I'm not sure how to begin. I want you to know that I'm glad I came to England, glad of the life I've had, and glad of you."

"I know." Sara frowned. "But that's not an answer. I need to understand what happened on the bridge. You know, I miss him so much, my baby, all his imagined futures. And Dad thinks you're not coming home. He can't even bear to be in the house anymore. I don't know what any of it means, if there are more secrets. It makes the past feel like it might be a lie, as if nothing was as I believed."

"Don't say that."

"Why not? Give me a reason."

Ice fringed the water's edge, frozen twigs and skeleton leaves trapped below the surface. "Yes, all right." Maryam shivered. "Let's walk. It's cold, and the shrine isn't far."

As they made their way back toward the village along a different path, the snowfall grew heavier, settling on their eyelashes and pricking their cheeks with cold. It misted the way ahead, great wings of cloud shutting out the day. Maryam bent into the wind, keeping her eyes on the smooth dome of the shrine as Sara looked back at the trace of their feet. She thought of how Saeed would love it, building snowmen in the park if they were lucky and had a white Christmas.

"They're the walls of the old fortress." Maryam pointed to mud-brick remains, crumbling on one side of the shrine. Behind it stood the stone woman. The wind sighed as they walked toward her, pocked and yellow with lichen. She had been there for ever. Maryam let her fingers run over the edges and holes as she had when a child.

"Why's it here?" Sara asked, and rested her palm on the icy surface of the weathered rock as she looked into the chiseled eye sockets, blind to the world. She felt the cold seep through her thick layers of clothes.

"People used to leave offerings, a sacrifice, for good fortune, health, peace. The village used to be up here when my father was a child, when they needed protection from attacking tribes from over the border. It's moved down into the valley over time, as the land's grown more peaceful." Maryam saw Sara shiver along her jaw, a grind of teeth. "Come on, let's get out of the wind." She looked up at the sky, but saw only glimmering flakes that stung her eyes.

They walked round the edge of the single-story building. Its door faced the plains, green paint peeling away in long curls to show the wood worn smooth beneath. They pushed hard with their shoulders to edge it open, slipping inside before it slammed shut behind them. The air was cool and still inside. Thin light floated through cracks in the dome and walls, where the mountain air sighed as if the land breathed. Sara felt a movement in the air like a flutter of wings, and covered her face.

"It's just the curtains in the breeze." Maryam's voice came from another corner and Sara followed with careful footsteps. The space was small, only a few metres across, and swimming with dark green shadows.

"Do people still pray here?" Sara asked.

"No, not really. You see these hangings?"

All around them, swathes of green fabric billowed down from the ceiling. They were hung with other small bundles of cloth and cotton rags, tied and knotted together. Sara touched one, like a small sling with an egg shape inside.

"It's superstition," Maryam said. "The young girls come here from the village. They make these small cloth cradles, cloth babies, and hang them here. It's supposed to make them fertile."

As Sara's eyes grew used to the flickering dark, she saw the cradles hanging everywhere, roping round and round the shrine, twisting from the floor to as high as hands could reach. "But this is a dark, horrid place." She wrapped her arms around herself. It felt as bleak as the churn of the Thames, like being swallowed by it, the suck of icy air like the murky river currents. "It's like a tomb. Why did you bring me here?"

"It's just bits of cloth, old folklore." Maryam reached out, but Sara pushed her away.

"It's too much, Maman. I lost *my* baby." She backed against the wall and sank to the ground. She should be with her family, with Julian, anywhere but this dark, abandoned place.

Maryam knelt beside her. "Forgive me, Sara, I didn't mean to upset you." She leaned to stroke her daughter's cheek, but Sara took hold of her wrist.

"You keep saying you're sorry and that you'll explain, but I don't know if you mean it. Do you know what you're doing? My life isn't yours to play with; neither is Dad's or Saeed's." She stared into the gleam of Maryam's eyes.

"No." Maryam quietly pulled her wrist loose and they both waited as their breathing slowed. She looked up into the dome and its cracks of light. "You know it's always frightened me as well, this place," she said. "I remember how the village girls used to call up to me in the summer nights as I slept on the roof, to creep up here with them—'Maryam, Maryam.'" Her voice sing-songed around the chamber. "I never came. I didn't want a baby back then, or a husband. But my father wouldn't let me have that freedom. I had to do as he said: marry or leave. He was so ashamed of me."

"Why?" Sara asked, hugging her knees for warmth.

Maryam shook her head. She'd talked to no one about that time, not even when she'd visited Doctor Ahlavi in London. They'd somehow agreed that it would be as if those events had never happened. "Well," she began, "he thought I had slept with Ali."

"And did you?" Sara remembered Shirin's story of the night of riots.

"No. But my father didn't believe me, so I had to leave."

"Run away?"

"No. Thrown out like so much rubbish." Maryam gestured to the cloth and clutter on the ground, shuddering as a gust of wind blew beneath the door.

"But he sent you all that jewelry, every year. The boxes in the loft."

"I don't know why he did that. He never called. He never wrote." The cloth cradles rocked, and Maryam thought of the last time she'd seen him. "He no longer wanted me as a daughter, he said that. I had disappointed him so much."

"And what happened to Ali?"

"He was punished, beaten." Maryam felt sick saying it. She remembered Fatima's words, how she'd found Ali curled like a wounded animal on the floor. She felt that part of herself had been buried back then, hidden in her own bones, and was still trembling there, waiting and frightened and wanting to scream. She looked up again into the dome. In her nightmares she had been unable to look away or reach out for help, waking with the taste of blood in her mouth.

"He was beaten by your father?"

"By my father's men." Maryam's own voice felt far away and she stretched out her hands where she crouched, running them over the floor, its dust and dirt.

"What are you doing?" asked Sara.

"There may be rats hiding." They had been in her dreams, in the gashes of wounds. She held her hands to her face. They were freezing, blue, so she put her fingers in her mouth for warmth.

Sara reached to take them in her own hands, feeling a clammy sweat or maybe tears on her mother's face. "It's all right," she said, trying to soothe.

"They were terrible days, Sara. We were so young." She wanted to cry, but it came out as laughter instead. "He should have protected us, my father, as you said I should have protected Saeed. But he treated us like dirt. He made me feel like a whore."

"Why? How?" Sara asked, but somehow she already knew a part of the answer deep in her bones. It was a little how Fatima had made her feel all those years ago, tutting as she ran barelegged in the garden, as if her girl's body was a thing of shame.

Maryam could scarcely bear to think about what had happened to her on the day in the barracks, how they had pulled her apart, and how she had learned to hide it away in the depths of her mind. "The jewelry," she said, floundering to keep Sara from the truth. "He was paying me to stay away."

"Maybe. You don't know that for sure."

They sat in the quiet, and Maryam scratched at her neck, as her own mother used to do in the house in Mashhad. Sara reached again to hold her hands still.

"So, after all that happened," she continued, "and you came to England and met Dad, did you still keep in touch with Ali? Were you in love with him?"

Maryam felt Sara's hands warm her. "No, I didn't keep in touch with him," she answered, frowning hard to herself in the dark. "I left him behind in my past. I was young. In Tehran, I made new friends and then I went to London. I needed to settle somewhere, and knew it couldn't be here. Your father was kind. But still I always knew Ali was back here. Often I found myself thinking about him—how he might be spending his days. So I suppose while we never kept in touch, he has been in my mind all along."

Sara was quiet. "And you kept Dad in the dark about all this," she eventually asked, "even though he tried so hard to support you and to understand?" She felt confused more than angry. It had not been an infidelity, but her mother had kept a hidden life.

"Sometimes it can be hard to know where to begin to talk about one's past. Your father and I, we had a life, and he had an idea of me with which he'd fallen in love. I didn't want to spoil it, to be a disappointment again, and make him feel second best."

"But don't you see, Maman, how you *have* torn that life apart? And Dad has always known you had something hidden. He's lived with that secret as much as you."

"I didn't want to hurt him."

"But still you did. All those times, when you lost your temper—when you chopped off my hair, do you remember? And when you hit Saeed. And now, leaving Dad with no clear reason. I love you, Maman, but a bit of you has been heartless."

Maryam tugged her hands free of Sara's and covered her face. She remembered seeing a documentary about a black hole: how a star might implode into a tiny pin-prick of destruction in the universe. Stars, suns, and planets would fragment and collapse in its force field. The day in the barracks had somehow punched a black hole in her mind, and however hard she tried to turn her back on it, it still wreaked its havoc.

"I wish I could turn back time." Maryam looked at her daughter.

"How do you mean?" Sara returned her gaze.

"Oh, undo all the bad things."

"But why did the day on the bridge happen? Why did you hit Saeed?"

"I'm sorry I did." Maryam's tears fell. "You would still be pregnant."

"I know, and I hated you for a while. But now I just want to know why."

"Yes, of course." Maryam looked for an answer in the dark, her fingers running over each other. "You know how you felt when you came in this place?" she asked.

"Yes. Sorry if I overreacted."

"Don't be," Maryam said. "You felt lost, disoriented, scared. Sometimes it can be hard to know where you are. When I first went to London, it was so different from here. I would lie in bed some nights and bite the side of my hand to make sure it was real. I think I was trying to wake up in a way as well, back here in the time before it went wrong. Sometimes you can rattle so hard between places, it's like your bones should break. You'd do anything to make it stop—slap a child even, who reminds you of a world that feels lost for ever."

"So that's why you came back here—to see it wasn't lost, that world?"

"I suppose so. I didn't want to cause more hurt."

"And does Ali want you to stay here now?"

"To tell the truth, Sara, I don't know what to do."

"Dad wouldn't want your pity. He deserves better."

"I know." Maryam listened to the wind rush around the dome. She didn't know how much time had passed. "I think it's getting late," she said. "We should go back."

"But I still want to know about Ali."

"Let's talk more when we're warm." Maryam's voice was tired.

They helped each other stand and went to heave open the door. Outside, they found the snowfall had swollen into a blizzard, a swirling veil of white that blanked out the path; they could see no more than a few yards ahead.

"We'll have to wait here till it passes." Maryam raised her voice above the wind as they were blown back inside. The door slammed shut and they caught their breath. "Noruz knows where we are if it gets worse."

They huddled side by side again on the floor and Sara held her head in her hands. For a little while she tried to take her mind somewhere else. She thought of Julian, Saeed, then Mara, and a long-ago Christmas when she'd been about Saeed's age. It had been a few years after the Revolution and Mara had visited with her husband, Ahmed, before Saeed or their other children were born. They had arrived late on Christmas Eve, holly and ivy on the front door, and Sara had woken with the noise of their arrival and padded down the stairs in her dressing gown.

She'd sat at the kitchen table eating mince pies and listening to their crescendo of Farsi as Ahmed set upon her father's drinks cabinet, the clink of vodka, gin, and whiskey bottles, winking in the lamplight. Edward had laughed about it years later: the perils of traveling from a dry country. When they had drunk enough, Ahmed took a kitchen knife from the drawer and set about attacking the heels of his shoes, levering them off and brandishing rolled notes of money he'd smuggled from Iran. They had clapped as if it were magic, sweat on his brow as he turned to their suitcase and the other shoes inside. Her mother had laughed as Sara had never seen before, her mouth open wide and head flung back, as heel after broken heel was brandished in the air. There had been a massacre of shoes on the kitchen floor in the morning.

Now she leaned against her mother in the dark and asked if she remembered.

"Of course. We played Go'goosh and Elvis and danced around the sitting room."

Their breath misted the air. Night was falling and Sara looked up into the dome, where lonely snowflakes spiraled through the gaps and the dim light. She swallowed her rising sense of panic.

"How do you think Ali feels about the life you've lived?" she asked. "Did he marry?"

Maryam shook her head. "No, but I think he's had a good life. He sees the children he teaches grow up and live around him. There is continuity and memory—a greater sense of lives shared. I think I had to be away my whole life to recognize it."

"But you've had a shared life at home in England." Sara shuddered with the cold.

"Yes, I know."

"And does Ali know?"

Maryam nodded in the dark. Home, she thought, and recalled a Saturday afternoon one springtime, when Edward had asked to meet her at the top of Richmond Hill, by the balustrade that looked out to the meadows below. It was before they were married, and daffodils were growing along the path. She sat in her red coat, watching the people pass and feeling the breeze in her hair, trying to be just where she was. He had come and led her along the quiet roads until they came to an iron gate, and then he'd covered her eyes with his hand so that she almost cried out. "It's a surprise," he reassured her, guiding her along a path. "Keep your eyes closed." She heard him fumble with some keys before a door opened and they walked over creaking floorboards, with a smell of paint in the air and bright light on her eyelids.

"Now you can look." She'd blinked her eyes open then, to find herself in a large, empty room with windows all along one side, overlooking a rose garden, and she'd glanced down to see Edward on one knee. "Maryam, will you come and live here with me as my wife?" he asked. She hadn't felt quite present and had turned and walked away from him, slowly, through the other rooms, past the heavy oak doors and beside the leaded windows. He was still kneeling when she came back. "Will you marry me, Maryam?" "Yes," she'd said, as if she were in a dream, and bowed her head in the bright sunlight, thinking of Ali, tears breaking as Edward stood and kissed her, and still she smiled.

"You do know I tried to love your father, Sara, as much as I could."

"I suppose so," Sara whispered. She was beginning to feel numb with the cold, with no more energy to persuade, argue, or fight. She didn't know if she was shivering anymore. She just wanted to sleep and for it to be warm when she awoke. Her eyes kept looking for shards of light in the dark and she stared up into the moving shadows of the dome. "I think a bird may be trapped up there, Maman."

Maryam followed her gaze. "It's an old wives' tale about this place: that wings beating above your head is a sign of pregnancy." She tried to see Sara's face, the gleam of her skin. "Noruz thought you might be pregnant, because of the sickness."

Sara heard the care and trepidation in her mother's voice. She had stopped herself from wondering the same thing. "It's too soon to say." She was afraid to hope, crouched on the ground in the freezing dark.

"Try to stay awake," Maryam whispered.

"Someone will come, won't they?" asked Sara, thinking of Julian and how much she wanted to see him.

"Yes, of course." Maryam tried to sound more assured than she felt.

In each other's arms, they fell into a dark sleep, as outside, the stone woman cried and the snow continued to fall. It gathered against the walls and door and entombed the dome in white.

Much later, Maryam awoke blind in the dark, at the sound of a muffled thud at the door. She heard Ali's voice calling over the noise of the wind and tried to move her legs, stiff with cold. She nudged Sara, who stirred from her own fearful dreams of sinking beneath icy waters, as the latch lifted and the door swung open. It was a black night beyond, but the wind had dropped, although the snow still fell heavily.

Ali had Bijan on his shoulders and shone a torch into the dark, revealing the glimmer of their white faces. "They're here." He went to kneel beside Maryam and Bijan slid to the ground as Farnoosh followed. "Are you both all right?"

Maryam nodded and Sara blinked awake, not quite following their whispers.

Ali heaved a rucksack from his back and pulled out a thick blanket to wrap around their shoulders. "Farnoosh has a thermos from Noruz and some food. We came as soon as we could—and Bijan would not be left behind." He reached to warm Maryam's hands with his own before turning to take Sara's. She watched him breathe on her skin, burning as the blood returned. She tugged her hands free of his, still shivering in her bones, and tucked them in her armpits. Ali raised his eyebrows. "You must eat and get warm," he said. "When you're strong again, we can go. The storm's passing." He tipped out some kindling and small logs from the bag and cleared a space on the floor. "Let's get rid of these rags before they catch alight."

They covered their faces as Ali walked round the shrine, tugging down the drapes and cradles in a whirl-wind of dust. Pale blue and white mosaic tiles were hidden behind, and a grimy window rimmed with snow. Sara felt as if she were putting her head above water again. Firelight and shadows soon flickered against the walls and the spiders scuttled away into the crevices. The smoke was drawn up into the dome and out through its cracks like a chimney. Sara held her hands to the flames and watched Ali carefully, as Bijan sat on Farnoosh's knee in the corner.

"You're having quite an adventure," Ali said, handing her some bread.

"I think we could have frozen here in the cold."

"It was good you stayed inside. You don't know the landscape and the snow has hidden everything. It would have been easy to get lost and hard to survive the night. Farnoosh brought bandages in case one of you was hurt."

"Thank you." Sara smiled across at her.

"Still, tomorrow we will close the school," Ali continued, "and the children will play and build snow-lions in the square that are large enough to climb."

They sat quietly. His words made Sara think of the lions beneath Nelson's Column and Christmas shopping one year with her parents. A thin blanket of snow had dusted the bronze manes and her father had lifted her to sit on one of the paws. There was a photo of it somewhere. She asked Maryam if she remembered.

"Nelson's Column," Ali repeated. "It must be a sight to behold."

"Yes," Maryam replied. Wrapped in the blanket, she recalled their walks through the stony orchard and the stories he'd once told her from her father's books. "But it's not as wonderful as the sight that once lived in our imaginations."

Sara watched them smile together and frowned. "Would you have liked to see London, the rest of the world?" she asked Ali, almost as a challenge.

"Your mother asked me that once."

"And what did you say?"

"I told her she was a naive, spoiled girl, who knew nothing of my life or its choices."

"And what have your choices been?" Sara asked. "What would you choose now?"

Ali heard the anger still simmer in her voice, and saw it in her eyes as her cheeks grew warm. He looked into the fire. "You do not ask a simple question," he replied.

Sara rubbed her forehead, and thought of how he had come through the night for them. She tried to ask more gently. "I suppose I want to know what's mattered to you in your life," she replied, "and how you can have been so important to my mother—even from so far away and after so long. And I want to know what you want from her now. I want to take her home to my father, to where I grew up. What *do* you want?"

Ali pressed the palms of his hands together and met Sara's eyes. "So you ask more than one question," he replied. "Partly you ask what hold I have over Maryam, as if I might be her keeper. Well, I am not, and nor do I want to be. Maryam must be her own person, as I'm sure you'd wish. *I* have not brought her here, and *you* cannot take her home. She must choose to come or go as *she* wishes—to be herself. If we put our own needs aside, the important thing is for Maryam to know her own mind, when it is not driven by fear or guilt or obligation. That is what she always wanted as a girl—she should have that freedom as a woman, should she not?"

It was not an answer Sara had expected, and she looked at the ground, thinking.

"And then you also ask about me and my life, and why it might mean something to your mother, and how I might behave now. Well, my life surely speaks for itself. I have spent it in the school in Mazareh, where as you see I have grown old. I spend the days with children like Bijan, who have only a few years of schooling to learn to read a little, write a little. Then they usually become farmers or shepherds and stay nearby. Some go to the cities and do well enough. A few may die of heroin beneath a park bench, or go to fight in a holy war, a *jihad*—of which we have more than enough these days. God willing, some have children of their own, and so life goes on. For a short time, I try to give them some care."

Sara glanced up to show she was listening, and Maryam's eyes ran from her daughter's face to Ali's, knowing her life was stretched somewhere in between.

He went on. "I think you also wish to know what your mother means to me. Well, Maryam and I, we were young together, and maybe we thought we would always be young and that we would always be together—although that was never said, and, truth be told, could only ever have been a daydream. I was a servant to her father, after all. Still, for a short time we did weave our own world back in Fatima's kitchen. They were our golden days, when we didn't know what we had to lose." He looked at Maryam, at her smile and the wrinkles round her eyes. "And then it was gone, and maybe we each thought that it was lost for ever. But decades later, here Maryam is, and for however long she chooses to be here, I am grateful. But I would not keep her here against her wishes. I know she has a family on the other side of the world."

"And you don't resent that?" asked Sara.

"No. Maybe once I would have done, but not now. I am glad to meet you, Sara," he spoke emphatically, "and now may I ask a question of you?" Sara nodded, tears in her eyes. He was a good man, and for some reason that made her feel so sad. "Tell me then: what is Iran to you, having grown up so far away?"

Sara looked from him to her mother and thought of

the world of her childhood: it had been as full of opium poppies and music as it had been of long-distance phone calls and the violence of the Revolution played out in their sitting room. It was a myriad of moments, letters read over hot chocolate on an autumn evening, bright sunlight and the fullness of her mother's voice, which Sara only ever heard when she spoke Farsi. "It's hard to know where to begin," she said. "I've never felt English but I know Iran isn't my home. I have relatives here who I've never met, who I may never meet, who may be dead and buried. Still, they exist in my head—the conversations I might have had, all I might have learned from them. It's like a thing that hasn't quite been born for me—Iran. It's an idea in my mind that I may never understand, but that will always be part of me. I would fight for that idea, although sometimes I've hated it—my mother's empty eyes, when I knew she was somewhere that I couldn't follow. Mostly I've loved it—summer evenings dancing on the patio to Persian music." Sara put her head in her hands.

Maryam smiled at the memory of dancing with Mara and reached to hug her daughter. Quietly, she started to hum Mara's favorite refrain, a lullaby. The words played in her mind: *Go to sleep little girl, beneath the blossom of the apple tree. Go to sleep, my darling, in the plum tree's shade. Go to sleep, little girl, my flower, close your eyes.* They listened as the wind grew gentler outside.

Maryam stopped. "Do you dance, Farnoosh?" she asked her in Farsi, and Farnoosh shook her head in reply, with a shy smile. "What about you, Bijan?"

He looked at her and then into the fire. "My arm dances," he replied, and Sara looked up to see him moving the shoulder, elbow, and wrist of one arm like a twisting snake in the firelight.

"And what about the other one?" Ali asked, breaking into a laugh.

The little boy danced both arms on either side of his still and serious face.

"Come and dance away this sadness, Sara," Maryam said, pushing herself to stand up from the floor of the shrine, but her daughter shook her head.

"I don't feel like dancing," she replied quietly. She ached all over.

"Farnoosh, please dance with me." Maryam urged her as she had Mairy, all those years ago, to roll down the hillside with her.

Little Bijan reached for Maryam's hand and Farnoosh stood as well, and with slow steps they moved in the firelight, humming as Ali clapped gently in the shadows. Their feet shuffled on the ground, brushing against the dirt.

Maryam's scarf slipped back and her hair fell across her face, her arms held open as Bijan moved slowly before her, doleful, like a funeral march. Maryam looked at Ali and felt that the ghosts of Fatima and her sisters were nearby. The little boy turned to tug at Sara's arm and reluctantly she stood as well, Farnoosh taking one of her hands and Maryam the other. Together, they moved round the shrine and the fire.

Sara closed her eyes. She felt as if she was falling through space, out of time, in the strange shrine on the foothill's edge, so far from anything she knew. She saw her mother smile through her tears.

When they sat again, Farnoosh knelt beside Sara. "Don't be sad," she said, and reached to take her hand. "Life's not so bad." Sara looked away, down at the ground. "Tell me, what was it like to grow up in England?" Farnoosh persisted.

Sara wiped her eyes and smiled. "A little crazy," she answered with a shrug.

"Were you free to do whatever you wanted?"

"Free enough, within reason."

"The papers here, they say that England has the highest rate of teenage pregnancy and abortion in the world. Is that true?"

"I don't know." Sara frowned kindly. The drill of questions made her feel a little like a schoolteacher again. "In some places, I guess. Everyone's different."

"But you can wear what you like?"

"More or less . . . Maybe you'll visit one day?" Maryam and Ali watched each other as the two young women talked. "You just need to get a visa. I can try and help."

"I can go to London." Farnoosh beamed at Maryam.

"I hope so," she replied, knowing how difficult and expensive that would be, but not wanting to spoil her hopes.

"But tell us, Maryam," Ali asked, "what has England been like to you?"

Maryam looked at Sara and then into the flames. "It's where I've watched my daughter grow up, and where I found safety when there was no place for me here." She stroked Bijan's hair as he rested on her lap. "I suppose it's a place where, although I wear no headscarf over my ears, I must concentrate so hard to work out what's being said and thought—even after all this time. And as I've grown older, I've missed having no one to share my memories of this place, of reading tea leaves with my sisters." She smiled, as much to herself as Sara and Ali. "It can be a strange loneliness, to be loved by people who will never come to Mazareh. But I'm grateful for all England has given me. There were no earthquakes and no one ever hesitated to shake my hand."

Ali pressed his fingers into the dust as he listened.

"And Dad?" asked Sara.

"You know I love your father as much as two people can from different worlds."

They watched as the fire died down.

"So, did I answer your question?" Ali asked Sara. "Do you have more?"

She shook her head. "No. I'm just glad you came to fetch us."

He held out his hand to her. "Well, we should go back now."

He helped Sara stand. "I'm sorry, Ali," she said, "if I've been abrupt or rude."

"You shouldn't apologize for saying what you think," he replied.

She bent to pick up a small cloth cradle that had fallen just beyond the fire, before rising to face him again. "The thing is," she said, "I think I know it's not your fault my mother's here; that it was her choice to come back." She put the cradle inside her coat.

Ali looked at her, the daughter he might have had. "Well, with those words you set us all free, Sara Mazar—including yourself—each to be as we wish."

Sara frowned, not so sure, as he turned to help Maryam stand as well, before fetching armfuls of snow from outside to douse the embers. Steam hissed up into the dome, and at last, the door to the shrine closed behind them. They made their careful way back in the moonlight to where the village appeared at the base of the foothills, surrounded by shimmering plains of snow.

Sara and Maryam slept heavily through the rest of that night and into the next morning, when they awoke to the shrill cries of a child beyond the compound wall and hurried to dress and go outside. Noruz and Hassan were already standing on the doorstep, as a truck with snow chains on its wheels waited with its engine running in the square.

"It's the dead woman's relatives," whispered Noruz. "They've come from the next village. Ali has taken them to fetch her body."

The shouts came from Bijan Ku'cheek, who clung to a hole in the wall as a stout woman tried to drag him toward the truck. Meanwhile two men staggered across the square beneath the weight of the woman's corpse, wrapped in a shroud between them.

Maryam ran to Bijan. "Stop, stop, please," she called, and as the women turned toward her, Bijan slid free and ran to hide behind Maryam's legs.

She knelt to hold him, his eyes hidden in her coat, as Ali followed after the two men. They heaved the body on to the back of the truck, and Sara turned her face from the contorted shape of limbs laid alongside bits of wood and metal.

"Bijan doesn't want to go." Maryam looked to Ali. "Must he leave?"

"He's a bastard," one of the men muttered. "But he can work as hard as the next boy." He stepped toward Maryam and Bijan, but Ali stood in his path.

"Not today, my friend," Ali said. "Leave Bijan here. He will be safe and has his schooling to finish. It's what his mother would have wished." He stood firm as the man circled him.

"I've heard the old stories about you, Ali Kolahin," he spat. "And you, Maryam Mazar, the outcast."

Sara looked at her mother's face, its shadows of gray, but Maryam merely shook her head. She would have no more humiliation, not from this man, not in front of her daughter. She walked to stand beside Ali, Bijan still clinging to her side, and Hassan stepped forward, too.

"Mazareh won't be on your side today," said Ali. "Go."

The man circled them again, swearing beneath his breath, before turning back to the truck. They watched him climb inside with the others, before the wheels kicked up a fresh flurry of snow and the truck lurched away over the potholes and ice. As soon as it was out of sight, Bijan ran to Ali, who picked him up and swung him high into the sky. As he hugged Bijan, Ali held Maryam's gaze, her face flushed in the chill. Sara knew her mother had never looked upon her father in the same way that Maryam smiled at Ali in that moment, jubilant and strong. She felt her father turn away in her mind and walk away, his head bowed.

They returned inside for breakfast, and Noruz gossiped to fill the silence that had fallen after the confrontation and the dark hours of the previous night. She said that the phone lines had come down in the storm.

"So we can't phone Julian or Dad?" asked Sara.

Maryam shook her head. "I think I'd prefer to write to your father anyway."

"Hassan says more snow is still to come," Noruz went on, passing round warm bread and cheese. "He says the mountain peaks are heavy with it."

"Maybe Ali and I could borrow Hassan's truck to drive Sara back to Mashhad tomorrow?" suggested Maryam.

Sara looked up. "You'll come back with me?"

"To Mashhad? Yes. I'd like us to go to Haram to see your grandfather's tomb."

That night, they ate early as a freezing wind blew over the plains. Bijan walked close to Ali as they crossed the square, muddied by the events of the day. Beyond the blue door, the courtyard was dark aside from the bright square of light cast from the window of the main room. It was Sara's last evening in Mazareh.

Inside, the heater was on high and Farnoosh and Noruz served bowls of steaming broth, their kind eyes on Bijan as he joined them cross-legged on the floor, twisting his black woolen hat in his hands. They ate quietly as the television flickered in the corner. Sara saw the White House and its lime green lawns. She frowned, peering into what seemed like an artificial world—the one to which she would have to return.

Maryam sat beside Noruz and watched the other faces. They were safe, she thought: Noruz with her family and stories of saffron and shit, Farnoosh caring for them all. She would make sure that one day Farnoosh would stretch her wings to the teashops and bridges of Isfahan, maybe further. Ali watched her across the white cloth and the hungry hands reaching for bread and cheese. He had seen her spirit fully alive again that morning and had wanted to swing her high into the air as he had Bijan.

Sara also tried to imprint each of them on her mind: strong farmer's hands bunched round the thin handle of a spoon, the red ridge of a scar in the light. She saw the look spun between her mother and Ali, and understood that it must have always been like that for them, from their very beginning, long before she was born.

As their plates grew empty, Noruz turned to Ali. "As it is Sara Mazar's last night," she said, "and as we have a new addition to our family"—she smiled at Bijan—

"I hope it isn't too much to ask you to tell us a tale of the plains and mountains. I would love to hear 'The Story of Gossemarbart' again."

"Doctor Ahlavi's story?" Sara asked, and Noruz nodded. Sara whispered to Maryam of how Doctor Ahlavi had given Saeed the faded leather folder with the booklet hidden inside, and Maryam replied that she had never heard the story herself.

"It would be my pleasure," said Ali.

Noruz smiled her thanks as Hassan went to prepare the hookah and Farnoosh brought fresh glasses of tea from the samovar. Finally, they all sat in the quiet and Ali began. Sara recognized the story's beginning and remembered Saeed's voice and his quiet concentration, turning the pages. As Ali spoke, she imagined Saeed reading it as well, with Julian by his side.

"Once upon a time," he began, "long ago, a girl child was born to the family of a shepherd living on the saffron slopes of Gossemarbart, and so the mountain gave the small girl her name. Her mother and father loved her dearly, for they had several sons, and longed to be blessed by a daughter. Now"—Ali paused and held their eyes, his forefinger in the air—"the land was ruled by a ruthless and powerful khan, who each year demanded that the villagers pay him a tenth of their living. But the year of Gossemarbart's birth saw a terrible drought, and one by one the shepherd, her father, lost his flock so that when the khan's men came for their due, he had nothing to offer. The khan was angry, and one dark night he came and knocked at the shepherd's door." Ali clapped his hands loudly three times, and Bijan Ku'cheek smiled, moving closer.

"The khan stood in the candlelit room and would not listen to the poor man's protests. 'What would you give me instead?' His eye fell on the shepherd's wife, soft curls slipping from her scarf, eyes dark as night. 'Do you have a daughter who will grow to be as beautiful as this woman?'

"'She's only a baby,' the mother cried. 'Take me instead.'

"The khan sneered. 'I would not break up this happy home, but I will return when the child is fourteen and take her to be my bride,' and with that he closed the door and disappeared into the night.

"Fourteen years seemed a long time, and so life went on more or less as before. The girl Gossemarbart grew up to be as beautiful as her mother, who taught her all she could, but because of her birth on the mountain, Gossemarbart also had the flame of a wilder spirit in her bones, and so could never be kept inside for long. On hot summer days she would leave her headscarf tied to a branch, golden-brown hair floating about her like a cloud and bare feet running through the coarse grass.

"Each day she ventured further afield, until one day, a few months before her fourteenth birthday, she came upon a deep, dark cave in the mountain's shadows, and because she had more spirit than fear, she stepped out of the sunshine's warmth and into the cool dark. She heard the gentle lap of water underground and followed its music deeper and deeper into the shadows, until she came to a mighty cavern, lit by a single beam from a crack high in the mountainside. The light gleamed off dripping stalactites, circling a turquoise pool. She knelt to drink, letting the water splash her face.

"'Gossemarbart,' the pool whispered, and as she looked up, in the water's reflection she saw a very old woman, as gray and haggard as the rocks, with watering eyes and long hairs sprouting from her nose and chin.

"'Who are you?' Gossemarbart asked, running her fingers through the water.

"'I am you as you will become, if the world is kind to you and you live for ever. So ask me what you will.'

"Again Gossemarbart reached her hand out to the ripples and the old woman's face stared back, although when Gossemarbart glanced by her side at the pool's edge, she was all alone. She looked back into the pool and the old woman's eyes. 'I would like to know what I should do if the world is not kind,' she said, and the old woman returned her smile.

"'Empty the water carrier at your side and fill it from this spring. If ever you are in mortal danger, you may pour some on your hands, and I will come and make you as strong as the stone of this mountain and as free as the air. But beware, you can do this only once. And it is better that you never do it at all.' With that, the old woman's face disappeared and Gossemarbart was alone again.

"She did as she had been told and returned home by dusk. She tried to tell her mother what had happened, but she just dismissed it as a young girl's daydream. But from then on, Gossemarbart kept the flagon by her side and under her bed at night.

"Time passed and her fourteenth birthday approached. Her father, in good spirits, was sure the khan would have forgotten about the dark night and his debt, and so did nothing, until the eve of her birthday, when there was a loud *thud, thud, thud* on the door."

Little Bijan clapped his hands, his fingers wide apart.

"There stood the khan," Ali continued, "grown hoary and gray with age. 'I have come to collect my debt: the hand of your daughter, Gossemarbart.'

" 'What is this?' Gossemarbart cried, standing up. 'What debt?' She looked at her father with his head in his hands, and toward her mother, arms outstretched.

" 'Take me instead,' her mother pleaded, just as she had all those years before.

" 'No, I will have the young, fresh Gossemarbart for my bride,' said the khan, and he grabbed her by the hair, but not before she had time to seize her flagon of water from the floor.

"The khan rode with her far from her beloved mountain and the plains where she had grown up, and Gossemarbart grew desolate with their loss. From the tower where the khan imprisoned her, she looked up at the clouds, orange and red with the sunset, and wished she could fly high and away with them, but she did not think this was yet mortal danger that she faced.

"As the day of the wedding approached, Gossemarbart's determination to be free grew. She would look out of the high tower for a means of escape, but the rock walls were smooth and high. She was strong, but she did not want to fall and die on the boulders far below. She tried to reason with the khan, but he had no time for her pleas and persuasion. 'If you do not shut up, I will cut off your hair,' he threatened. But Gossemarbart was not vain, so soon her hair lay shorn about her on the ground. She held it to her face and remembered the mountains where she had once run free in the teasing spring breeze, but still she was not sure that it was mortal danger she faced.

"If the khan would not listen to her, he might read her petitions, so she started to write letters deep into the night, until he again grew weary. 'If you do not stop this, I will cut off your thumbs.' But because Gossemarbart was starving for her freedom, her family, and the mountains, she did not stop writing until the guard held her hand against the wall and sliced it in half. 'No more then,' she cried, thrown back in her tower. Gossemarbart's sorrow filled the air and she wished she was as strong as the rocks, but still she was not sure if she was in mortal danger. She cried into the night.

"As the day of the wedding grew ever nearer, the khan decided once and for all that he'd had enough of her lamentation. He said to his guard, 'I will not have these tiresome cries when she becomes my wife. Take her away and cut out her tongue.' The guard did as he was commanded. When Gossemarbart was returned to the tower, she tried to cry, to pray, but all that came from her lips was a sound like the wind in a cave. Now she knew this was mortal danger, so, her hands shaking, she took the flagon of water and poured it into what was left of her hands. Through her tired, swollen eyes, she saw the old woman she would never be staring back at her: the woman she might have become if the world had been kind. 'Why have you left it so long?' the old woman asked.

" 'Hope,' Gossemarbart wanted to say, but she just grunted an animal sound.

" 'You wish to be free?' the old woman asked, and Gossemarbart nodded through her tears. She would be as strong as the stones and as free as the clouds. 'Then drink this water and wish.' And so Gossemarbart did, and when the khan stalked toward the tower to claim her for his own—his shorn, tamed, and mute bride—he found she had gone.

"Gossemarbart smiled again. Her spirit danced with the stars. And in the foothills near the mountain of her name, her body chose to rest as it does to this day, a stone woman, kissed by lichen, sun, and snow, looking out over the land she loves. The villagers make their sacrifices to her, and she grants the wishes of those who are good. And in the lonely night, the breeze of Gossemarbart blows down from the clouds, across the plains, and through the holes and gaps of the stone woman. She sings, an echo of her name, sometimes sweet as a flute, sometimes angry as a drum, reminding families to keep their loved ones safe and close, to heed what they say, and forever guard against the barbarian knock and the wolf at the door."

The room was quiet and Ali looked up at Maryam in the hush. He knew Doctor Ahlavi had written the story for her, because of what had happened all those decades before.

"Thank you," Maryam said in the stillness. "All of you. For your kindness and care, for waiting for me." They sat quietly as the smoke from the hookah wound through the air and curled among the wood beams.

As Maryam and Ali stood in the snow later that evening, they remembered Doctor Ahlavi as he in turn, far away, looked out over his narrow garden of weeds and thought of his homeland. He heard the song from Haram's minaret again in his mind, and pictured evening shadows falling across the bazaar. He closed his eyes to see his wife's smile in the days when she'd been young and her skin had been warm.

For a moment Maryam and Ali waited alone in the courtyard while Sara helped Bijan Ku'cheek to put on his warm clothes. "Will you walk with me to the village edge?" Ali asked, and so they wandered past the compounds glowing with light, their footprints behind them like commas in the snow. They looked out across the black plain and Maryam remembered the night she had arrived, sitting on her bags in the dust, sensing Fatima's ghost in the breeze.

"I hope I know you until the end of my days, Maryam," Ali said, reaching for her.

"I hope so too," she answered, turning to him, and he held her close, out of sight in the dark.

They awoke early the next day and prepared to leave. Sara moved around the small spaces of the compound and bent to kiss Noruz and then Bijan farewell. She didn't know if she would see any of them again. Noruz chuckled gently. "If you have a little girl, name her after me." With a gentle bow, Sara stepped back from Hassan, his arms held tight across his chest. He straightened his shoulders and nodded to Maryam as well.

The truck doors slammed shut after they climbed inside and Ali started the engine. "I'll await your return," Noruz called from the doorstep as they pulled away, and Farnoosh ran from the clinic, her hand held high in the air as they lurched across the snow.

They left Mazareh behind. Sara and Maryam turned in their seats until it was gone, a haze of white where the wind flurried over the land. Sara remembered driving home from Norfolk one winter afternoon, the fields flooded and glassy brown as far as she could see from the winding lanes. She had thought it beautiful then, puckered with rain. It seemed small now, dark in her memory. She wound down the window to a rush of cold and sound, the silence of the plains and the heater's rattle.

Maryam thought of the courtyard behind the bright blue door that had become her home. In her mind, she began to compose the letter she would write to Edward. She saw him taking off his glasses, hands held before him, listening.

You will understand. Whatever I do, husband of mine, you have always known there is a world I must choose to live without, not an inaccessible past, but another country where flesh-and-blood people breathe and go about their day. As I look at my wedding ring, I see the years of our marriage together, years I would not change, although I know they have not been easy. Our one roof has not always seemed strong enough for all the different lives and places it had to hold. You know I do not regret my return to Mazareh, and maybe—as you say—it was something that I would always have needed to do. You will smile, I hope, that I have grown reaccustomed to unrolling my mattress on the floor each night, and to breathing a freezing mountain air that seems to bring new strength and purpose. I fear now I would be more lost than ever in London, the polished tables and silver cutlery, polite conversation of this and that. But you say that you are by the sea again, and part of me hopes you would no longer choose to return to those trappings either. There is a relief, is there not, in packing it all away, the house—it gives us the freedom to breathe, to choose again the lives we would live, although I do not know if I will be here for ever, through the winter of my days. The next week or month is far enough for me to see, to choose, unconstrained by the future and its fears. Of course, I look at Sara and think of the children she may have, our grandchildren, and long to be there for her, to watch them grow, to give them the grandparents she never had. But I do not wish to be near her in a way that would cause more harm than good.

And so for now, today, tomorrow, as far as I can see from this point, I will wake in Mazareh and work in the school beside Ali, where the horizon is endless and the playground has no walls, where I can be of some use to the villagers who have given their lives, generations, to my family's land. Sara will tell you about Ali, and I hope you will see it is a good friendship. We knew each other from our beginnings, the first stony pathways that made us as we are, and where I find I now need to tread again. I also know, only husband of mine, that whatever I do—stay or go, choose one home or another, one country or the other—I must cause hurt somewhere to someone I love, and that is the reparation I will pay for ever. I would wish it on no one. Forgive me these days.

You are in my thoughts, my prayers,
Maryam.

The morning passed as they made their way across the plain.

"We will come to the motorway soon," said Ali.

Maryam reached for Sara's hand. "So, you are glad you came?" she asked, and Ali turned to hear her answer as well.

"It has changed everything." Sara looked through the

window. "I wouldn't have lived without it."

They sat in silence as the land beyond Mazareh, its curving foothills, the mountains of Gossemarbart, Tomor, and Shilehgoshad, disappeared in the muddied wing mirrors, and the whisper of a stone woman ebbed away. The motorway roared into view, its impatient speed scarring the land.

They reached Mashhad at dusk, the snow far behind and a fog of pollution soaking up the last of the daylight. Maryam felt its weight sink over her, the town now a city, as they drove through its fringes, the dusty cars slowly nudging ahead, bumper to bumper in the rush hour and falling dark.

"How often do you come back here?" Sara asked Ali.

"As little as I can: once a year to pray at Haram and buy some books. Mashhad isn't how it was. It has no community anymore. They're even building an Underground. I think a way of life ends when people must travel in the dark, beneath the trees and the sky, to go about their day."

"I know." Sara frowned and thought of London, the Piccadilly Line from Heathrow, its shuffle and squeeze of tired, anxious faces—Knightsbridge, Hyde Park, Covent Garden, the creeping city. She shook her head, not wanting to think of it yet, wishing to keep the wide-open plains of Mazareh as a place to run in her mind.

Maryam showed Ali the way to Shirin's house, through the smart outer suburbs, and along a deserted road. "These were open hills when I was a child," she said to Sara. "We would walk here and could see across to the mountains on the border. I would dream of lying in Afghan poppy fields. Now all you see is smog and construction, a new dome for Haram that will eclipse the sun."

"It's the way of things," Ali said as he pulled in to the curb.

Sara climbed down and glanced at the row of elegant houses set back from the road with their security lights, wrought-iron grilles, and white stucco walls. She rang the buzzer beside the driveway.

"*Salaam?*" She heard Shirin's voice through the intercom.

"It's Sara," she replied. "I've brought my mother back."

There was a short pause and then a buzz releasing the gate, lights automatically flashing on alongside the house as Hassan's battered old truck pulled up behind Hameed's silvery four-by-four. Sara followed before the gate closed, and Maryam climbed out and turned where she stood, still in her long Afghan coat, smelling of sheep. She straightened her scarf as Shirin appeared, immaculate, kissing Sara on both cheeks, then Maryam.

"We've been waiting for you too long." Shirin smiled her most charming welcome. "The samovar is ready. You must both want hot showers."

"Ali is here too." Maryam turned to the truck.

Shirin stopped and stared at her. She frowned, her fingers clasped beneath her chin. "I'm so happy to see you here, *Khonoom* Mazar. You are welcome in my home, my aunt, but please tell me what I should do. We're a good family. You know the stories. I'm sorry, but I cannot have Ali here, under the same roof as my children, as you. My husband won't permit it. Please do not ask it of me." Her eyes were beseeching beneath their black mascara.

Maryam looked up at the sky and its yellow moon. "So the world does not change."

Sara watched her mother's face and saw her weary despair. "Where will he sleep?" she asked Shirin. "We've been driving all day. He can't stay in the truck. He's a schoolteacher, like me. He's older than my mother. What are you so afraid of?"

Shirin rested her hand with its neat, manicured nails on Sara's arm. "Forgive me." She didn't meet Sara's eye. "Customs die hard here as elsewhere. Judgments are made for good reason and are difficult to change, however much time passes. They are the boundaries we must live within." Her shoulders hunched in the cold.

"Shirin," Sara whispered angrily. "Don't be like that. Don't judge my mother and Ali from old stories told by the dead and gone. See them with your own eyes. Do they look like outcasts, criminals? Please give them a home, just for a few nights. Then you may never see them again."

Shirin closed her eyes. What would her mother have done? She would not have turned them away. She had loved her sister, cried for her. She looked again at Sara.

"Please know how difficult this is for me. It's not much, but there's a room at the back of the garage. It has a bed and a sink. He can stay there. We have enough food."

"I guess it will have to do." Sara turned to Maryam, her eyes a sheen of tears. "Come on," she took her mother's arm, "let's take Ali inside."

Shirin walked away, back into the warmth of her home, as Maryam turned to the truck where Ali sat, still and silent. She opened the door. "Forgive me for bringing you here." He looked at the eyes he had held in his mind his whole life, and straightened his back, bracing himself against a feeling of shame that he had thought long in his past. She took his arm and they walked to the back of the house, Sara beside them, stepping through a side door into the garage and dusty workshop. Beside the trestle bed and sink there was a rusty heater on the floor. Maryam sank on to the edge of the mattress. "I'm sorry, *joon-am*." She put her head in her hands.

Ali looked up at the bare light bulb. "This is nothing," he said, his skin taut. "It is others' ignorance. Think of the things we have seen, Maryam. All we have lived through and survived." He stood before her in the bare room, his face tired and lined in the harsh light. "Who needs finery, this prison of gossip, when we always have Mazareh and the mountains?" He knelt before her, taking her hands in his.

Sara turned away and walked back through the garage, its smell of oil and petrol. Outside, she looked up at the fattening moon. She knew Julian was waiting for her far away. If her father had let her mother go, so should she. She made her way into the house to face Shirin.

"It will drive me mad to stay here." Tears ran down Maryam's face.

"Just a night or so. All will be well." Ali pinched her cheek tenderly and lifted her face to his. "Go now. Tomorrow will come soon enough." He watched her leave and then lay back on the rough blanket, and waited for the day.

Dinner was quiet. Shirin, tired behind her smile, talked mostly to Sara about her trip, asking if Mazareh had been dirty, cold, lonely. Maryam ate little, feeling her breath rise and fall. When they finished, the maid took a plate of food out to Ali and the women retired to the drawing room, an empty space of marble and carpet. They looked at each other across the bow-legged tables and gold doilies. Maryam sat on the edge of her chair, embroidered with a woman in blue on a swing. She remembered it had once belonged to Aunt Soraya as Shirin handed over a small glass of amber tea. She held it tight in her hands, almost burning her palms as she looked at the drawing board of photographs, faces pinned like butterflies. Her father stared back.

"Are you all right, Maman?" asked Sara.

Maryam's eyes focused on the carpet—twisting fig leaves and a leaping gazelle in the weave of silk—as dark tea leaves floated, then sank in the glass in her hand. She spoke slowly. "You know Ali stands for so much that is good in my life that the world has tried to take from me and make bad. Do you understand, Sara?"

They held each other's eyes.

"I see how hard it would be for you to leave Ali alone again."

At that, Shirin coughed delicately before smoothing the hair from her face. She stood and left quietly to fetch the maid, to tidy the tea tray and turn out the lights.

"You will still come to Haram with me tomorrow?" Maryam asked. "I want my father to see you at his tomb. And Ali. It would bring some peace."

"Yes, of course. But you should rest now."

She helped her mother to her feet. Maryam seemed older and more fragile away from Mazareh, and Sara wondered if it had always been so. They crossed the marble hall to the room Shirin had prepared on the ground floor, then curled on the twin beds, side by side in the dark, too tired to wash or change. Sara watched her mother fall asleep, the gray light of imagined shapes and shadows swimming across the room. Lying there, it was as if she saw all Maryam's ages pass across her face on the pillow: the infant, girl, woman, and even the corpse she would become, when there would be a time for her to rest at last, beneath the pink shale and silver birches by the dark spring. She placed a finger in her mother's palm and Maryam's hand curled around it like a child's.

• • •

The next day Sara woke early, longing for her own home. Shirin had driven her boys to school and gone to visit a friend, so Sara helped herself to tea and bread before wandering outside. She found Maryam sitting on the steps beside the pool with Ali, under a winter-blue sky, the air cool and smelling of fallen leaves.

"Have you been waiting for me?" she asked.

"Just watching the morning," her mother replied. Sparrows swooped through the bare branches. "Come, let me find you a chador for Haram."

She stood and they made their way back inside. There was a tall walnut cabinet in the room where they'd slept, and Maryam pulled out a drawerful of clothes, neatly folded and left behind when she had gone to Mazareh. She brought out a charcoal gray silk for Sara, swirling dark as a shadow as she shook it open, floating up through the air and over her hair and shoulders. Maryam smiled, choosing another for herself: black cotton with shiny beads. "This used to be my mother's. They've spent a lifetime in the loft in London." She wrapped it around herself, broken stems of lavender falling to the ground beneath their feet, then bent to the drawer again, reaching for a primrose yellow chador with polka dots. "You won't remember this."

"Yes, I do." Sara took it from her. She held it to her face, chiffon that smelled of home. "May I keep it?" she asked. "It reminds me of Fatima, and I'd like to show it to Saeed. I told him about us going to Haram years ago."

"Of course." Maryam rested her hand on Sara's arm.

Sara looked at her, with the bright morning sunlight streaming through the window. "I know you're not coming back," she said.

Maryam shook her head. "No. Not yet. I wrote a letter this morning to Edward, for you to take." They sat on the edge of the bed together, their faces side by side in the mirror, hair hidden beneath their silk scarves. "Are you all right to look after Saeed?"

"Yes. He gets on well with Julian. The little brother I always wanted."

"Did he ask you to bring anything back for him?"

"Some saffron earth, but I don't think he meant it. We painted the kitchen saffron, and he told me about their villa at Torbat, the red earth. I'll think of something."

"Let me see." Maryam reached for the bag she'd brought from Mazareh. Tucked in the corner, as she'd hoped, she found the fox-head stone, and handed it to Sara.

Sara turned it in her palm, pointed ears and snout in silhouette. "He'll like it a lot. I'll let him know you found it for him."

"Tell him how sorry I am," Maryam said quietly.

Sara nodded and leaned to kiss her mother's cheek.

"Come then," Maryam said. "Let's go and meet your grandfather."

They stood and checked themselves one last time in the mirror: the same eyes, younger and older, staring back.

Outside, Ali was waiting in the driveway. He wore

the same clothes as the day before, his stubble as dark and heavy as the lines round his eyes. They climbed into Hassan's truck, reversed through the gates onto the dusty road, and began the short journey toward the heart of Mashhad, where all roads converged on Haram. Sara watched the streets pass by—Kheyabun Shahid, Esfahani, Sanabad, Hashemi—as she thought of her grandfather's photo, his hooded eyes and their gray shadows.

"What do you remember of my grandfather?" she asked Ali.

He kept his eyes on the road, looking beyond the mud-flecked windshield. They moved slowly along a wide avenue of grimy cars, passed brown buildings with dark shutters. Ali had wrapped his arms around his head, he remembered that, as cigarettes burned his back, the smell of his own smoldering flesh, bound in the dark, a boot in his gut, in his groin, lying there until Fatima found him, as Maryam fell away out of reach. Sara waited, hearing only the window's rattle and car horns outside, and Maryam turned to watch the side of Ali's face. "He was a powerful man," he said, still looking straight ahead. "He was driven by tradition and duty. He prized respect and obedience above all else. I think, for him, to be loved was to be feared."

Maryam looked at her hands, and saw again her father's footprints on the sand by the Caspian Sea, how he had once lifted her in the air in the sunlight, in her memories or in a dream. "He was kind sometimes," she added.

Ali shook his head. "No, Maryam, forgive me, but he took back and destroyed as much as he gave. He was cruel and barbaric; to you, to me, and to many others. You know this. It's all right to forgive him, but don't deny his crimes and the scars you carry."

Sara looked at her mother's face as they crawled along the busy road, and Maryam blinked back the darkness. It sank over and she remembered the sound of saliva in the army doctor's mouth, his hand punching up inside her. In the truck, she felt short of breath.

"You did tell me everything at Mazareh?" asked Sara.

Ali spoke gently. "Doctor Ahlavi told me something of what happened in the barracks, years ago, so that I wouldn't set my heart on your return."

"What do you mean?" asked Sara.

"Stop, stop, please," Maryam begged Ali. "I need some air."

He pulled over, and Maryam clambered out over Sara and walked along the pavement beside a small bazaar selling paintings, rugs, and charms. She turned round where she stood and remembered the road from when she had been a child, much narrower then, more carts than cars.

Sara followed her. "What is it, Maman?" she insisted as Ali parked up on the curb; car horns blaring. He climbed out and went after them.

Maryam stopped and touched her daughter's face where she stood, tracing from her brow down beneath her eyes and round to her temples. "It's all right because you're here."

"What is?" Sara searched her mother's eyes.

"I can't take this back when I've told you."

"I know. It's all right," said Sara. "What can be so bad?"

Maryam reached for Ali's hand, as he joined them there in the street. "My father," she began and felt herself shudder. "I've never told anyone this. Before he sent me away, he ordered an examination." Maryam's breath came harder, as if she had climbed to a high plateau where the air was too thin. She remembered how Doctor Ahlavi had slipped her sandals from her feet and helped to undress her. "It was a punishment more than anything, to see if I was a virgin, 'intact,' I was only sixteen." Maryam's voice was a whisper. "It was done by a stranger, a soldier, forced really." She remembered Doctor Ahlavi pleading with the soldiers: *For pity's sake, have you not mothers and sisters?*

Sara looked into her mother's eyes, and she could almost see the young girl that Maryam had once been, straining toward her. "They did the test. That was bad enough. I thought it was over. The soldier in a white coat said I was intact, that I could go home." Maryam closed her eyes and remembered herself as a child. Her tears fell. "But then they treated me like a rag doll. All my clothes torn and thrown on the floor. I remember their spit on me, the smell of their sweat, their rough hands. I did not think it was possible to be hurt so much." She could not remember how she had got home, just that dark shapes had crawled into her mind and stayed there. Doctor Ahlavi's hands had been shaking as he wrapped a blanket round her shoulders. "I was no virgin after that day."

"Maman." Sara took her mother's hands and, in a flood, it all suddenly made sense: the moments of blankness in Maryam's eyes as if she'd lost herself; her flashes of anger through the years which had been fear as much as rage; slamming shut the turquoise door in vain against her ghosts; emerging with exhausted apologies before retreating to the garden, its solace of bonfires and roses. She had been caged by secrets. "You've hidden this, all this time, even from Dad. Why?"

"Shame," Maryam breathed, everything aching. "I was spoiled. My father took me for himself, in a way, that day." She bent her head back to the empty white sky.

"But you have nothing to be ashamed of." Sara felt her tears spill. "It's your father who should be ashamed, not you. You must see that."

"And you have never been anyone's to take." Ali felt Maryam lean all her weight against him. Her breath was heavy.

"The most important thing is that you're both here now," Maryam whispered. "If that terrible day hadn't happened, maybe none of us would be here at all." She rested her hand against her daughter's face. "Maybe you wouldn't have been born, Sara. Maybe I would have married some man with brown shoes. Maybe Ali

310

would be a tutor to some other family." They leaned together on the pavement, the shouts of the bazaar and the busy road all around them.

Ali let his cheek rest against hers. "So, we're here," he said. "Good comes from bad. Let's finish what we came for."

He led them back to the truck, where Maryam rested her head on his shoulder for the rest of the journey. She was exhausted.

Sara laid her head against the grimy window as they drove. She realized now how her father had really never stood a chance. In a way, her mother had never let him anywhere near her. She wiped her face on her sleeve as they parked near to Haram, and drew her chador close, feeling safe in its dark folds.

As they walked to the mosque's entrance, they passed cripples, beggars, and peddlers squatting on the ground, reaching out their hands for money, with black nails and torn clothes, hungry eyes in their lost, dirty faces. Maryam and Sara went through a curtained security check, separated for women and men, and waited for Ali on the other side, at the top of a sweeping pathway to the main courtyard.

"I have some good memories of my father too, you know." Maryam searched Sara's face. "I always want to believe that he didn't know how terrible it would be."

A call to prayer sang out from the minaret, echoing off the marble courtyards and mosaic domes. They walked down the path and Maryam retreated to a friendlier past. She thought of her sisters and the hot summers when they would come to Haram, chadors wrapped lightly over their nightdresses. They would hurry to pray beneath the black sky, to the floodlit mosque with its shimmering fountains, splashing cool on their skin. And now Sara was there as well. They heard the lonely sound of prayer being called, a single male voice across the courtyard, where lines of men bent to pray beneath the turquoise and gold curves arching across the pale sky.

They walked to the main door, Maryam and Sara separating from Ali again to go through the women's entrance, with its noise of chatter and gossip. Maryam smiled, hearing Mairy and Mara's whispers grow louder in her mind: *What if they find out we're just wearing our nightdresses underneath?* Sara watched her mother's face, calm again in the sea of black. Ali rejoined them then and led the way past crowds of sick people crouched and lying on the floor, waiting for healing. Sara felt lost as they looked for somewhere to kneel in one of the cavernous rooms, filled with the whispers of families praying. At last they found an empty space of red carpet and sat side by side.

Sara knelt as Maryam and Ali prayed. She remembered her primrose polka-dot chador and how she'd felt all those years ago, the strangeness of the place and her mother's cry. A small, dark-eyed girl walked toward her between the groups of worshippers. She wore a yellow scarf and carried a cloth toy in her arms. They smiled at each other, and Sara thought of her father, how he had visited her in hospital, bringing the small rag dog of her childhood. She missed him, her home, the family that would now only exist in her memory. When she looked again, the little girl had gone.

As she knelt there, Maryam felt the world turn, gentle and fierce winds in her mind. She thought of Edward's eyes, his kindness, their child, and Ali by her side—the house of fragments that was her home.

"I have a memory of my father," she told Sara when they were outside again, sitting beside a fountain of shimmering turquoise tiles. "He liked to walk in the garden late at night. In the summer, it would have been watered and swept at the end of each day. The air would smell moist, of the earth, jasmine flowers and honeysuckle. He would sit on a bench by the pool in our courtyard. It would be very dark, just a sliver of moon reflected in the water. I'd only know he was there by the red glow of his cigar. I'd sit there and wait for it sometimes, in the blackness, the smell of tobacco."

"It sounds lonely," said Sara as Ali joined them.

"Come then," he said. "Let's go to where he is buried."

They stood and walked together, passing from court-yard to courtyard, until they came to a black wrought-iron grille in the ground, cool in the mosque's shadow, near to a square of bare trees.

"He's in the catacombs below. You can't go in any-more," Ali explained.

Maryam knelt down, looking up at Sara from the cracked gray marble. Her eyes glistened, sad and hopeful like a child's. She rested her hands in front of her and bent to pray. Sara stood beside Ali. She had not expected such emptiness, such loneliness beneath the white sky as people walked past. Her mother crouched on the ground. When Sara's father died, she would bury him knowing he had loved her and kept her safe.

"Come," whispered Ali, helping Sara kneel by Maryam's side.

And so she touched her head against the cold stone and remembered how she had fallen on Hammersmith Bridge that day. It felt like another lifetime. There had been enough hurt. She thought of Julian and Saeed and prayed for them, and for her own father and mother, longing for the possibility of a new life beginning inside her as well.

Maryam felt calm, resting there, thinking of all she would say to her father if she could see him now, still alive, in a garden somewhere, flooded with soft yellow sunlight. They would sit side by side on a bench, watching leaves fall from the trees and the glow of his cigar. "I have missed you, Maryam," he would say. "I'm sorry it's taken so long, and if you've been sad and alone. Come and tell me your stories, how far away you've been and all you have seen."

"I have a daughter," she would begin, and turning her head where she knelt, Maryam saw Sara beside her and smiled.

5. Home

We shall not cease from exploration
And the end of all our exploring
Will be to arrive where we started
And know the place for the first time.
                                        —T. S. Eliot

I t was Christmas Eve and I was home. Through the kitchen window I watched my father and Saeed on the bench at the bottom of the garden. The trees were bare, and Creswell rolled in the leaves on the grass. I saw Saeed hold up the foxhead stone as he showed it to his uncle Edward. My father had arrived from Robin Hood's Bay that morning and would stay for a week. As he smiled at me across the lavender and rosemary bushes, he seemed just a little thinner and grayer than the last time I'd seen him. I waved back and turned from the window to put the kettle on as Julian came downstairs. "Want some tea?" I asked.

"Sounds good." He put his arms around me.

I was pregnant again, and felt a careful, fragile joy as we leaned there together.

The small cloth cradle from the shrine hung beside Fatima's charm above the door. It was a bundle of ragged green cloth that I'd reach up to touch now and again, to reassure me that Mazareh hadn't just been a dream of snow in the night.

The last time I saw my mother was at the airport in

Mashhad. Ali had stayed in Hassan's truck, and I'd shaken his hand. "I'm glad we met," I said. "You will look after her?"

He nodded and said farewell. "Be strong, Sara Mazar. This life is yours to take."

My mother and I waited together in the departure lounge. "So, tomorrow you'll be in Mazareh again," I said, and we smiled, both now sharing the place in our minds, its gentle foothills and whispering space. We held each other as my flight was called, and I closed my eyes on her shoulder. Then we stepped apart.

"I have something for you." She lifted a bag from the floor with a bolt of rose pink silk inside. "It's your color," she said. "It's from the bazaar. Make something beautiful."

I held it tight. "I'll never forget, Maman. I'll remember for ever, I promise."

"Go, Sara, be free." She kissed each of my eyelids. "You're always my daughter."

With that, I had walked away.

I turned again to Julian as the kettle came to the boil. "I wish we could go there."

"One day, with our family." He stroked a curl of hair from my face.

That evening, we sat by the fire and my father watched the flames through his glass of wine. "You could go and see her for yourself," I suggested, but he shook his head.

"My family's right here. Maybe you can all come and visit me in the New Year."

He had decided to stay in Robin Hood's Bay for good, in love again, in a way, with the open space, the heather, and the green sea. He was going to rent out the old house in Richmond. Julian and I had driven past it on our way back from the airport and seen the TO LET sign at the end of the black-and-white path. The windows were gray and lifeless now. I had walked round the garden on my own, just once, fallen leaves cluttering the paths and borders. I had looked inside the greenhouse, dried poppy pods in a bowl on the side, their tiny black seeds fallen out through the holes. I put them in a plastic bag and took them away with me. On the floor was a cardboard box of hyacinth and crocus bulbs beginning to shoot. I took them as well.

I closed my eyes by the fireside as winter breathed outside.

"Shall we read some more 'Gossemarbart'?" I asked Saeed, and he ran upstairs to fetch Doctor Ahlavi's folder.

My father and I exchanged a smile at the jump and drum of his feet. He'd changed. We all had. Something gone, something found. Saeed would start his new school next term, and I would be back at work, for a while at least. He half slid down the banister and flung himself in front of the fire, his elbows resting on the bolt of rose pink silk. "Come on," he called out to Julian, who was still in the kitchen.

I went to find him, pouring a brandy. For a moment we stood alone beside the dark window, a Christmas quiet with just London's low rumble beyond. I reached for the jar of *zaferan* on the sill and undid the lid, breathing it in. "I'm so glad you're back," Julian said, and we leaned against each other in the shadows and the candlelight.

*F*ar away, the stone woman sighed out across the land, a flute, a drum, a song, a whisper, and Maryam walked alone into the foothills beyond Mazareh. She looked up at the sky where clouds tore apart in a slipstream of wind. Soon the seasons would change and coarse grass would grow again through the melting snow. Then there would be new knots for her to tie in the desert straw strands, and fresh wishes to be made, along with other stories to be told of the dead and gone, and of lives just begun.

Center Point Publishing
600 Brooks Road ● PO Box 1
Thorndike ME 04986-0001 USA

(207) 568-3717

US & Canada:
1 800 929-9108